THE TIME RIVER

Feng Junke

 FOREIGN LANGUAGES PRESS

First Edition 2013

ISBN 978-7-119-08530-2
© Foreign Languages Press Co. Ltd, Beijing, China, 2013

Published by
Foreign Languages Press Co. Ltd
24 Baiwanzhuang Road, Beijing 100037, China
http://www.flp.com.cn

Distributed by
China International Book Trading Corporation
35 Chegongzhuang Xilu, Beijing 100044, China
P.O. Box 399, Beijing, China

Printed in the People's Republic of China

CONTENTS

vi	Preface
viii	Introduction

1	The Burning Cornfield
15	Tan the Fourth, Leader of the Eighth Production Team
28	Ma Xi, Leader of the "Prairie Fire Combat Unit"
36	Wu Musan, the Ball-biting Louse
44	Wang Gubo
54	Gangquan's Ma
60	Gouwang, the Scoundrel
68	Niu Xiaofang, the Pig Castrator
75	Guo Jun
81	My First Taste of Beef
86	Mr Liu's Henan Cuisine
91	Old Pao, Leader of the Ninth Production Team
98	The Tragic Life of Wang Zeng

104	Ding Mao, an Urban Youth Back in the Village
114	Jiang Yue, a Revolutionary Veteran
121	Blackie's Ma
129	Maiduo, Chairman of the Peasant Association
138	Wang Laobiao, Village Calligrapher
146	Grandpa Wang, a Daring Fellow
153	Son
162	Heaven Kills "Heavenly Law"
167	Chang Gen, a Crippled Fan of an Actress
175	Great Leap Forward Nights
182	My Grandfather's Goats
186	Bathing
192	Spring Festival in the Countryside
202	Accusing the Old Society
211	The Iron-rod Yam
217	Dividing Up Vegetables
225	Village Nights
234	Village Smoke
240	The South Yard and the North Yard
247	Concerns about the Land, the Water and the Trees
257	The Weeping Pagoda Tree
263	The Yellow River Flood Land
272	Undying Love
277	Father's Burial
289	Mother and Beijing

PREFACE

A collection of succinct sketches of the native soil and a nostalgic symphony of emotional attachment, *The Time River*, delineated with the liveliest and most unsparing strokes of the pen, reintroduces the unbleached beauty of China's villages, once considered backward, ignorant and rude. In the calm yet powerful narratives of the author, the small villages of Central China, along with their inconsequential inhabitants and their simple stories, radiate a vigorous sheen of life and etch themselves into our memory as treasures for us to cherish.

The Time River is not only a collection of fine essays. It is also a literary creation that has made a return to simplicity. From the perspective of a modern city dweller, the author delves directly into the heart of China's native soil with faithfulness and without exaggeration, seeking no moral high ground and avoiding any overstated criticism for its own sake. Exploring the various dimensions of humanity, the author employs traditional sketching techniques just as capably as he manages to illuminate the nature of man through the depths of modern literature.

He serves us with an opportunity to discover the open-minded nature of good Chinese writers, who are confident but not boastful, humble but not self-abasing. They depict the genuine faces of China, the true historical facets of the Chinese and their collective character. A genuine reflection infused with emotion, this work is more than a recollection of the past or a collection of memories relived. It is a creative rediscovery that embodies the author's greatest respect for the period of unforgettable history in which he has immersed himself.

A quality literary work in its own right, *The Time River* also presents the remarkable progress made in China after the country initiated its development program for rural areas. In this sense the work serves not only as literature, but also as a sample of social observation teeming with vivid detail and sentiment.

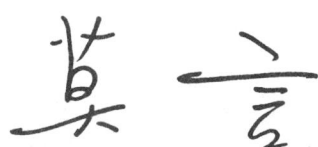

Mo Yan, born Guan Moye, is a contemporary Chinese writer. Emerging to prominence in the mid-1980s with *Frog*, *Big Breasts and Wide Hips* and other native-soil novels, he won the Nobel Prize for Literature in 2012.

Introduction

Wen County, Henan Province, is located north of the Yellow River and south of the Taihang Mountains. It is the birthplace of Chen's tai chi boxing and many well-known historical figures, such as Bu Shang, one of Confucius' 72 disciples, Sima Yi, a renowned statesman and strategist of the Three Kingdoms period, and Sima Yan, Emperor Wudi of the Jin Dynasty.

In the early 1950s I was born in an ordinary village in this county, and there in the following 18 years I experienced the anti-rightist campaign, the Great Leap Forward movement, the establishment of the people's communes, the three years of natural disaster, the Four Clean-ups movement and the Cultural Revolution. These have great impacts on the course of China's development in the following decades, and have left with me unforgettable impressions. This collection is a microscopic reflection of China's rural life during that period.

The village I was born and grew up in was small, with about 1,000 people. With the exception of a few brick ones, most of the houses were structures of sun-dried mud-brick walls and a thatched roof. There was not even a paved street to speak of. To the people living there, the village was their world. Although it was only a little more than a mile from the county seat, my grandmother had not visited the town many times in her life. My maternal grandfather's home was about six miles from the town, but in his village there were people who had never in their whole life set foot there. Before Deng Xiaoping led the Chinese people onto the road of reform and opening-up, the ordinary people spent their entire lives in the village, working and sweating on the land, marrying, and begetting children.

When I was young, the village Party branch secretary, the head of the production brigade and the leaders of the production teams were the "big guys" in the village, such as Tie An, Wang Laoman, Old Pao, Ma Xi, Tan the Fourth in this collection. And the most powerful person was no doubt Old Jin, the leader of the workgroup stationed in the village. The villagers regarded these people with fear and shuddered at their words, because in the village those guys were as powerful as the emperor, and their words were as good as imperial edicts. They could decide the fates of the villagers. The tragedies of Wang Zeng, Guo Jun, Blackie's Ma and Grandpa Lin the Eighth were directly caused by them. For no more than a handful of wheat grains, a sweet potato, a few corn ears, or some vegetable that could have saved lives, ordinary peasants were criticized and denounced, paraded through the streets, driven insane or even driven to an early grave. And yet, despite their humble status, ordinary peasants are hard-working, candid and kind-hearted, and are ready to sacrifice themselves at critical moments. My pen tries to reflect their pains and sufferings, their noble efforts and their helplessness.

Apart from those swaggering big guys, there were people who were upright and ready to uphold justice, such as Wang Chongshui and Grandpa Lin the Eighth, and there were others who were selfish and mean, for example, Tan the Fourth. The story "Tan the Fourth, leader of the Eighth Production Team" depicts a brutal person riding roughshod over the villagers. His copulation with a sow forcefully brings out his sick and perverted mind. I'm trying to bring alive and present to the readers a spectrum of personalities worthy of contemplation.

After more than thirty years of reform and opening-up, my hometown has changed in many ways. As I'm portraying these changes they also reveal to me something deeper. Every step forward in natural science, in a certain sense, is a step backward. While Man conquers Nature, he must look out for Nature's revenge. For instance, when the large cities are limiting the development of fertilizer, plastics, chemicals and cement plants, and paper mills, the villages are inviting them over in the name of introducing new technology to speed up the local economy. In little more than a decade the amount of arable land has shrunk sharply, the water table has dropped alarmingly, old trees have been cut down and the air has become seriously polluted. Both the number of cancer patients and that of deformed or disabled newborns have increased. People in the smaller towns are blinded by short-term interests, and that has brought about catastrophic consequences. The harsh realities in "The Weeping Pagoda Tree" and "The Yellow River Flood Land" are warnings of what this nearsightedness leads to.

I can never forget the love between my maternal grandfather and grandmother, and my parents. They were honest and hardworking. They went through poverty, wars, natural disasters and various political upheavals. They gave me life and led me through my most difficult years. My mother turned her life into tiny bits of love and care, and selflessly devoted herself to her children, and she is still doing so though she is approaching 90. My father worked on the yellow earth all his life, but at the time of his death he could hardly find a final resting place, because farmland is so scarce that the loss of a tiny plot of land can affect the interests of the whole village. If father should know about this in Heaven, I wonder what he would think.

Zhou Daxin, a renowned author and winner of the Mao Dun Literary Award once remarked, "The most soul-touching works of Mr Feng are those about his love of his people." As he has had a similar life experience, he can feel an emotional affiliation. After reading this collection he said that the stories reveal "genuine feelings in an unaffected way," the language is "witty and humorous" and "as heart-touching as that of fairy tales," and "one can enjoy reading it as much as if exploring a new world."

Soon after the publication of the Chinese version of this book by the People's Literature Publishing House, *Beijing Times* on November 18, 2011, *The Beijing News* on December 17, 2011 and *Writers Digest* on January 6, 2012 carried full-page commentaries under the titles of "Feng Junke's Indigenous Description of

His Native Soil," "Feng Junke: Folks, History, and Memories of His Native Place," and "A Passionate Retrospection of a Bitter Past." Many stories in this collection have been reprinted in such magazines as *Chinese Writers, People's Literature, Selections from Chinese Literature, Xiao Shuo Xuan Kan, Beijing Literature, October* and *Readers*.

The Time River won the fifth Bingxin Prose Award in August 2012.

The readers comment on the Internet that "The book depicts the daily events of ordinary people in a small village in the heartland of China in an almost rustic and indigenous way. The events are true to the very details. They show the diligence and endurance of the Chinese peasants, the simplicity of their lives and the nobility of their minds. The power behind the seemingly placid narration touches the heart and strikes an aesthetic chord. In these times of impetuosity, vulgarity and utilitarianism, that power can warm and console our hearts."

I would like to thank the readers for their attachment to this book.

Feng Junke
Beijing
May 15, 2012

The Burning Cornfield

Grandpa Lin the Eighth was a childless widower. His wife had died long before. Therefore he qualified as a five-guarantees household, that is, he was guaranteed food, clothing, medical care, housing and burial expenses. He never thought that at the age of 63 he would be granted an "official position" by the production team – crop watcher.

The crop watcher's duty was to guard the crops – to prevent the ripening crops from being stolen before they were harvested. In the late 1950s and early 1960s when peasants had their three meals at collective kitchens they were almost always hungry, so hungry they would not hesitate to steal food directly from the production team's cropland. In those days, hunger even made people do crazy things. They would steal whatever they found edible, depending on the season. When wheat was ripening, they would sweep their hands over the wheat ears as they walked past the field and come away with a handful of grains, give them a rub between their palms, blow away the chaff, pop the seeds into their mouths, and, without much chewing, swallow the whole thing down. When the tubers of sweet potatoes were just swelling, some people would shove aside the vine, give a few hard kicks at the root, pull out a few tubers from the loosened earth, and then push back the earth to cover up the hole so no one would notice that anything was missing. In autumn the fields offered a greater variety of things to eat: corn, sesame, soybeans, mug beans, turnips, eggplants, cabbages and much more. In fact there was nothing people did not steal.

Some people, however, refrained from stealing from their own production team but would pilfer the crops of other production teams. Some would avoid stealing from their own village, but go to other villages to steal. It's no exaggerating to say that stealing was rife and thieves ran amuck. That was why Old Jin, the leader of the work group from the county government, would berate the commune members.

"Look at you!" he would growl. "Do you look like commune members of the new society? What you are doing is no different from what the bandits did in the past!"

Tan the Fourth, the leader of the Eighth Production Team, suggested that the militia be deployed to guard the crops.

"Then who's going to work in the fields?" Old Jin retorted. "Better appoint one person to watch the crops. He can patrol the fields with a gong, and beat it to summon the militia when he spies a thief."

"Isn't that the old trick we used to warn people that the Japs were approaching the village?" someone blurted out.

"That's the spirit the higher-ups want to see," Old Jin

responded gravely. "Let's select one now."

As watching crops was considered an easy job, and the watchman himself had a chance to filch some extra food, people usually vied for the position. After arguing back and forth the majority finally agreed on Wang Chongshui's nomination of Grandpa Lin the Eighth. The reasons were that Grandpa Lin the Eighth was too old for heavy work and should enjoy some privileges. Since he didn't have family, he was more likely to spend time in the fields rather than at home. More importantly, without a family to feed, he wouldn't squirrel things home. As the saying went, when he had eaten his fill, his whole family would no longer be hungry.

Tan the Fourth exploded. "That's a ridiculous choice," he yelled. "Lin the Eighth is so meek and weak thieves could tear him apart and eat him up!"

Indeed, Grandpa Lin the Eighth was a soft man. It was hard to say whether he was born so or whether it was because he had no one to back him up. He always wore a smile that made him look humble, and even servile. He never spoke loudly, and his voice was soft as drizzle.

Every day ever since Grandpa Lin the Eighth assumed his new position, he patrolled the fields with a gong and little hammer in one hand and his long pipe in the other, puffing tobacco smoke out while walking along the ridges and footpaths between the fields.

Reports of theft started to roll in from one production team after another even while the corn ears were still in the milk, but throughout the first ten days there was not a sound from the gong of the Eighth Production Team.

At the general meeting of the village Old Jin praised the Eighth Production Team and Grandpa Lin the Eighth. He also said that the crop watchers must be more vigilant in the days ahead, for the ripening corn was going to attract more and more thieves, and corn was the most widely cultivated autumn food crop. From now on, he emphasized, crop watchers must stay in the fields around the clock to put a complete stop to the stealing. Any watchman who allowed ten ears of corn or more to be stolen would be publicly criticized, and, moreover, he'd be given no rations for three days!

The autumn sun was like a ball of fire, scorching the cornfield. Day by day, as the corn ears grew bigger and firmer under the blazing sun, stealing and filching became more and more frequent, and Old Jin's curses increased in frequency too, as well as in volume. He ordered the radio station at the production brigade headquarters to make daily announcements of each production team's loss of corn ears. Before long, two watchmen were each deprived of rations for two days. In another few days, it became obvious to the leaders that the third production team was suffering the heaviest losses of corn and sweet potatoes. The team's watchman Wang Maochi, nearly 60, was brought to the brigade headquarters for a public accusation in front of the whole village. His face dark as death, Old Jin proclaimed that if one more case of pilfering should occur in that production team, he'd dismiss the team leader from his post. Shamed and enraged, the team leader,

"Then who's going to work in the fields?" Old Jin retorted. "Better appoint one person to watch the crops. He can patrol the fields with a gong, and beat it to summon the militia when he spies a thief."

Wang Hezhou, rushed forward and gave Wang Maochi several slaps in the face. Wang Maochi was discharged and punished with deprivation of rations for three days. The other watchmen walked away with frayed nerves and leaden hearts.

To maintain his own and the Eighth Production Team's good reputation, Grandpa Lin the Eighth diligently patrolled the cornfields despite the blazing sun, his arms and legs badly scratched by the corn leaves. He even had his three meals sent to him in the fields. At night he kept walking his beat under the moon and stars. Exhausted, he would doss down on a patch of grass beside the fields to take a nap, only to spring to his feet again before long. Every time Old Jin and Tan the Fourth came checking, they would find him dutifully guarding the cornfield.

In those days, the banging of gongs could often be heard, night and day, and corn ears were stolen, but never was there a thief caught, not even one. Some speculated that it was the watchmen themselves who were the thieves, and they struck the gong only after they had the booty properly stowed away. If that was the case, how could the thief ever be caught? Surprisingly, only Grandpa Lin the Eighth's gong never sounded, and only the Eighth Production Team's corn was never lost.

Old Jin considered Grandpa Lin the most dutiful crop watcher. He should be set up as a role model and his dedication propagated, he decided. So, with slogan-shouting young men leading the way, Grandpa Lin was put on the production team's clapped-out old donkey, and paraded through the village streets with a big red flower on his chest and a corn-flour bun in his hands (awarded to him by Old Jin himself). The rattling of gongs and the crackling of rifle fire filled the air as if it were a welcome celebration for the return of a triumphant hero. When Grandpa Lin was finally able to dismount from the donkey, he was immediately surrounded by a swarm of little kids, crying out that they were hungry and reaching out for the corn-flour bun in his hand. Their sallow faces and the craving in their eyes caused him a pang of distress. Without a moment's thought, he shared out his reward among the children.

Grandpa Lin the Eighth was nominated "Model Crop Watcher" by the commune and subsequently by the county government. His feat was broadcast over and over on the PA, and he became a celebrity in the county.

One morning his patrol route led him to the cornfield at North Low, a place he seldom visited, because it lay far from the village and main roads and was the village's traditional burial ground. Wild animals used to haunt the tall weeds and bushes among the tombs, and people tended to shun the place. Suddenly he noticed that there were scattered footprints on the ground. Someone must have been here! For what? To steal corn ears? His heart raced. But he quickly composed himself and looked more carefully at the corn. On the stalks the ears were all growing in their places, swaying slightly in the breeze. His heart calmed down, but he still felt a tinge of unease. He went closer, reached out and pressed a corn ear. It felt empty. He peeled back the husk and found that the entire cob was gone! So someone had snatched off the cob and carefully furled back the husk to make it look intact. In a panic, Grandpa Lin pressed one ear after another, and found that several dozen had been stolen. He drew several sharp breaths, and sat down with a thump on the ground. He wanted to wail, but no sound came; he wanted to curse, but he did not know whom to curse; he wanted to beat the gong to summon people, but he couldn't remember where he had left the gong and hammer. His mind was filled with one horrible thought: What if Old Jin and team leader Tan the Fourth learned of this? They would skin him alive! Who on earth could have stolen the corn? He figured that there was only one way to clear himself, and that was to catch the thief. Since so many corn ears had been plucked off, it couldn't have been done in one night, and so the thief was most likely to come back. I'm going to catch him, he thought.

He found his legs watery, his eyes veiled in mist. He managed some ten or twenty stumbling steps and hid himself among the tombs of the Liu family cemetery. There he lay prone behind a tomb mound, his dim eyes fixed on the site of the theft. From morning to afternoon, from afternoon to evening, from evening till midnight, there was not a sound. Perhaps the thief wouldn't come back after all? Then how could he redeem his reputation? The fiendish face of Old Jin floated up before his eyes. He could see himself sitting proudly on donkeyback with that big red flower on his chest and the corn-flour bun in his hands. He could see the contorted face of the leader of the Third Production Team, Wang Hezhou, slapping the face of Wang Maochi. He thought of the leader of his own team, Tan the Fourth....It was as if his stomach were filled with fluffy cotton; he couldn't spit it out, and neither could he swallow it down.

A chill creeps out from the earth on autumn nights. Crickets chirp and trill, but to Grandpa Lin that night it was a sad tune, plaintive and helpless. As he listened, he shuddered at the coldness of the night. He raised his eyes toward the east, and found that the morning star had risen above the horizon. Day was about to break. The thief is not coming tonight, he thought. He wanted to get some sleep, but as soon as he closed his eyes, he imagined that there was a rustling of corn leaves. He pricked up his ears. No doubt about it! There was someone there stealing corn. He jumped to his feet and dashed toward the sound.

He found a little girl about eight years old. She didn't cry when the old man suddenly appeared, neither did she make any attempt to run away, but instead, she dropped to her knees and begged in a whisper, "Grandpa, please spare me. This is the last time and I'll never do this again."

The sight of the little girl had assuaged his anger. He squatted down on his heels and looked kindly at the girl in the starlight. She was very lean. A pair of big and frightened eyes were gazing at him.

She was from the neighboring village, she explained. In the famine her father suffered dropsy and died last winter. Her mother tried a kind of white clay for food, and now her whole body was swollen and she too was dying. A rumor ran round her village that there was a chance to steal corn ears from fields near the Liu family cemetery if one could sneak there in the small hours. So here she was, hoping to bring back a few ears for her mother. She had lost her father and now she didn't want to lose her mother. While speaking, she prostrated herself before the old man, and knocked her forehead against the ground, pleading for mercy.

This scene took Grandpa Lin back to 1943. That autumn the entire province of Henan was swept by a plague of locusts. All the crops were chewed to the stalk by the locusts. Family after family ran out of food and countless people died of starvation. Back at that time he too had a daughter almost the age of this little girl before him. His daughter was too hungry even to move. She lay on the ground and kept stuffing handful after handful of dirt into her mouth. He was an able-bodied young man then and had thought of stealing, just to get some food for his daughter. There was a saying among the older generation that "Hunger makes bandits." And it was certainly better to be a bandit than starve to death. But all the crops had been consumed by the locusts. No family had food, and people were dying everywhere. Even if he wanted to steal there was no food to steal. He had no one to turn to and Heaven did not respond to his pleading. In the end he wasn't able to save his daughter.

A look at the little girl stirred a ripple of sadness in his old heart. "Don't be afraid, sweetie," he muttered as he pulled the little girl into his arms. "Grandpa is going to pluck corn ears for you. You can take them home and eat them with your mummy."

He stood up, took off his shirt and spread it out on the ground. Pretty soon there was a small pile of ears on it. He wrapped them up in his shirt, and put the bundle onto his shoulder. Holding the girl's hand, he took her home.

On autumn nights, the sky turns pitch-black just before the dawn. "Do you know why the sky turns so dark just before the dawn?" he asked the girl.

"Tell me, Grandpa."

"A long, long time ago there was an emperor called Zhu Yuanzhang. He almost died of starvation when he was young. One night, he and his cronies stole an ox from a rich family, but after they butchered it they realized they had no vessel to cook the meat in. So he went back to 'borrow' a pot. By the time they finished eating and he was going to return the pot, the day was about to break. What to do? Zhu Yuanzhang pointed at the sky and commanded, 'Go dark again to give me time to return the pot.' And guess what! Although the petitioner was a thief he was destined to be an emperor, the Lord of Heaven granted his wish and immediately turned the sky pitch-black. Now the sky has darkened again, because it wants you to get safely home. You must be a blessed person."

The little girl's face beamed. She held Grandpa Lin's hand tightly and followed him.

Soon they crossed a ditch, and turned onto a barely visible footpath in the fields. Since it was rarely used, he thought, there was little likelihood of coming across anyone. But before they had gone far, they saw a shadowy figure walking straight toward them, with a parcel on its shoulder too! It was too late to dodge. All Lin could think of doing was walk bravely ahead. Any person who appears at this time of night and in this place is, nine out of ten, a thief. When a thief meets a thief, neither is put to shame, as the saying goes!

When they bumped into each other, Grandpa Lin was surprised to find that the other was none other than the leader of his team, Tan the Fourth. Without question, Tan was a thief, too. He must have gone to the neighboring village to steal.

When Tan the Fourth realized the other one was Grandpa Lin, he hissed in a low, harsh voice, "Old Eighth. So you're stealing what you're supposed to guard!"

"What about you?" Lin retorted.

"Me? I went to that village over there to retrieve stolen corn. This is proof of theft. Tomorrow a criticism meeting will be held in our village. You just wait!" Tan stalked off, leaving a menace in the air.

The little girl clung to Grandpa Lin's leg with tears in her eyes.

"Sweetie, never mind him. He is a thief, a hardened thief. He must have been to *your* village to steal."

When Grandpa Lin the Eighth got back from taking the girl home, the day was already bright. The sun, red as blood, had climbed high in the east, driving away the nocturnal moisture from the earth and turning the fields into a huge steaming pot.

That day, instead of going on his usual patrol around the fields, Grandpa Lin went straight to the scene of the theft at North Low. He stamped down the earless cornstalks to create an open space. Then he went over to the Liu family cemetery to fetch some dead branches and dried grass which he had prepared to take home for firewood or to feed his ox. He spread them on the ground to sit comfortably down, and took out his long pipe. As he puffed on his pipe, he looked around. It was only then that he realized that the corn was already ripe. The leaves had started to wither, the stalks had turned from yellow to brown, and some ears had cracked open. They were ready for harvest. His sight was then caught by the hollowed ears, and the torn open husks which were his doing. They looked like wilted flowers hanging limply on the stalks, conspicuous and offending to the eye. These were proof of his stealing, and Old Jin and Tan the Fourth were ready to denounce him for it. Having lived so many years and seen so much of life, what could he be afraid of? Criticism? No way.

The image of the little girl from the neighboring village reappeared to him. Her father had passed on and her mother was dying. He could see her prostrate on the ground making kowtows to him, begging for mercy. He remembered the locust plague and famine of 1943, his own daughter starving to death in a shallow pit. He had thought of stealing then, but there had been nothing to steal. It felt liked a knife was slashing at his old heart. Tears cascaded down his cheeks. He looked at the boundless cornfield all around him. Isn't the corn raised by the pain and sweat of the peasants? Then why can't the peasants and their children eat it? Why must the corn growers and their children die of hunger? He just couldn't figure it out.

At noon the commune members were gathered in the courtyard of the collective kitchen with bowls and jars in their hands waiting to line up for lunch. Suddenly Old Jin's voice barked from the PA system: "Attention, all members of the commune. The crop watcher of the Eighth Production Team, Grandpa Lin the Eighth was caught last night stealing corn. We have decided to rescind his title of Model Crop Watcher and stop his rations for three days. This evening there will be a meeting to criticize him. Your presence is required."

Old Jin's voice rolled like thunder over the village. The very air seemed thick with foreboding, and a dead silence fell over the courtyard of the collective kitchen. No one moved; no one uttered a sound. It was learned later that at that announcement the entire village of more than one thousand people all stood motionless and silent, not just those of the Eighth Production Team.

Just then there came a shout of "Fire! North Low! Eighth Production Team's cornfield!"

There was a stampede toward the field.

Ripe corn baked by the fiery sun is as dry as tinder. A cloud of dark smoke hovered over the field. Flames shot up and spread in every direction, swallowing more and more corn. Corn seeds popped like fireworks.

When Tan the Fourth and the commune members finally beat out the fire, they found in the smoldering cornfield the charred corpse of Grandpa Lin the Eighth.

Tan the Fourth, Leader of the Eighth Production Team

Tan the Fourth's house was the best one on the main street of the village. Upon a foundation of granite slabs, gray bricks rose all the way to the eaves, and the entire roof was covered with gray tiles complete with six auspicious animals of carved brick squatting on each of the five ridges. In the 1950s, when most houses in the rural areas had mud-brick walls and thatched roofs – even houses of the better-off families couldn't afford more than a few layers of brick at the base – such a house couldn't but be eye-catching.

It was said that Tan the Fourth's family had been very poor before liberation, and this grand house which he occupied used to belong to Ma Fei, the village landlord. It was allocated to Tan the Fourth during the land reform movement, for he was an enthusiast in publicly denouncing landlords and toppling on local despots. Not only was he rewarded with the best house of the village but also appointed team leader of the militia. In the socialist campaigns after liberation, such as organizing the mutual aid team, the cooperative transformation, the establishment of the people's commune, he was always in the lead. He was outspoken and daring, and as a result, was appointed the leader of the Eighth Production Team.

In 1958 the upsurge of the Great Leap Forward movement spilled over into the countryside. "Go all out, aim high and gain greater, faster, better and more economical results in building socialism," "Surpass UK, surpass US, and dash toward communism!" Slogans like those were inscribed on walls and stuck on trees all along the streets.

One day Tan the Fourth summoned Wang Laobiao, and ordered him to paint the Great Leap Forward symbol of a winged steed on the back wall of his house.

"But that's a beautiful *brick* wall!" Wang protested, "If I spread mud over it, won't it look the same as the mud walls beside it?"

"Shut your face! Just do what I tell you."

Wang clammed up and slunk away. In no time a layer of mud was smeared over the wall. Now, if one didn't glance up at the roof, the house looked no different from its neighbors, except that the mud was somewhat fresher.

Some people grumbled under their breath, "It looks like Tan the Fourth is going to make a big leap forward himself. It's a pity he's making a mess of such a grand brick house."

The mud and whitewash dried up in a few days. In another two days Wang Laobiao finished the painting. In the upper left-hand corner there was the sun, big as a washbasin and red as blood. At the center of the picture was a galloping winged horse. Riding on the horse was a man holding a fluttering red flag bearing the slogan "Long live the Great Leap Forward!" In the lower right-hand corner there was a fat sow, its sagging belly almost scraping the ground. Judging by its short legs and weight it wouldn't be able to move very fast. A man was sitting astride its rump, his legs clutching tightly, his hands pulling back the pig's ears. Coming out of his mouth were the words "Slow down! Slow down!" Everyone at that time knew that this figure represented the "sluggard," meaning backward people, and there was the slogan "Sweep away sluggard!" Almost every village had paintings of this kind – a most popular phenomenon back then.

One morning, people found inscribed on the pig rider the name of "Tan the Fourth." Nobody knew who did it or when, but the news soon spread through the village. At lunchtime nearly half the villagers gathered in front of the wall with their lunch bowls in their hands, winking and gesturing while engaged in hushed conversations.

"How can team leader Tan be the sow rider?" someone wondered aloud.

"He should be the one holding the red flag," another asserted.

"Somebody's got a nerve!"

It was really incredible for anyone to paint Tan the Fourth as a sluggard riding a sow, for who didn't know that he was the most eager beaver in the whole commune – even in the whole county – in the Great Leap Forward movement? He took the lead in door-to-door searches for grain; he smashed people's cooking vessels and took away their tables and chairs; he bent over backward to set up the socialist collective kitchen; he insisted that each *mu*

($^{1}/_{15}$ hectare) of land could produce five tons of grain and more. Had he ever lagged behind? His most renowned feat that helped him make his name in the county was the "big socialist family" he advocated and put into practice. All school-age children were gathered into one compound to take classes during the day and sleep there at night, and not allowed to go home. They were told to abandon their family names and adopt the new unified family name "She," meaning socialism, and the compound was therefore named "the youngsters' socialist big family."

As for women, they would work together in the fields during the day, and have their three meals at the collective kitchen. Instead of going home in the evening they were ordered to live together in one designated compound called "the women's socialist big family." Men were also ordered to live together in "the men's socialist big family." Sentries were set up at the gates of each of the three compounds, and no one was allowed to visit the other compounds. Not only would the kitchen stop providing food for those who dared to violate Tan's rules, the offender would also be publicly criticized and denounced.

Although people were seething with anger, no one dared to come out openly in opposition. In the end they persuaded Wang Chongshui, an ex-soldier of the People's Liberation Army, to speak up, for he had been wounded in wars and won medals for bravery.

"Old Fourth, what do you think you're doing?" Wang walked up to Tan and said. "What's the purpose of separating man and wife, parents and children?"

It was allocated to Tan the Fourth during the land reform movement, for he was an enthusiast in publicly denouncing landlords and toppling on local despots. Not only was he rewarded with the best house of the village but also appointed team leader of the militia.

Tan the Fourth brushed aside the question in scorn. Through the years he had savored the advantages of being an activist. In his bloated high spirits, he dismissed Wang as a had-been. It was true that he had been a war hero, but except for his free-tongued bluntness what had he actually achieved in recent years?

"Don't you know," Tan said haughtily, "in the communist society small families will be abolished and people will all live in big families? Now we've turned our private kitchens into collective kitchens, we're going to live in big families. This is what is meant by 'dashing toward communism.' When you were in the PLA, did you ever live with a woman?"

That made Tan the Fourth and the Eighth Production Team an advanced model of the Great Leap Forward throughout the village, the people's commune, and the county.

In that evening people from both the men's and women's socialist families were gathered into the courtyard of the collective kitchen to attend an "accusation meeting." The entire yard was filled with people sitting or squatting around a wooden table at the center. A battered barn lantern on the table shed a feeble yellow light over the dark crowd. Old Jin, leader of the work group, sat in a wicker armchair at the table, looking dignified and intimidating. From time to time, without a word he swept his eyes from the lifeless barn lantern to the crowd. Tan the Fourth sidled over, bent low and whispered in his ear, "Old Jin, shall we start?"

Old Jin nodded without saying anything.

Tan the Fourth immediately straightened up.

"Tonight's meeting," he barked, with his hands on his hips, "is to find out one thing: Who wrote my name on the sow rider? Tell me, and you're dismissed. Who did it?"

The sparrows under the eaves were alarmed and fluttered away, but the crowd remained dead silent.

Tan the Fourth's temper rose. They were the same people, but what had happened to the enthusiasm they had expressed in the gatherings denouncing the landlords, dividing the land, toppling despots, and exposing traitors and Japanese collaborators?

"If you had the guts to write it, why are you afraid to admit it? You're nothing but a coward! Now, who did it?!"

The crowd remained silent.

The evening air seemed to have frozen solid, and a ghastly quietness fell over the yard. Suddenly Old Jin stood up, and banged his fist on the table.

"You all know team leader Tan well, don't you?" he blared in a strong Shanxi accent. "If he is a backward element riding a sow, then what about my work group? Anyone who attacks our team leader is attacking the government work group. Attacking the work group is attacking the Great Leap Forward movement. Attacking the Great Leap Forward is attacking socialism itself! Do you understand?! Who is responsible for this? Come forward! Don't get others into trouble. Who did it? Speak up!"

Nobody spoke.

Old Jin felt his authority slighted, and that was no less than a challenge, opposition! If so many people should give him the cold shoulder, then where was the authority of the work group leader? How could he carry on his work in this village and push forward the Great Leap Forward movement in the future? The thought irked him.

"This meeting will not be dismissed until we find out the culprit," he said with a determined wave of his hand. "Militiamen, block the gate. No one shall leave this yard until the culprit owns up."

The team leader of the militia, Ma Dada, rose up from the shadowy crowd with his rifle, stood at attention before Old Jin without a word, and led a few militiamen to the gate to stand guard.

The night grew deeper, and the air became colder. At first there were whispers among the gathering, but soon the noise died down and was replaced by sporadic snoring, which grew louder and infectious.

"You villains! Don't even think of sleeping until we find the culprit!" Tan the Fourth yelled. He went into a side room, and returned with a fowling piece in his hand. He filled it with gunpowder and lit the fuse. The blast and flash shocked the sleepers awake, and flushed the birds out from their nests, fluttering away from the village.

There was a commotion among the crowd, and before they realized what was going on they saw Tan the Fourth filling the fowling piece again.

"I'll keep shooting till someone speaks up. See if you still can sleep then!"

No one had the courage to step forth to reason with him. They turned to Wang Chongshui.

Wang stood up and went over to Tan the Fourth, "Old Fourth, calm down. If they knew who it was they'd certainly tell you."

Tan the Fourth stared at him for a long moment without replying. One couldn't tell whether he didn't want to reply or he didn't know how to reply.

"Old Fourth," Wang entreated, "why take that picture to heart? Who doesn't know you're an advanced model?"

"What! Don't think that just because you've been through wars and won medals you can defy me. I also won honors in the struggle against landlords and despots in the land reform movement. Tell me, was it *you* who did that? Well, was it?"

Totally unprepared for this counterblast, Wang was caught tongue-tied.

With a demonic gleam in his eye, Tan the Fourth raised the fowling piece again. The crowd broke out in a murmur of protests, "We're exhausted. We've been working all day. You Old Jin and Old Fourth only talk and talk about the Great Leap Forward, but you never work in the fields. Tomorrow we have to hoe the fields, to pull the harrows, to carry manure. How do you think we can keep awake all night after a day like that?" But rebellious as they might feel, no one dared to speak out loud, and no one knew how to pacify Tan the Fourth.

"If you're going to fire again, shoot at me!" Wang's temper also rose. "What weapon haven't I seen on the battlefield?"

"Shoot you? Why not? Since you oppose this accusation meeting, it must have been you who scribbled on the painting.

Why don't you confess?" Tan the Fourth raised the fowling piece and pointed the muzzle at Wang's chest.

Wang tore open his shirt and patted his scarred chest. "Shoot me! If you don't, you're simply a cowardly wretch." As he spoke, he pressed his chest against the muzzle.

Tan the Fourth flew into a helpless rage. He blew at the smoldering incense stick he was holding in one hand, and made as if to light the fuse of the fowling piece. Afraid that a life might be lost, the crowd was horrified.

"Calm down," some implored. "This is no big deal. Just scrape your name off."

Some tried to pull Wang aside, saying "You escaped many a hail of bullets on the battlefield. What a pity it would be to be killed now by accident."

Some went to plead with Old Jin. In such a situation, Old Jin's attitude was crucial. Even in his fit of temper Tan the Fourth had kept making sidelong glances at him to guess what his attitude was.

"Wang Chongshui," Old Jin stood up and walked to Wang with murder in his eyes, "don't think you can sabotage the Great Leap Forward and the Three Red Flags movement simply because you've been wounded in wars and won medals. Many people have been through more wars than you, received more wounds, won more honors. Look at me. I joined the revolutionary ranks in 1938, and what battles haven't I been through? What honors haven't I won? I have more scars than you can boast of. If you don't know who did that scribble, just shut up and sit down."

Since Old Jin had made his attitude clear, Tan the Fourth was more than encouraged. He blew again at the incense stick and assumed the posture of lighting the fuse.

"If it was not your doing, why risk your life to offend him?" someone reasoned.

"I don't care if that son of a bitch is offended or not," Wang shouted. "I can't let him bully the whole team simply because someone put his name on the sow rider. I'm not the one to back down yield. Never in a million years will he make me so much as blink, gun or no gun!" Far from flinching, Wang grew even more aggressive.

"Team leader Tan, I wrote it!" a voice came from the crowd.

An almost palpable silence gripped the whole courtyard. People looked around and saw that the speaker was none other than Wang Chongshui's son, Wang Sanmao. His admission gave the team members a real surprise. Why admit it? Isn't that as good as seeking death? He shouldn't have been so foolish, even to save his father.

"Team leader Tan," Sanmao continued, "would you swear to all the people here that sow rider isn't you? Do you think I should tell them what happened the night before?"

Tan the Fourth was taken aback and to everyone's surprise he immediately calmed down and threw the fowling piece to the ground.

"Nephew Sanmao," he muttered quickly, "forget it. Forget it."

He turned around, and said to Old Jin, "Let's call it a day."

Wang Chongshui was bewildered by this abrupt change.

Old Jin was also bewildered.

The whole gathering was bewildered.

This was really too weird to believe.

"Tell us what happened," Wang Chongshui said to his son after a moment's silence.

"Don't ask, Brother Chongshui, don't ask," Tan the Fourth said hurriedly. "The meeting is dismissed. The meeting is dismissed." By now he had become as soft as a pile of mud, holding his clasped hands before his chest in humble apology.

"No. We must get to the bottom of it," Wang Chongshui insisted as he turned back to his son and demanded, "Now tell us."

Sanmao shifted his glance from his father to Tan the Fourth and then back to his father. He opened his mouth but made no sound. Wang Chongshui raised his arm and gave his son a loud slap across the face.

"Tell me, or I'll give you another slap!"

"When I passed by the production team's pig sty the night before," Sanmao sobbed with his hands covering his face, "I heard the pigs screaming. I looked over the wall and saw team leader Tan, all naked, mounting a sow from behind. He was clutching the sow by the ears and fucking it. The way he screwed the sow was so much like the painting on his wall I couldn't help thinking he's the sow rider. So I wrote his name there."

The crowd boiled up like a huge cauldron of bubbling water ready to scald a butchered pig. People yelled, cursed, clapped and stamped. Wang Chongshui picked up the fowling piece, snatched the smoldering incense stick from Tan the Fourth's hand and lit the fuse. The boom in the night sounded like thunder and woke up the whole village. People grabbed their clothes and ran toward the Eighth Production Team's meeting place.

"What in Heaven's name is going on? Is Team Eight going crazy? What can they be doing at this hour of the night? Has Tan the Fourth lost his mind?"

Ma Xi, Leader of the "Prairie Fire Combat Unit"

During the Cultural Revolution Ma Xi was the team leader of the "Prairie Fire Combat Unit." He took the lead in opposing Old Pao, the leader of the Ninth Production Team. He claimed that Old Pao was leading the production team down the capitalist road, and therefore a capitalist roader in power and a loyal progeny of the prime capitalist roader Liu Shaoqi in the countryside.

One day, another meeting was held to accuse and denounce Old Pao, who was stood on a bench with his hands tied behind his back and a small blackboard, the type students used to chalk on, hanging round his neck. On the blackboard was inscribed the slogan, "Down with the capitalist roader Wang Lishan!" He had a dunce's cap made from old newspaper placed on his head, his back bent, his eyes half closed, his mouth shut. The imperious look that used to adorn his face had long gone. Now he seemed docile and obedient.

Ma Xi held a copy of *Quotations from Chairman Mao* in one hand, and with his other hand he tugged on the blackboard to make the string sink deep into Old Pao's neck. Old Pao made no complaint.

"Old Pao has been ruling us for so many years, and now Chairman Mao is calling on us to overthrow the despots," Ma Xi began. "Who wants to take the lead in exposing and denouncing his crimes?"

Not a sound from the audience.

"Who's going to take the lead?" Ma Xi asked again.

Still no response from the crowd.

"What's the matter with you? Are you all dumb?" Ma Xi screeched in exasperation.

"I know what you're up to," Erwang's mother muttered under her breath. "You're getting your own back because of your mother."

Her hushed comment created a ripple of giggles around her, for most people in the village, except perhaps Ma Xi's father, knew that Ma Xi's mother had had an affair with Old Pao. Having a job in Xi'an City, Ma Xi's father seldom came home, and his mother had to raise her four children all by herself – Ma Xi, a younger brother and two younger sisters. It's easy to imagine how hard life could be for a rural family without manpower but with so many mouths to feed. Since Old Pao was the team leader, he had the chance to steal food from the production team, which he gave to Ma Xi's mother. And Ma Xi's mother offered her body in return, just one of Old Pao's many mistresses.

Ma Xi had found this out himself. Coming back home late one night after a day's work dredging the irrigation canal, he saw a figure beyond the courtyard wall of his home. The figure threw something over the wall and hurried off. As the shadow passed by the dark corner where Ma Xi was hiding, he saw that it was Old Pao, no doubt about it. As he entered his courtyard, he was just in time to see his mother picking up a cloth bag from the ground. In it were a few ears of corn and some sweet potatoes. There was no need for an explanation.

Although Ma Xi's father was away from home year after year, his mother didn't stop giving birth. Besides the four of them, his mother had another four or five babies, who lived no more than a couple of days. The young Ma Xi had seen his mother wrap up the little bodies in straw and discard them in the graveyard under the cover of night. Just like throwing away a bundle of straw, his mother never cried when she did so. Once he caught sight of someone pointing at one of his little dead brothers there, and heard the man say, "Another of Old Pao's." The words pierced his heart like needles.

From then on he started to watch his mother carefully. He made a habit of getting up several times during the night on the pretence of going for a pee, in order to check if his mother was sleeping at home. Soon he discovered that she would get up and slip quietly out if someone gave a few kicks at the back wall in the small hours. She was always back just before daybreak and would pull out from her blouse a few sweet potatoes for him and his brother and sisters, but she herself would never eat. She always said she was not hungry.

Once he followed his mother out, and discovered the secret.

The production team had a large collective courtyard, which was surrounded by high rammed-earth walls. He saw his mother push open the gate, walk in and bolt it behind her. He climbed onto the top of the wall and saw her entering the sweet potato cellar. He knew the cellar well. It was a pit more than three yards deep, about seven yards wide and ten yards long. The roof was constructed by a layer of sorghum stalks above the beams, then a thick layer of wheat straw and finally plastered over with a layer of mud. As an entrance, a vertical shaft was sunk beside the cellar, and every year the harvested sweet potatoes were lowered down this shaft into the cellar. Two wooden bars were placed at right angles to each other over the mouth of the shaft, with a small hole in the middle of each. A short iron rod that had a loop at one end and an eye at the other was inserted through the hole. A padlock was fixed through the eye of the rod, and the key hung on Old Pao's belt. Without him unlocking it, nobody could get into the cellar.

When Ma Xi descended on the other side of the wall, his mother had disappeared. He peeped down the shaft. It was dark and the cross bars were placed at the mouth intact, except that the padlock was not there – a sure sign that someone had entered. But he didn't dare to follow, for he could not imagine what was going on inside. He circled the cellar thinking hard, and suddenly noticed the air vent, a pipe made from used tinplate. He placed his ear to the hole and could clearly catch the flirting and cooing of Old Pao and his mother. He thought of his father, who lived far away in the city of Xi'an and had practically abandoned his children; he thought of the expression on his mother's face every time she discarded his dead brothers and sisters; he thought of the finger-pointing and gossip of the villagers. He felt his heart bleeding with pain and his chest exploding with wrath.

A few nights later, he found his mother and Old Pao in the cellar again. This time he fetched a bundle of hay, lit it with a match and dropped it down the shaft. That was the way the Japs used to flush out villagers hiding in cellars, his grandma had told him when he was still very small.

In a moment the cellar was filled with choking smoke. Old Pao and his mother frantically stamped out the fire and climbed out through the shaft. After that, his mother never again went out at night.

Then Old Pao started to condemn his mother at meetings of various sizes, asserting that she was as lazy as the pampered and spoiled girls from the landlord class, for she would either excuse herself from collective labor or simply loaf away the time. Therefore, at the end of the year, rather than receiving dividends of staple grain and money like other families, his family had to pay cash to buy their grain quota. Working far away in the city of Xi'an, Ma Xi's father seemed to have clean forgotten he had a wife and children, and he seldom sent any money home.

Helplessly, Ma Xi's mother even went down on her knees to beg Old Pao for a credit on the grain. Her children had been without food for days, she told him.

He simply spurned her with his foot, barking, "Don't come to me complaining you've not enough to eat. You shouldn't be so

Members of the "Prairie Fire Combat Unit" said that their team leader had joined the International Red Guards and gone abroad to carry out revolution in Vietnam and Thailand.

lazy!" And stalked away.

Ma Xi wished he could beat up Old Pao, but at that time he was too young to be his match, and could only bury the hatred deep in his heart. As he remembered all that, he felt a fire burning in his chest.

"Down with the capitalist roader Wang Lishan!" he shouted and gave the little blackboard a hard pull.

Old Pao fell headlong onto the ground, and before he could turn over Ma Xi stamped on his back and cursed, "You'll never get a chance to rise again."

It suddenly occurred to someone that Old Pao wasn't moving. "Let him up, or you may kill him," he cried out.

"Kill him? He's just pretending." Ma Xi went over and gave Old Pao a few more kicks. Old Pao remained motionless.

A few people ran forward and helped Old Pao to his feet. They found that he was unconscious. Blood was trickling out of his mouth. Ma Xi grew frightened.

"He's faking! I didn't kick him hard. How could he be so weak?"

"Ma Xi! You Villain!" a voice burst out from the crowd. "How could you treat him so savagely?"

Ma Xi turned around to see the eldest son of Old Pao rushing toward him brandishing a kitchen knife. As he raised his arm to fend off the blade, his little finger was hacked off. Blood squirted out immediately. Erdan and Gouwang gripped Old Pao's son by the waist, and wrested the knife from his hand. Ma Xi's younger brother scooped up a handful of plaster from the wall to cover the bleeding wound. He then looked around for the severed little finger, but couldn't find it anywhere. Someone said he saw Erwang's dog running off with something in its mouth.

The news that the capitalist roader's crazy son had maimed a member of the Red Guards shocked the village, the commune and the whole county, and was splashed in headlines across the provincial newspapers. An incident like that in the early days of the Cultural Revolution was an unpardonable felony, and Old Pao's son was arrested by the security forces that very day.

A few days later, he was tied up like a bundle and taken to the wasteland outside the south gate of the county town and executed by shooting. Old Pao died the very evening his son's corpse was brought back.

A few days later Ma Xi disappeared from the village. Members of the "Prairie Fire Combat Unit" said that their team leader had joined the International Red Guards and gone abroad to carry out revolution in Vietnam and Thailand.

Wu Musan, the Ball-biting Louse

Ball-biting louse is the peasants' curse for a man who always pins the blame on others or slings mud around when he gets cornered – a stinging nuisance like a louse in one's pubic hair. And Wu Musan, who once lived at the southern end of the village, was one of the kind.

When I was young, I often heard the village kids sing a rhyme to ridicule him. It went like this:

> *A louse biting balls*
> *Is Wu Musan.*
> *Bite but don't crush the balls,*
> *Or he's no longer a man.*

I guess it was the adults who actually composed it, and since it was somewhat vulgar for them to say that in public themselves, they egged on the children to spread it around. By the time I joined the other kids in chanting it Wu Musan was already in his 50s. He had a small face, connected by a long, thin neck to a skinny body, but there was a cunning in his eyes, and when he snapped at someone he used to have his head on one side, his neck twisted till the blue veins stood out so that the words seemed to be darting out from his mouth.

In fact there is another story behind this nickname. He was orphaned in infancy and was raised by his grandmother, for his father died before he was born and his mother died soon after. His grandmother carried him in her arms from door to door, begging for milk and for food. Years later when his grandmother died, he took a spade to the family graveyard to dig up the bones of his long-gone grandfather so that the couple could be buried together. Curious to see what a dead man's bones might look like, the village kids tailed him to the grave and flocked around the pit to watch him dig.

"Get lost!" he growled as he dug. "There's nothing to see here."

The kids giggled and backed off a few steps. But as soon as he bent down to dig, they closed in again. He was irritated. As he had just excavated his grandpa's skull, he held it up in both hands and thrust it right into the crotch of one of the nearest boys with a blood-curdling yell, "Bite your balls! Bite your balls!"

The kids scattered horror-stricken, but at the same time spread the belief that his ball-biting habit was inherited from his grandfather and it must have been a trait ingrained in his family line.

When the nationwide Cultural Revolution started in 1966, Wu Musan had no intention at all to "make revolution." His eventual involvement was forced by Ma Xi, the team leader of the "Prairie Fire Combat Unit." Ma was then the man of the hour in the village, always wearing an old army uniform with a red armband around his left sleeve, which had the words "Red Guard" printed in yellow. With a cigarette rolled up from old bits of newspaper between his lips, he led his group in the revolutionary campaign of "destroying the four olds (old ideas, old culture, old customs and old habits) and establishing the four new ones."

One day he led his group to the house of Wu Musan. "Old Biter," he said as a greeting, "it's time to make revolution, to rebel against the old. You are a member of the poor-peasant class. How can you still have that picture of a god hanging up on the wall behind the altar table? Don't you know it's one of the four olds? It must be burned! And the candlestands, the incense burner. They've got to be smashed! And this brick house you're living in. It once belonged to the landlord, Wang the Eighth. Look at those carved-brick animals on the ridges! Day after day, they stare defiantly at the sun. The red sun is our great leader Chairman Mao. How can you allow this? Knock them off!"

No sooner had he finished his lecture than his gang stormed into the room. They shredded the picture of the god, hurled the incense burner to the ground and squashed the candlestands. Ma Xi himself climbed a ladder with a hammer in his hand and smashed the brick animals on the roof ridges with a few determined strokes. The raid was about to blow over when someone found that Wu Musan was clutching the wooden memorial tablet of his grandmother close to his chest. How

Years later when his grandmother died, he took a spade to the family graveyard to dig up the bones of his long-gone grandfather so that the couple could be buried together. Curious to see what a dead man's bones might look like, the village kids tailed him to the grave and flocked around the pit to watch him dig.

could he do that? Revolution must be thorough! The tablet must be destroyed!

"Fuck your mother!" Wu snarled in defense. "You can't pick me out to make revolution. What about Ma Bing, Old Qiu, Hongshui and Ma Mingyi? They all have this kind of old things at their places. Why don't you go there to destroy the old things?"

"Fuck!" Ma Xi said. "It's only a matter of time. But first of all, we must destroy that thing in your arms. You are a member of the poor-peasant class. You should take the lead in destroying the four olds."

"No way!" Wu retorted. "You destroy theirs and then I'll destroy mine."

"Done," Ma Xi said. "You motherfucker, that's a piece of cake!" Having said that, he turned around and led his gang to the other households to destroy the four olds.

Wu followed, and when Ma Xi had the other households' old things destroyed, he had no choice but to throw his grandma's memorial tablet into a bonfire. However, he felt himself unfairly treated. So to make every family in the village suffer what he had, he decided to join Ma Xi's combat unit in door-to-door searches of old things to destroy.

One evening, the production team's meeting room was ablaze with lights. Ma Xi was conducting a criticism meeting to denounce their former production team leader Old Pao when someone accused Old Pao of making use of his position to steal grain from the production team. He not only satisfied the needs of his own family, but also dished out some to Old Biter's grandma.

"Fuck your mother!" Wu jumped up in anger. "My grandma is not the only one he gave grain to. I heard my grandma say Goudan's mother, Ma Erwang's mother and Ma Xi's mother also received favors from him!"

The heat of his indignant criticism was still seething within Ma Xi when he heard this. He leaped up in a rage and slapped Wu several times across the face. "Fuck your mother, Old Biter!" he roared. "How dare you bite *me*! When, if ever, did Old Pao give my mother favors?"

"Fuck!" Wu cursed, holding his stinging face. "How dare you slap me? He did! He did! If you don't believe me, just ask *him*!"

Ma Xi turned to Old Pao. "Did you?" he asked.

His face expressionless, Old Pao made no reply. Just at that moment Goudan, Ma Erwang and their brothers dashed onto the stage in a cacophony of curses and laid into Wu Musan with fists and kicks. For a long time he lay sprawled on the floor unable to get up, while Old Pao was pushed aside, completely forgotten.

Wu Musan's ball-biting habit actually ended up costing him his life. It was the autumn of 1968. Someone had put up a big character poster accusing him of cuddling Simple Jun in the cornfield. Well, that was no doubt sexual harassment, and Ma Xi was quick to take the law into his own hands. At his order, Wu was brought to the threshing ground to be interrogated.

"You know she's retarded," Ma Xi said. "How could you think of taking advantage of a half-wit? You are a shameless old bachelor!"

"I'm not the only one." Wu retorted.

"What do you mean? Who else?" Ma Xi pursued.

"Wang Chongshui, for a start."

"You saw it?"

"I caught wind of it."

Wang Chongshui was an ex-PLA soldier who had lost two fingers in the Korean War. As he was of good class origin, a war hero, and had a fiery temper, the villagers usually refrained from provoking him.

That accusation surprised Ma Xi and his gang, for they had no way of telling whether it was true or false or whether it was a wise thing to confront Wang with it. While the assemblage was thus engaged in whispers and speculations, someone shouted, "Old Biter, run! Wang Chongshui is coming for you with a shotgun!"

The crowd swirled around and saw Wang stalking over with a rabbit gun, his eyes glaring like fire.

Wu took to his heels and Wang, with his gun, chased after him. The whole village turned out to watch.

"Come on," someone tried to dissuade Wang. "You know what kind of person he is. Just a mad dog who likes to bite people."

"He can bite anyone he likes, but he's not going to bite *me*! I'm a veteran revolutionary. How could he accuse me of embracing Guo Jun? I'm going to kill him if it's the last thing I do!"

Since many of them had been bitten by Old Biter, there were plenty of people ready to let Wang know where he had hidden himself, and before long, someone pointed out to Wang that Wu was hiding in the crown of the ancient pagoda tree. The tree must have been centuries old, for its trunk was so thick that four adults with extended arms could hardly encircle it. Since it was popularly believed that the tree had divine powers, Old Biter must have thought that Wang, however fearless he might be, would not dare to fire at this sacred tree.

Wang circled the tree several times with his gun, but the dense branches and leaves blocked his view. It was not known whether he panicked or was simply awed by the tree, but people saw him close his eyes tightly, raise his gun and fire.

In response to the crack of the gun, something heavy fell from the tree. It was Old Biter. "What a sharpshooter!" people exclaimed admiringly. No wonder he had gained such honors in the Korean War, or how could he have hit the target without even looking? However, it was found afterward that there was not even a single bullet wound in Wu's body. He must have been too scared to keep his hold.

Ball-biting Louse lingered for several days in a coma before he died.

Wang Gubo

Wang Gubo's family was extremely poor before liberation, for they had neither shelter nor land. It was liberation that completely changed their fates, when they were allocated farmland and houses, but Wang Gubo stubbornly refused to take up any post in the village leadership.

I heard village elders say that in the land reform movement no matter how the government work group tried to persuade him, he just declined to accept a position. He argued, "I grew up in poverty. I can't read and I can't make a good speech. How can I lead others? I'm happy enough with a house to live in and a piece of land to farm."

However, some others, who were not as poor as he had been and lacking in seniority, were happy to accept leading posts, and one of them was later promoted beyond the village level to become a high ranking official, but Wang Gubo remained an ordinary peasant all his life.

Wielding his poor-peasant family origin, Wang Gubo was "an awkward customer." He came straight out with whatever he wanted to say. While most of his fellow-villagers dared not contradict the village leaders or members of the government work group, he had no fear. People agreed that poverty had puffed up his pride, for it seemed true to say, "the poorer, the more contrary."

Take the land reform for instance. The work group said that the property of the landlords and rich peasants should be completely confiscated and given to the poor, but Wang Gubo said that if they were stripped of everything, they would become the poor, and wouldn't they bring in a new land reform movement in the future? It was further rumored that he had even covertly given grain out of his own share to the former landlord Wang the Fourth, who had been denounced and stripped of all his possessions.

When setting up the collective kitchen the village work group proclaimed that the collective kitchen was "paradise." Sitting on a clod of earth, Wang Gubo tapped his porridge bowl with his chopsticks and said, "If the collective kitchen *is* paradise, how come there's so much water in the rice I can see my face in it?" Some people claimed they saw him steal the production team's corn and sweet potatoes in the night.

When the government work group came to his village at the beginning of the Four Clean-ups campaign, he was heard to say, "If water gets too clean, there'll be no more fish and turtles in it, and now you want *four* cleans!" Some members of the work group and village leaders thought of teaching him a lesson, but the idea was immediately opposed by others, because Chairman

Mao had said, "Without the poor peasants there would be no revolution. To attack them is to attack the revolution." Since he was a poor peasant, how dare they attack him? Better forget it. So in the decade or so after liberation and through the successive mass movements and political campaigns no one dared to lay a finger on him. Not until 1966, when the Cultural Revolution started.

At first he was as awkward as ever. Then one day a group of Red Guards arrived in the village to "destroy the four olds and set up the four new ones." They barged into people's houses, and burned the ancestral memorial tablets; they climbed up onto roofs to knock off the brick animals; they even wrenched off the brand tag from the *Forever* bicycles, accusing it of symbolizing an evil spirit biting into the red star – if you looked at it upside down. Such craziness enraged Wang Gubo.

"You little brats!" he cursed them when the Red Guards came to his place to destroy his ancestors' memorial tablets. "Without ancestors where did you come from? Did you just spring out of a crack in the earth?"

That was no less than courting disaster, and attracted to the village the joint forces of two Red Guard organizations – the "February Seventh" and "Rebels Headquarters" – of Number One High School from the county town. A Red Guard leader jumped onto Wang Gubo's altar table and shouted, "Wang Gubo is a secret counter-revolutionary with a long history of sabotage! He sympathized with the landlords and rich peasants in the land reform movement, he brazenly attacked the 'Three

Red Flags' in the Great Leap Forward movement, and he tried to undermine the Four Clean-ups campaign. The Communist Party and government have offered him many opportunities to serve the Party and people, but owing to his reactionary standpoint and his long-time anti-Party, anti-socialist political stance he simply refused. And now he openly and viciously curses the Red Guards, and tries to sabotage the Great Proletarian Cultural Revolution. We must criticize and denounce him till he's beaten flat and never, never be able to rise again!"

So saying, he jumped down from the table and pounced on Wang Gubo with a shower of blows and kicks. The other Red Guards joined in the beating, and in less time than it takes to smoke a pipe he was beaten black and blue, his face covered with blood and his hair all messed up like a chicken's nest. For a long time he was too dazed to speak. Finally he was taken away by the Red Guards.

Wang Gubo's arrest evoked sharply different reactions among the villagers. Some were glad; some were sad.

"He has been bullying us for too many years. See if he can still do that," said those who were glad.

"No wonder he was against the Party in every movement," said others. "So he was a counter-revolutionary all that time!"

The most worried person was his wife. She called together their four sons, and asked, "What can we do about your father, boys?"

Her sons were young and hot-blooded, for they had their father's "awkwardness" running in their veins too.

"Screw them!" said the eldest son. "It seems we have no choice but to make revolution too. Chairman Mao says, 'Either the East Wind prevails over the West Wind or the West Wind prevails over the East Wind.'"

"He who is not afraid of death by a thousand cuts swears to bring Father home," said the second son.

"Perhaps we can organize a Red Guard combat unit or combat corps ourselves," said the third son after some thought. "In that way we'll be comrades-in-arms with those Red Guards in the county town. And since we are fighting in the same trench they'll have no reason to hold our dad in custody."

"Will that work?" said the fourth son hesitantly.

Unexpectedly their mother clapped her hands sharply. "That's a great idea," she exclaimed. "Let's do it."

So very soon the four sons set up a revolutionary organization called the "Jinggang Mountain Combat Corps" and persuaded some other young guys in the village to join them. Then they went to the county town, and after talks with the Red Guards of Number One High, they successfully brought their father home.

Wang Gubo seemed to have completely changed when he returned to the village. His pride and arrogance had gone, and he became taciturn, saying very little when meeting people and shying away from expressing his own opinions. Although many things happened in the village during the remaining years of the Cultural Revolution, there was hardly a word of comment from him. It could be said that the pounding waves of the Cultural Revolution made him a completely different person.

On the other hand, his sons grew more radical with their "combat" experience. In the course of time they succeeded in uniting most of the rural Red Guard groups in the county into an umbrella organization called "The Peasants' Rebellion General Headquarters (PRGH)," his eldest son the commander-in-chief. The PRGH mobilized the country youth to go to the county town to criticize and denounce the capitalist roaders, and even took over the county government. For a period of time their posters and slogans filled the streets of the town. One day they might read, "Deep fry so and so!" Another day they would say, "Chop so and so to pieces!" Later on, when the Red Guards united to set up the county's "Revolutionary Committee," his eldest son was elected a deputy director.

Deputy Director Wang often returned to the village in a faded green army uniform with a Mauser pistol at his waist and a cigarette between his lips. He spoke as brashly as his father used to speak.

"Who's that guy who passed by our gate just now?" an old woman asked her grandson. "Is he that Liu who was an interpreter for the Japs? Has he come back again?"

Those who heard her laughed up their sleeves.

Although his eldest son had attained such an admirable position, he was still unmarried at the age of nearly 40. His parents went all out to get matchmakers to find him a wife.

One day Wang Gubo heard about a young woman in a village not very far from theirs. She was pretty and yet unmarried though approaching 30, because, besides being picky, she was the daughter of the second wife of a former landlord, certainly not considered of a good family origin. That very night he made a secret trip to the village with a bag of roast peanuts. There he located the family, and paid the landlord's second wife a visit.

"You should be aware," the mother said after learning the purpose of his visit, "that your family enjoys a good class status while mine has a bad status. Wouldn't it be wise to avoid any contact with us?"

"What's class status? It was stuck on us by outsiders. Our ancestors didn't know what class status was, but didn't they marry and raise children? We peasants care no more than our daily lives."

"Your son is a member of the revolutionary ranks and a high official," the young woman said. "I'm a descendant of the five bad elements. Aren't you afraid we may drag your son down?"

"High official!" Wang Gubo hooted. "If I had wanted to, I'd have been an even higher official long ago. The purpose of life is not to climb the official ladder, but to live a normal life – get a wife and beget babies."

So, at his father's insistence, the deputy director of the county revolutionary committee from the poor-peasant class married the daughter of a former landlord.

The news shot round the county like wildfire. And Deputy Director Wang's opposition faction was quick to take the opportunity to hand in a report to the higher authorities, asserting that Wang's father was not a poor peasant but a long-term counter-revolutionary who had kept up an adulterous relationship with the landlord's second wife even before liberation. The fact that Deputy Director Wang had swerved from his class alignment by marrying a woman from the landlord class could only prove that he had completely lost the class stand of a revolutionary proletarian official. Subsequently, Wang was dismissed from his post and driven out of the revolutionary ranks, to become an ordinary peasant again.

In the last phase of the Cultural Revolution, the tide of revolution gradually ebbed. Wang Gubo had grown hoary and old by this time. He became even more taciturn and seldom joined others in chatting, but there still seemed to be a pronounced trace of reactionary zeal running in his blood.

When the "Learning from Dazhai" and "annihilating the remaining tail of capitalism" movements were in full swing and the commune members were challenging heaven and earth to reap bumper harvests, he declined from collective labor on the excuse that he was old and feeble, but would rather go out with a basket on his back to cut fresh grass. He was often seen sitting in the shade of trees at the edge of the village proper and gazing nonchalantly at the crawling ants. But pretty soon some people noticed that he was actually "restoring capitalism" – he was covertly selling peanuts!

Nobody knew where he got the peanuts. His method of roasting them was to heat up an iron wok half-filled with sand, and then mix the peanuts in the hot sand and stir fry them till the shells turned golden brown. Peanuts roasted this way are crisp and tasty.

To prevent the village leaders from discovering his secret, he would hide the roast peanuts in his basket beneath the fresh grass and watch the passers-by closely, trying to sniff out potential buyers.

He never used a steelyard to weigh the peanuts but would use an old enamel mug as a measuring cup. Five cents for a mugful. When he found a customer, he would first look around to ensure there wasn't anyone watching before he took the money and measured out the peanuts with the mug. But when he sensed the approaching person was somewhat suspicious or was a team leader, he would cover up the peanuts with the grass.

In case of being discovered and having his peanuts confiscated, he would only keep a small portion of the peanuts in the basket while hiding the major part of his stock in a cloth bag in the crack of a wall somewhere nearby and cover the crack with straw. Later on, someone must have discovered his little secret and taken away his bag from the crack. That made him furious.

"You little brat!" people heard him holler in the streets. "If you eat *the thing* you've stolen it will eat away at your bowels and kill you."

"Who stole what from you?" some asked with a twinkle in their eyes.

"Don't ask if you don't know," he answered roughly. He must have felt like a dumb man who had taken some bitter herbs – there was no way to tell others of his bitterness.

Nobody in the village could tell for certain how many years he was engaged in that peanut business, how much he earned, or how he spent his earnings.

When I came home for the Spring Festival many years afterward, I accidentally brought up the topic, and asked my mother about Wang Gubo.

"He died last year," she said with a sigh. "No one knew the exact date, for his family had him secretly buried. As you know, nowadays the government is advocating cremation instead of burial. His family didn't want him burned up, so they buried him in the dead of night. No one knows where."

Gangquan's Ma

Ever since she gave birth to her son Gangquan she became known as Gangquan's Ma, her real name virtually forgotten. And yet, that didn't prevent her from being a well-known figure in the village.

She was of medium height with matronly looks and was rather careless about her wear. In summer she went around almost naked, except for a pair of shorts and a pair of wooden slippers. She used to carry a worn palm-leaf fan with her and her flabby flesh quivered in rhythm with her gait and fanning. Her neck had barrel rings and her cheeks were muscular, the making of a loud, thick throat. She talked fast, and when she talked her voice, punctuated with laughter and obscenities, could be heard halfway down the street.

Although she was a crude person, she liked to pose as an educated one. In fact her education was limited to two trips to the night school during the rural anti-illiteracy campaign of the 1950s. On the third day people saw her sitting on the granite stone block at her gate reading out a newspaper in all seriousness, and her voice would grow louder as people approached. School over, pupils on their way home were surprised to see her reading. They swarmed around her and found that she was holding the newspaper upside down. When a loose-tongued kid tactlessly pointed that out, she retorted, "Bullshit! I've turned it over for *you* to read!"

She also loved to sing the numbered musical notation of a song, but she could manage only "1, 2 and 5." With these three notes, however, she was able to hum the complete tune of *The East Is Red* and *Sailing the Seas Depends on the Helmsman*. She could also sing a nursery rhyme, which goes like this:

> *Seven Door Burg,*
> *Eight Cao Ville,*
> *Ride on Square Head to He Ville.*
> *East Woods Zhao,*
> *West Woods Zhao,*
> *Between lies Temple to River Ji.*
> *Ji-a-Ji,*
> *Pee-a-pee,*
> *the piss flows down to Bull Woods Zhao.*
> ...

It was many years later when it finally dawned on me that the lyrics were composed of the village names within the vicinity of a dozen miles of my home. The song was to help children remember the place names.

She was daring, carefree, and even "shameless," as you may put it. Once, her son was engaged in a fight with Fatty Liu, a neighbor's son, when the latter cursed, "Fuck your mother!"

Hearing this, she undid her belt and ran over. She caught hold of Fatty's head and pushed it into her crotch while bellowing, "You fuck me? Try it! See if you don't get drowned in the hole."

The boy was scared shitless.

On another occasion, the production team members were digging up land after the autumn harvest. One of her cousins stood pissing with his back toward the team. Holding his penis, he called out, "Third Sister, come quick and see what I've got here."

She went over with a smile on her face and a spade in her hand, and gleefully announced that she'd like to cut off that thing to have a better look at it. Her cousin ran as fast as his legs could carry him as she chased him with the spade. The other team members hopped in delight and whooped in encouragement.

As to farm work, she was physically stronger and tougher than quite a number of men. In winter she didn't hesitate to jump barefoot into the chilly river to dig up the silt. In spring she was not afraid to descend into the depth of the earth to sink a well. In summer she worked on the threshing ground naked to the waist and pulled the heavy stone roller like a draft animal to husk the wheat. In autumn she was a good hand at plowing the land, carrying manure and steering the drill barrow.

Once in the Great Leap Forward movement in 1958, Old Jin, the leader of the work group from the county government, organized a cart-pulling contest. Xinmin, a member of the Fifth Production Team, stripped to the waist, drew a red sun on his belly, suspended a large firecracker on each ear, grabbed the shafts in his hands and pulled the cart along the street like running. Just as he was thinking no one could challenge him, he saw Gangquan's Ma coming head-on toward him. She was also pulling a cart, half naked, with a winged steed painted on her belly, two red silk ribbons floating from her ears, and, most eye-catching of all, two big red flowers hanging from the nipples of her balloon-sized boobs. With her hands holding the shafts, she sang as she pulled:

> *Socialism is like a giant cart;*
> *I pull it faster than a horse with wings.*
> *In one day I can run a thousand miles*
> *And reach the Lord's palace in a wink.*
> *The Lord greets me with big smiles,*
> *And says he'd like to come to pull the cart.*

Old Jin decided to award her the championship, for Chairman Mao had said women can hold up half the sky, and besides pulling the cart, drawing the winged steed and making red flowers, the most impressive thing was that she sang the praises of socialism.

During the Cultural Revolution Ma Xi, the team leader of the "Prairie Fire Combat Unit," came up with the idea of holding a contest to see who could recite the most quotations from

Chairman Mao. Since many commune members were illiterate, they couldn't even read, not to mention recite, the quotations. But Gangquan's Ma walked up to Ma Xi and declared that she only needed him to read a quotation out once and she would be able to remember it forever, because what Chairman Mao said was what she had felt all along in her heart. She was from a poor-peasant family and had a deep class feeling for Chairman Mao.

"Really?" Ma Xi asked in disbelief, and she made an affirmative reply.

"Chairman Mao teaches us," Ma Xi intoned, "Policy and tactics are the life of the Party."

"Chairman Mao teaches us," she echoed, "Please eat and taste it are for life and party."

The audience erupted in laughter.

"You've got it wrong," Ma Xi said.

"How could I get it wrong? Chairman Mao has put it wonderfully."

It was only after Ma Xi explained the meaning of the sentence that she admitted she was mistaken. But she was undaunted. "That one is a bit too long," she conceded. "Read me a shorter one and I'll get it correctly."

"Chairman Mao teaches us," Ma Xi said, "Serve the people."

"Chairman Mao teaches us," she repeated, "Serve Di potato."

"Chairman Mao is really great," she wondered aloud, "or how could he even know the Old Monk in our village had a little boy named Di? And he reminds us to feed Di in case the boy goes hungry. Chairman Mao really lives heart to heart with us poor and lower-middle peasants."

The commune members split their sides laughing, but with a proud look of victory on her face she stood unaffected.

Ma Xi's countenance suddenly darkened. He accused her of viciously altering Chairman Mao's quotations and was therefore an active counter-revolutionary. She must be severely criticized to eliminate her pernicious influence. So a recitation contest turned into a criticism meeting.

The criticism had hardly begun when she said she needed to relieve herself. Ma Xi refused her plea, saying she was looking for an excuse to avoid criticism.

She looked Ma Xi straight in the eye and suddenly pulled down her pants, revealing a huge white bottom. As she squatted down to urinate, the embarrassed gathering dispersed in all directions, including Ma Xi himself, who ran with his hands over his eyes and cursed her as a "shameless bitch!"

"However revolutionary you are, you can't stop people from pissing, can you?" she said as she did so.

From then on, whenever Ma Xi started to criticize her, she would either say she needed to pee or poo, and that frustrated all Ma Xi's efforts right to the end of the Cultural Revolution.

When I went home last year, my mother told me that Gangquan's Ma had passed away at the age of 103.

Gouwang, the Scoundrel

"Gouwang ... Gouwang ..."

A bright moon was shedding her soft light on the vast rural land that had just quieted down from the din of the day. The shouts, however, rolled like thunder from the north to the east, then to the south of the village.

The shouts came from Gouwang's father, a man in his 50s, tall and lean. At that moment he was shuffling onward with his hands behind his bent back. When the thunder rolled to the western side, a dark figure rose from behind a waist-high rammed-earth wall and bellowed out in a deep voice, "What for?"

"To get you killed!" the father snarled back and turned away without taking a second glance.

The figure emerged from behind the wall and followed. It was Gouwang, a notorious scoundrel in the village. He was a wild one, the ringleader of a gang of young hooligans who roamed the village from day to day like ghosts.

If someone tried to talk some sense into him, he would glare and rave, "Don't you discipline me! Go home and discipline your pigs. Be careful. They may escape from their sty tonight and gobble up the production team's sweet potatoes. Then your team leader Old Pao will have you criticized at a public meeting." And sure enough, the gate of the sty was thrown open in the night and the pigs swarmed out to wreak havoc in the village.

Gouwang had a bed-wetting problem, which he carried into his teens. Though exasperated, his mother could find no cure. One day when he was already 16, he wet the bed again. Worse still, it happened to be the rainy season. His mother raised the wet mattress with a pole and ordered him to hold it above his head to dry. Instead of taking the mattress from his mother, he grabbed a shoulder-pole and assumed a combat-ready squat.

"Come on, come on!" he threatened. "No more bullying me! You can dry it on *your* head."

In that way he vexed his mother to death. He didn't even shed a tear at her funeral, and it was only when several young men, offended by his unfilial insolence, threw him down and gave him a good beating that he whimpered, "Ma … Ma…."

For some time, gambling was rife in the village, and Gouwang was a regular at the gambling house. On the eve of one Spring Festival he lost again at the table. Infuriated and distressed, he slunk out and went straight to the commune police station. The police descended on the den and apprehended the gamblers.

Afraid that others might suspect he was the informer, he used his slyness to call together his gang to sing the theme song of the movie *The Handcuffed Passenger* as a send-off for the captives as they were led away from the village.

> *Our comrades-in-arms*
> *forward march.*
> *We in silence shed hot tears....*

The policemen stared severely at the gang, all of whom but Gouwang lapsed into silence. Gouwang alone was not intimidated.

"Don't stare at me like that!" he shouted. "I didn't gamble; I didn't break the law. What's wrong with singing a pop song?"

He turned around and called on his cronies to sing again:

> *Our comrades-in-arms*
> *forward march.*
> *We in silence shed hot tears....*

Well, the villagers sighed, if even the police couldn't handle that hooligan, who else could do it?

As soon as the police were out of sight, Gouwang clapped his buttocks in delight and cheered. "They've taken the top hands away. Now it's our turn." He and his pals returned to the gambling table.

But the police didn't go far away. In no time at all three plainclothes cops caught Gouwang. They ordered him to put his arms around a wire pole outside the production brigade office and handcuffed him there.

"Enjoy yourself here," one of them said. "If you feel like singing, go ahead. The day after tomorrow is the Spring Festival.

The warm breeze of reform and opening-up gradually spread from the coastal regions to central China. When most peasants were still tied to the earth cultivating the land Gouwang had packed up two boxes of yams and gone to Guangzhou, where he started to peddle his yams at a free market.

You can sing some pop songs to entertain your fellow-villagers." With that, they left the village, and left Gouwang in utter despair.

The warm breeze of reform and opening-up gradually spread from the coastal regions to central China. When most peasants were still tied to the earth cultivating the land Gouwang had packed up two boxes of yams and gone to Guangzhou, where he started to peddle his yams at a free market. There he waited from early morning till the sun was declining in the west, when finally a man walked by and stopped at his stall.

"Where do these come from?" he asked, pointing at the yams.

"Wen County in Henan Province. These are the famous 'iron-rod' yams of Huaiqingfu."

"Wen County?"

"Sure. It's the hometown of Sima Yi, the famous general of the Three Kingdoms. These are genuine 'iron-rod' yams. They cost a fortune in Hong Kong. Even Chairman Mao knows that. In 1963 when he received the first secretary of my county Party committee, he greeted him with, 'You're from Sima Yi's hometown.' I'm also from Sima Yi's hometown. If you don't believe me, look at this certificate."

The man glanced at the paper and bought the two boxes of yam without haggling about the price. In the twinkling of an eye, Gouwang made a net profit of more than 300 *yuan*.

"What an idiot!" he crowed. "'Iron-rod' yams? From their original production place? He might wear a tie and glasses but the fool didn't know that they came from Zhengding County, Hebei Province."

Now with money in his pocket, he bought a roast chicken and a bottle of liquor. Then he sat on a curb to eat and drink. When he'd finished he wiped his mouth with the back of his hand, dusted the seat of his pants as he stood up and belched loudly.

October in Guangzhou is a pleasant month. Gouwang strolled down a wide street flanked by skyscrapers. Cars flowed like water in a river; people bustled around in crowds. Fuck it, he thought. Guangzhou is much better than my hometown. Ma the Eighth said he felt dizzy just gazing at the three-story buildings in the county town. Dizzy? If he should come here and look at these skyscrapers, he would fall down in a faint.

As the evening progressed Gouwang started to feel a bit tired. Quite by chance, his eyes fell on a bikinied woman on a poster beside the cinema gate. The blood rushed to his head and reminded him that Guangzhou is an open city. What are the girls like in an open city? He had heard that you can go to bed with them as long as you have the money.

Once the thought occupied his mind, it wouldn't go away. To make himself look decent he spent 36 *yuan* on a suit and 50 *fen* on a necktie. Thus spruced up he entered a hotel.

"How many of you, sir?" the receptionist asked.

"Only myself. What are the rates for one night?"

"80 *yuan* for a single room."

"Single room then."

A twenty-something smiling girl led him up the second floor to a room and closed the door. She helped him take off his suit and filled the bathtub. He was going to slip out of his clothes but was embarrassed to find the girl standing right in front of him with no intention of leaving, and, without warning, she reached for his arm to help him remove his shirt. He cringed, but suddenly remembered why he was here in the first place. Fuck! I've paid for this service! he thought.

The thought calmed him and he stripped to his underpants. However, try as he might he couldn't undo the knot of his tie.

"I'll have to take it into the bath with me," he muttered helplessly.

"Isn't that weird?" the girl's voice sounded like she was singing.

"No problem," he said as he picked up his lighter. There was a pungent whiff, and the necktie came off with a tug.

"Damn it," he said as he threw the tie onto the floor. "I'll buy a better one tomorrow."

He went into the bathroom and found the water at a comfortable temperature. He couldn't switch his mind away from the girl. She's a real beauty, much more beautiful than Wang Mutou's daughter Suzhen, no matter how highly her mother had been boasting about her looks in the village. If she should come to Guangzhou, she'd be nothing but a pile of shit in comparison. Will the girl slink away while I'm in the bath? What if she's gone? His mind was tangled up. He quickly finished his bath, and came out of the bathroom.

Oh, heavens! His excitement almost escaped from his lips. The girl was sitting on the bed wearing only a bikini and smiling at him. She was more lovely and vivid than the one on the movie poster. The look in his eyes turned from amazement to greed, like the two greenish beams of a hungry wolf at night. He pounced and embraced the girl.

When he woke up in the morning, the girl was already gone. He searched the pockets of his pants. A chill swept through his body when he found his money was all gone. Cleaned out to the last cent. Damn it! He had been swindled.

He demanded to see the manager, who turned out to be none other than the yam buyer of the previous day.

"All the attendants at my hotel are men," the manager said gravely after hearing his complaint. "We don't have any girls or women working here. You must have summoned a call girl last night."

If it were not for the fact that he'd seen him selling yams, the manager added, and knew that he wasn't a vagrant, he would have him handed over to the police.

Gouwang fled from the hotel at the first opportunity. Fuck! The Cantonese are devils, he told himself. They swallow you whole and spit out the bones. There's no denying I cheated him yesterday, but I did give him two boxes of yam. Now he gets his revenge but won't leave me a cent!

Penniless, he returned home by stealing rides on cargo trains.

Niu Xiaofang, the Pig Castrator

Niu Xiaofang was from a village called Niugou. He was about five feet seven and well-built. The smallpox he suffered in childhood left his face pockmarked, and it glistens hideously in the sunlight. But more frightening than his face was his occupation – castrating pigs, a skill which was handed down in the family from generation to generation and which he started to practice at age 14. He has castrated so many pigs in his life that he's lost count of the number.

In the old days he used to go around on a shabby bicycle. A few strips of red cloth flew from a flagpole made out of a length of iron wire fixed to the handlebars of his bike. That was the signboard of the pig castrator. He always carried a greasy leather case at his waist. Pull open the lid and you could see a set of shiny knives. Children usually winced at the mere sight of the tools.

It was at my second aunt's place that I watched him castrate a pig firsthand. She had bought a piglet, a lively little thing that kept skipping around the courtyard. But two months of diligent feeding only added a dozen pounds to its weight. So one day my aunt called in Niu Xiaofang.

He stood his bicycle in the yard and pointed at the piglet, "Is it this one?"

My aunt nodded. Unbelievably, as soon as the piglet saw him, it crouched on the ground shivering, while on normal days it was so wildly naughty that two or even three young men could hardly catch it. That seems to prove the old saying "Everything has its conqueror." Of course, another explanation could be that since he had castrated so many pigs, the other pigs could catch the smell from him. Not only was this an instinctive awareness of the pigs but of the dogs as well. No matter how ferocious a dog was, it never dared to bark or snap at him, but would slide away with its tail between its legs.

He stared silently at the piglet and moved slowly forward. At about two yards away he suddenly stamped his foot and shouted, "Come over here!" Before the sound had died down he had already caught the pig in his hand, and despite its screaming he had turned it belly-up on the ground, put one foot on its neck and the other on its hind legs. He nimbly plucked off a few handfuls of fluffy hair from its belly, took up a knife, wiped the blade on the side of his shoe, and quickly sliced an inch-long cut on the pig's abdomen. With a squeeze a soft lump of something was pressed out and with a swing of the knife the lumpy mass was severed. He then scooped up a handful of earth and plastered it over the wound. The whole process took less than a minute.

In that way he made a living. Year in year out he went from

village to village, and was a familiar figure in the neighborhood. Though it was only 20 *fen* for castrating a pig, considering the prices at that time his annual income could be considerable. But for some reason he wasn't able to find himself a wife even when he turned 50.

One day, however, a piece of news exploded among those gathered for lunch under the big pagoda tree – Niu Xiaofang spayed Widow Liu of the neighboring village.

Widow Liu was in her 30s. Her husband had died in a coal mine cave-in, leaving behind a daughter, Xiaocui, who was then eight years old. Since the widow wasn't able to do heavy work in the fields, she made ends meet by raising three or four pigs every year. She was much obliged to Niu because he always refused to accept the castration fees. So instead of paying, she sometimes cooked him a meal or made him a pair of shoes. And understandably, affection sprang up in the course of time. She wanted to marry him, but her husband's brothers firmly opposed the idea because they thought Niu was a violent man and was prone to abuse Xiaocui.

Unable to marry, they made love in the cornfields, among the wild bushes, or behind the wheat-straw stacks. As contraceptives were not easily available in the countryside they had to be careful not to get pregnant, and thus every time they had to stop short of reaching orgasm.

It occurred to Niu one day that he could make use of his skills to have her spayed. But the bloody sight of the screaming pig was too scary for her.

One day, however, a piece of news exploded among those gathered for lunch under the big pagoda tree – Niu Xiaofang spayed Widow Liu of the neighboring village.

A few days later, however, emboldened by a pounding urge she asked tentatively, "Do you really think it's safe?"

"Why not? Humans and pigs are the same. Just look at the pigs I neutered. Do you find any of them still able to conceive?"

"Would it be painful?"

"'A sharp blade doesn't make a painful cut.' Besides, my hands are swift. It'll be over before you feel anything."

She smiled, and agreed to give it a try.

So one day after a careful bath, she lay on the bed ready for the operation.

Watching her naked body, he suddenly realized she was quite different from the hairy pigs which he used to hold down with one hand and stamp beneath his feet. His hands stroked her soft white belly, trying to locate the exact position. The caressing was tickling and made her giggle.

"Hold it," he said. "Your belly quivers when you laugh, and I won't be able to determine the spot."

Both seriously and teasingly, his hands brushed over her belly up and down, left and right. She was almost aroused when he said he had pinpointed the exact place.

He selected a knife, heated it over the flames of an oil lamp as a way of sterilization, and with a flip of his wrist, the belly responded with a shudder and blood spurted into the air. With a piercing scream she rolled back and forth on the bed in pain. After all, a human being is not a pig, least of all an innocent piglet.

He was appalled. He threw down the knife and grabbed some

cotton to press down on the cut. Neighbors, alarmed and invited by the screaming, lifted her onto a bamboo cot and rushed her to the hospital. Luckily, it was no more than a shallow cut and far from life threatening. The doctor stitched up the wound.

Alerted by the incident, her brothers-in-law agreed to their marriage – on the condition that the bride groom must marry into the Liu family and never abuse her daughter, a condition he happily accepted.

Twenty years had slipped past since then, and their life had been mostly peaceful and stable. The only pity is that they were unable to beget a child. Behind their backs people said it was probably because he had done too much evil by castrating and spaying pigs. Since he deprived them of their reproductive ability, Heaven must have decided to deprive him of having offspring.

During the years, their daughter, Xiaocui, had blossomed into an attractive young woman, a flame in the eyes of many a young men in the village, but she seemed uninterested in their attentions. Finally, as she was going on 30, she fell in love with a young pig raiser in a village to the west. Her mother agreed to their engagement on one condition, that is, instead of marrying her daughter off, the young man must marry into the Liu family, just like the condition once set for her stepfather.

On the day of the wedding, the bridegroom had just set foot in the door when his brothers steered a herd of pigs into the bride's family pigsty. Niu's eyes shone when he saw the piglets. He would have liked to take up his tools to do his old job, but he was too old even to climb over the low wall of the sty, not to say catch the pigs. As he leaned on the wall and watched, the pigs must have thought he was going to feed them. They looked at him fearlessly, their snouts raised in expectation. In their eyes, Niu Xiaofang was no longer the castrator of twenty years previously.

Guo Jun

In my childhood Guo Jun was a well-known figure in the village, and there was not a child who was not afraid of her. It was not because she was insane and dumb, or because she was dressed in rags and appallingly filthy, but because her hearing was incredibly sharp and she ran terribly fast. If a kid dared say "Insane Jun is coming" within earshot of her she would hurtle across and clutch the child in her arms in fits of giggles. Rather than beating or cursing, she kept implanting fervent kisses on the child's cheeks and wouldn't release her hold until the petrified child begged grannie or auntie's pardon and promised never to call her "Insane" again. So kids would flee pell-mell as soon as they saw her coming.

   My first close contact with her was on a very cold winter's day when I was going to Grandma's place with my mother. The snow on the ground had not completely melted away, and the wheat had not yet turned green. There were few travelers on the road, and the fields were void of activity. We were about to cross the bridge on the periphery of our village when someone in a tattered padded-coat and a thin pair of pants sprang out from under the arch. Her face was covered with grime. She walked barefoot and had in her arms a bundle of firewood, which she had probably collected from the frozen riverbed. She broke into a silly smile when she saw us.

"Second Sister," she greeted my mother loudly, "going to visit your ma?"

So it was Guo Jun.

"Yes," my mother smiled back. "Jun, it's cold out here. Hurry home."

"I'm not cold. I've collected some firewood for Old J, to swap it for some soybeans." She shuffled away with her armful of sticks.

The first couple of sentences of a lunatic may seem rather normal. And yet, her last sentence baffled me.

"Who's Old J?" I asked. "Which village does he live in? Why's she going to swap firewood for soybeans for him?"

"Old J was the leader of the government work group. He came to our village in 1959, but after so many years no one has any idea where he is now. Poor Jun, her mind is confused." Mother seemed lost in thought.

"Her insanity was actually caused by that Old J," she continued after a deep sigh. "It's a wonder she still keeps him in her heart though her mind is flaky. See what evil a man can do!"

Mother then told me her story.

Guo Jun was quite pretty when she was young. In fact, she was not a local but was married into our village to a poor orphan. In

In my childhood Guo Jun was a well-known figure in the village, and there was not a child who was not afraid of her.

the land reform movement they were allocated land and a house, and thereafter they lived much better. She gave birth to four children, but just as everything was going on well her husband died. With no relatives to fall back on you can imagine how hard life could be for a widow with four kids to feed.

In the late 1950s the "communist wind" of egalitarianism blew across Henan Province. Collective kitchens were set up in the countryside to replace the private ones. At first she thought it was paradise for her family, but within a year there was a shortage of grain and rationing was introduced – three ounces a day for an adult and two ounces for a child. That was far from enough to fill the stomach, and hunger lingered on every face. As more and more people suffered from dropsy, opposition to the collective kitchen started to spread and the commune members started to steal crops from the production team's fields. In order to stem this trend the government dispatched work groups to the villages, and Old J was the leader of the work group stationed in our village.

The production brigade leaders made arrangements to put up Old J in Guo Jun's house, for she was a warm-hearted and reliable person. Old J was very busy – holding meetings, making speeches and running hither and thither day after day. Since he didn't have his family with him and had nobody taking care of his daily needs, Guo Jun often helped him with the chores, such as providing him with hot water and washing his clothes. As time went on they became close to each other.

One night after the kids had gone to bed, she knocked on his door and handed him half a bowl of boiled soybeans.

"Old J," she said softly, "you must be hungry. Here are some boiled soybeans. Eat them now. No one is watching. You work so hard, and if you don't have enough food your health may suffer."

The team leader looked at the beans, expressionless.

"Where did you get these?" he asked.

"When they were organizing the production team and confiscating private grain storage," she answered candidly, "I saved some soybeans and buried them in a jar under my bed. I told no one about it. When the kids get too hungry, I give each of them a few beans. You're a high official and have a lot of work to do. If you don't have enough to eat, your health may suffer. Please take them."

"Leave the beans here," the team leader said after a moment's thought. "and you may go now."

In embarrassment, she withdrew to her room.

It wasn't long before she was awakened by an urgent knocking at the door. She opened it and saw the leader of the "Women's Shock Brigade" standing there with her group behind her. There was murder in their eyes. They charged in, pushed the bed aside and dug up the jar of soybeans. She was taken under escort to an empty storeroom of the collective kitchen and ordered to confess her crimes of hoarding grain and sabotaging the collective kitchen.

It was Old J who had betrayed her.

The shock brigade's interrogation lasted till the first cock crow but failed to uncover any new crime. They locked her in the room and went their separate ways home to make up for their lost sleep.

Old J had decided to make an example of her and had arranged for a public meeting the next day to have her criticized and denounced. But when they unlocked the storeroom door in the morning, they found her disheveled and filthy. Her clothes were torn into shreds, exposing her body here and there. The room stank of excrement. At the sight of the intruders she broke into wide-mouthed smiles and kept muttering, "Team leader Old J, here are some soybeans for you."

Guo Jun had gone mad! Really mad. People sighed sympathetically at her fate and the consequences to her family.

Years later, I heard a different version of her story from other elders in the village.

According to them, after Old J moved into her house, he made advances to her, but only met with repulsion. Then he thought that in her pitiful condition he could easily win her heart with half a bag of soybeans. She accepted the beans but refused to have sex with him. Shamed into anger, he framed her, and turned a young widow into a mad woman.

Many years have passed since her death. May her soul rest in peace!

My First Taste of Beef

It was at my grandma's place that I had my first taste of beef. She lived in Y Village, which lies about seven miles from the county seat. It is bounded on the north by a small river, and an ancient stone bridge links the village proper with the woods and graveyards on the northern bank. Amidst the woods was a courtyard enclosed by rammed-earth walls. There were three buildings there – a triple-roomed main house on the northern side and two thatched huts on the eastern and western sides, respectively. It used to be the grave keeper's residence, but was later turned into the production team office.

I was nine then. Hit by three successive years of natural disasters, the whole country was suffering from a severe grain shortage, and meat could only appear in one's dreams. But it was exactly then and in that particular courtyard where I had my first taste of beef. The scene, the taste and the sensation are engraved on my memory.

It was an early autumn night. I was lying in bed in the eastern room of my grandma's house tossing and turning with hunger when Grandma pushed open the door and entered.

"Get up quick, and keep quiet," she whispered. "We're going north of the river to eat beef."

Eat beef? Was I dreaming? But with only a moment's hesitation I jumped up, grabbed my clothes and rushed out.

A moon was hanging in the western sky, casting her dim light lazily on the sleeping village and painting it pale yellow. I followed my grandma out of the back door toward the stone bridge.

"Who goes there? What are you doing here at this late hour?"

A sudden low shout frightened me. Two old women were sitting on the stone drums at the head of the bridge, their walking sticks blocking the road.

"It's me. Cold night, isn't it?" Grandma answered in a low voice.

"Who is this?" one of them pointed at me with her walking stick, her aged eyes squinting hard.

"My grandson."

"Oh, you'd better hurry. The hungry wolves are gorging themselves!" the other raised her stick and pointed north.

Reaching the courtyard in the woods I saw a huge cauldron set in the southeastern corner over a fire. In the cauldron, the head, legs, ribs and offal of an ox were boiling. Accompanying the crackling of burning wood, the smell of beef and white steam from the cauldron permeated the whole yard. I saw Uncle Senlin, Uncle Zhonghe, Uncle Nao, and more than 30 others of the production team squatting in the yard, munching the bones and beef, which they held in their hands. None of them talked

The scene, the taste and the sensation are engraved on my memory.

or even coughed, and the whole place was as quiet as if it were deserted. Near the cauldron, my playmate Little An, Uncle Nao's son, was gobbling a piece of beef. He stood up at the sight of me, and was about to greet me when his mother slapped him on the back, and he squatted down immediately to go on gnawing on his piece of beef. Seeing me, Uncle Gen, the team leader, thrust an iron hook into the cauldron and pulled out a rib of beef. He wrapped it in two leaves plucked from the sunflower beside him and handed it to me. Then, without making a sound, he squatted down to continue eating. I cupped the warm beef in my hands and sank my teeth into it. How delicious it was! Thrilled by the delicacy, I guzzled the first mouthful down and took another bite. I could hardly tell whether I was dreaming or really eating.

Soon, the whole cauldron of beef was eaten up. The crowd of more than 30 people dispersed like phantoms. Uncle Twelfth, the custodian of the production team, picked up a spade and dug a pit by the wall of the yard. Then he dumped the leftover bones in it and refilled the pit. As a further precaution, he stacked a pile of firewood over the spot. As I wiped my mouth and watched, I was fascinated by the contrast between the dexterity of his hands and the tense looks on his face.

"What are you looking at? Go home now and keep your mouth shut!" Uncle Gen said gruffly.

I turned around, and slid out of the yard immediately.

At noontime the next day Uncle Tenth, the accountant of the production team, posted a "Lost Ox" notice on the wall outside the production brigade office. It read, "Our production team accidentally lost an ox yesterday. Anyone who finds it, please contact the Third Production Team."

"Gen's team lost another ox?" someone among the watching crowd wondered aloud. "Didn't they lose one just before the Spring Festival?"

"That's funny. The First Production Team lost an ox a few days ago. How could the Third Team lose another yesterday?" another added.

Confused by the notice and the comments, I was about to pipe up when someone gave me a spank on my buttock.

"It's lunch time. Go right home! Your grandma's waiting for you."

I turned around and saw Uncle Twelfth. He grabbed me by the collar and dragged me out of the crowd before I could protest. I looked up and saw his stern face. At that moment, everything clicked into place.

(Translated by Hu Liang)

Mr Liu's Henan Cuisine

Liu Yin had been a pig butcher when he was young. In the old days, a butcher in the rural areas did not demand a fee but would take the pig's offal as payment. If he had lots of butchering to do he would then have too much for even his whole family to consume. He therefore cooked the tripe and chitterlings, and put them out for sale. As that simplistic line of trade was not likely to blossom into a prosperous business, he tried to explore and expand the use of the offal by adding it to noodles, porridge, stewed cabbage, hot and sour soup, or as an ingredient in the stuffing of dumplings and steamed buns. He also learned to make pastry and appetizers. As his fame spread through the village and spilled over into other villages, he was often invited to cook wedding or funeral banquets.

Interestingly, his fame was not acquired by his culinary skills but by his adventurousness. There was nothing he would not cook, including mice, which he steamed, simmered, deep-fried, pickled, stewed or roasted. He was not only good at cooking them, but also good at catching them. His method was simple but effective. He would first catch several field voles, insert two soybeans into their rectums, which he would then stitch up. The bursting voles ran wild and would crawl into any opening they could find and attack the holed-up house mice, which were thus flushed out from their dens into his waiting net.

Not only were mice his food source, he also cooked wild cats, street dogs, hares, foxes, turtle doves, ravens, sparrows, cicadas, snakes, frogs, scorpions, grasshoppers, and even earthworms. In a word, he would, and knew how to, cook whatever he was able to lay his hands on, no matter whether it flew in the sky, ran on the land, burrowed in the ground, or swam in the water. And, most strikingly, whatever he cooked all looked and smelled mouth-watering. He bragged that he was using secret recipes passed down from his ancestors.

His fame also arose from his resourcefulness in difficult situations, with which he more than once saved the face of his employer. For instance, sometimes when a banquet was already underway, the host could be surprised and stunned to find more guests than expected were arriving.

"No worry," Liu Yin would say. "I guarantee there'll be enough to go around."

Having said that, he would ladle out a separate bowl from the wok for the distinguished guests, then grab the salt jar and drop handfuls of salt into the remainder. In that way, despite the excessive number of guests and the scarcity of food, there were always leftovers after the banquet.

If sometimes there was a short supply of cooking utensils, he would never trouble the host for this or that but would make use of whatever came within his reach. If there was a lack of large bowls, he would get the wash basin, the pigs' or the chickens' feed basins, give them a rough scour and a quick rinse, and put them on the table. Or if he failed to find a pot-brush to clean up the wok, he would use a broom, duster or scrubbing brush for the animal's feed basins. In an extreme case, someone had seen him use the brush for the chamber pot to clean the wok.

In his opinion, everything raised by Heaven and Earth was edible. Arsenic is poisonous, isn't it? But a small amount will not do any harm; on the contrary, it can cure diseases. The same applies to cooking. So the key to success is whether one can combine the ingredients into the most palatable dishes, and he proudly claimed that he was an expert at doing just that.

The sauces he made were also said to be prepared in accordance with secret recipes passed down from his ancestors. When he added them to the dishes their appetizing flavor would flow out from the kitchen and hover over half the village. And it was these sauces that covered up any unpleasant smells the dishes might have. People praised his dishes as creative, savory and unique in style.

And yet he was clear-headed enough to know that his so-called creativeness was the result of the three years of natural disasters between 1959 and 1961. At a time of grain shortage people were starving to death. Wouldn't they eat whatever they could? Besides, the rural areas were backward and poor. It was not a place for a cook or diner to be choosy about foodstuffs or utensils.

The livelihood in the countryside gradually improved after China's reform and opening-up policies were introduced in the late 1970s. Steamed wheat-flour buns, pork, poultry and fish were no longer rarities on people's dining tables, and a "creative" cook became less in demand. As he got older and more reluctant to go out cooking, his fame gradually faded from people's memory. But to the surprise of all, at the age of 60 he was again able to capitalize on his skills.

One day a car came to the village, and out stepped a middle-aged man fashionably dressed.

"Excuse me, do you know where the master chef, Mr Liu Yin, lives?" he asked everyone he met, in a strong southern accent.

He was told that Liu no longer lived in his old house. He had moved to the bank of the Yellow River, about four or five miles from the village, to help out his son running a pig farm there.

The man drove to the pig farm, and found Liu Yin cooking pig feed beside a stove. He was stirring the feed in a giant cauldron with a small shovel, his hair unkempt, his face greasy and his clothes stained with scraps of the feed. Piglets were nudging and squealing at his feet. Could this be the famous chef? The man hesitated at the sight, but his doubts were quickly swept away by the delicious smell seeping from the wok. He asked Liu a few questions about cooking, and then, with a pat on his thigh as if a bargain had been struck, he handed Liu's son 3,000 *yuan* and whirled Liu Yin all the way to Guangzhou City in his car.

Before long, a new restaurant opened up in Guangzhou. Above the gate hung a horizontal board inscribed in large characters:

"Mr Liu Yin, Famous Chef from Henan, Genuine Inheritor of Traditional Cooking."

Two years later, Liu Yin's family back home was able to pull down their old three-room house and replaced it with a two-story brick house, which then became the landmark building of the village. In another few years, Liu Yin opened his own restaurant in Guangzhou, which he named "Mr Liu's Henan Cuisine." Boasting inherited traditional dishes, the restaurant became legendary. His business flourished and money rolled in. With the money he bought a villa in the suburbs and brought his son's family to the city.

In another ten years, having turned 70, he retired and returned to his hometown. When some of his fellow villagers jokingly remarked that he had never been a choosy chef despite his fame, he replied with a knowing smile, "How could you be choosy in those days, when there was little to choose from? But look! People nowadays are really choosy. They put washing powder in the deep-fried dough-sticks, they use sulfur to bleach the steamed buns, they use red dye to pickle chili, they use formaldehyde to soak sea cucumbers in, and they add melamine to milk. Those chemicals are poisonous, and could do serious harm to a person's health. I never used those sorts of things."

Old Pao, Leader of the Ninth Production Team

Old Pao was the nickname of the leader of the Ninth Production Team, a man with a seemingly perpetual scowl. He was completely bald on top and his face was studded with dark moles that somewhat resembled the sesame seeds on a pancake. One of his eyes was larger than the other. The corner of the larger one was lifted toward the temple so he had to look sideways to get focused. Despite his short stature and short legs, he walked fast as if he were always chasing fires. His sturdy steps kicked up puffs of dust and left a trail of yellow smoke in his wake. People made up a doggerel to ridicule him:

A dwarf is soaring to the sky,
Trailing smoke as he passes by.

It was almost unbelievable that such a person could have run the production team for nearly 20 years.

As I recollect, he had an effective way to manage his team members, that is, by running around. And that's how he acquired his nickname Pao, meaning "run." Most of the time, he did not work in the fields like the other members. Rather, his short legs carried him from place to place, door to door, one street to another, one plot of land to another like an untiring, energetic sheep dog. When he saw someone, his greeting was fairly predictable:

> *"Why don't you hurry to the fields?"*
> *"Haven't you finished yet?"*
> *"Are you loafing again?"*
> *"Keep fooling around and there'll be no grain for you!"*

The team members were most afraid of his perpetual motion. Sometimes, they had hardly stopped working to swap a joke or two when he emerged from a nearby cornfield as if attacking from an ambush. On another occasion, he had just been seen inspecting the southern fields, but the next moment he was seen tongue-lashing someone north of the village. To avoid being caught unawares, team members would alert the others if they saw him anywhere near, "Look out! Old Pao's coming." At the warning, those who could slink away would get out of his sight and those who were loafing would pretend to be hard at work. Like a spirit Old Pao's erratic apparition was a great annoyance to the team members, and kept their hearts in their mouths.

Although his eyes were not aligned, he was a keen observer; although he was not a talkative man, he was a good calculator. In the evenings he would grade the performance of the team members according to his observation during the day and

Old Pao was the nickname of the leader of the Ninth Production Team, a man with a seemingly perpetual scowl. He was completely bald on top and his face was studded with dark moles that somewhat resembled the sesame seeds on a pancake.

transcribe it into workpoints on each member's attendance book. Well, that was the most effective way of control, because the amount of grain one received as a dividend at the end of the year depended on the total workpoints one earned during that period. If one didn't earn enough workpoints and wanted to get the full ration, one had to pay cash for the shortfall. On the other hand, if one's workpoints exceeded the amount needed for one's ration, one would be able to earn a few *yuan* pocket money from the production team.

Among all the members of the team, there was only one person who did not dance to Old Pao's tune. It was Six-Digits Zhang. He got this nickname because he had a sixth finger on one of his hands. He was a lazy but gluttonous bachelor. He refused to do heavy work, and was of no use when doing light work. So by the end of the year he was always the one with the fewest workpoints, and consequently received the least amount of grain. But that did not worry him, for he was capable of one thing – stealing without taking. That meant that he always ate up his spoils on the spot, whether it was sweet potato, corn, sesame, sorghum, wheat, soybeans, or cabbage, never taking anything away with him. Sometimes during work, people would suddenly notice he was missing, and when he reappeared a moment later, they could detect food stains on his lips.

"I've put them in my stomach already," he would say, pointing at his belly. "What can you do? Cut me open? Well, if I'm going to die I won't die of hunger at any rate!"

But once in his life he was caught red-handed by Old Pao. It was on the threshing ground during the summer harvest. After a hard day of pulling the stone roller, stacking up the straw, sunning the grain, winnowing the chaff, and finally piling up the year's harvest into a mound of gleaning seeds, the team members were finally able to take off their straw hats to fan their sweating bare chests and go home. But before he left Six-Digits deliberately stepped on the wheat mound and filled his shoes with the seeds. He hadn't gone a dozen yards when he was stopped by Old Pao and ordered to take off his shoes. The grain hidden inside weighed more than three ounces.

That very evening a criticism meeting was held on the threshing ground. The team members sat in a circle with Six-Digits standing in the center and the wheat he stole in a small heap beside his feet. Old Pao stepped forth and gave him a loud slap in the face.

"You villain!" Old Pao cursed. "Thank Heaven you've only got an extra finger. What if you've got an extra hand? You would have cleaned out the production team by this time!"

Six-Digits raised his eyes and stared at Old Pao. "So I stole something," he said nonchalantly. "What are you going to do about it?"

"People say thieves can only remember eating, not beating. Can you remember a beating instead of eating?"

"Old Pao, you mean I deserve a beating, right?"

"Right. Beat yourself. I don't want to hurt my hands."

"No problem," said Six-Digits, and with a shoe in each hand he slapped his face gently, as if patting a baby.

A few days after the meeting, Old Pao too was found stealing from the production team. That morning just as the team members were ready to go to work in the fields, Six-Digits suddenly pointed at a trail of millet grains on the ground and yelled, "Come over here! See these millet grains?"

The team members squatted down to examine the find, and then spread out in opposite directions following the millet trail. With Six-Digits in the lead, one group turned several corners, went through a few deserted yards and finally stopped at Old Pao's door.

"Aha!" Six-Digits patted his belly and said. "He's a thief too! How can he blame me for stealing?"

The other group followed the trail to the production team's storehouse. So that was where the millet had come from! The news that Old Pao had stolen from the production team's storehouse swept the village like a gale. Even the production brigade, the people's commune and the county government were notified.

The security bureau sent detectives to investigate the case, but no matter how hard they searched, they couldn't find a single grain of millet in Old Pao's house.

"Of course you can't find anything," Six-Digits said, "because he and his family have put all the grain in their stomachs."

The investigation lasted a fairly long time, but the case was finally dropped for lack of conclusive evidence. However, the ferocity had gone from Old Pao's face, and his pace became obviously slower. Never again did he mention the wheat stealing when he saw Six-Digits.

Old Pao died during the Cultural Revolution.

A few years later, Six-Digits confessed on his deathbed that the millet incident was his doing.

The Tragic Life of Wang Zeng

Wang Zeng was doomed as the son of Wang the Sixth, who, by the social classification of the time, belonged to one the "four types of bad elements."

Wang the Sixth had joined the reactionary society "Yiguandao" before liberation. And this had been an erasable scar to him and his family. At the very start of the Cultural Revolution he was ordered to sweep the streets by the village revolutionary committee, and two streets were assigned to him. So every morning at about four o'clock the swishing of his broom would wake up the people in those two quiet streets, and grandmothers would call to the schoolchildren: "Wang the Sixth is sweeping the streets. Get up for school." The swishing of Wang the Sixth's broom had taken the place of the rooster and become the students' alarm clock, because at that time all the chickens and dogs had been killed as part of the "annihilating the remaining tail of capitalism" movement.

Wang Zeng was two years my senior. He was an intelligent boy, and his grades were excellent. Teachers often read out his

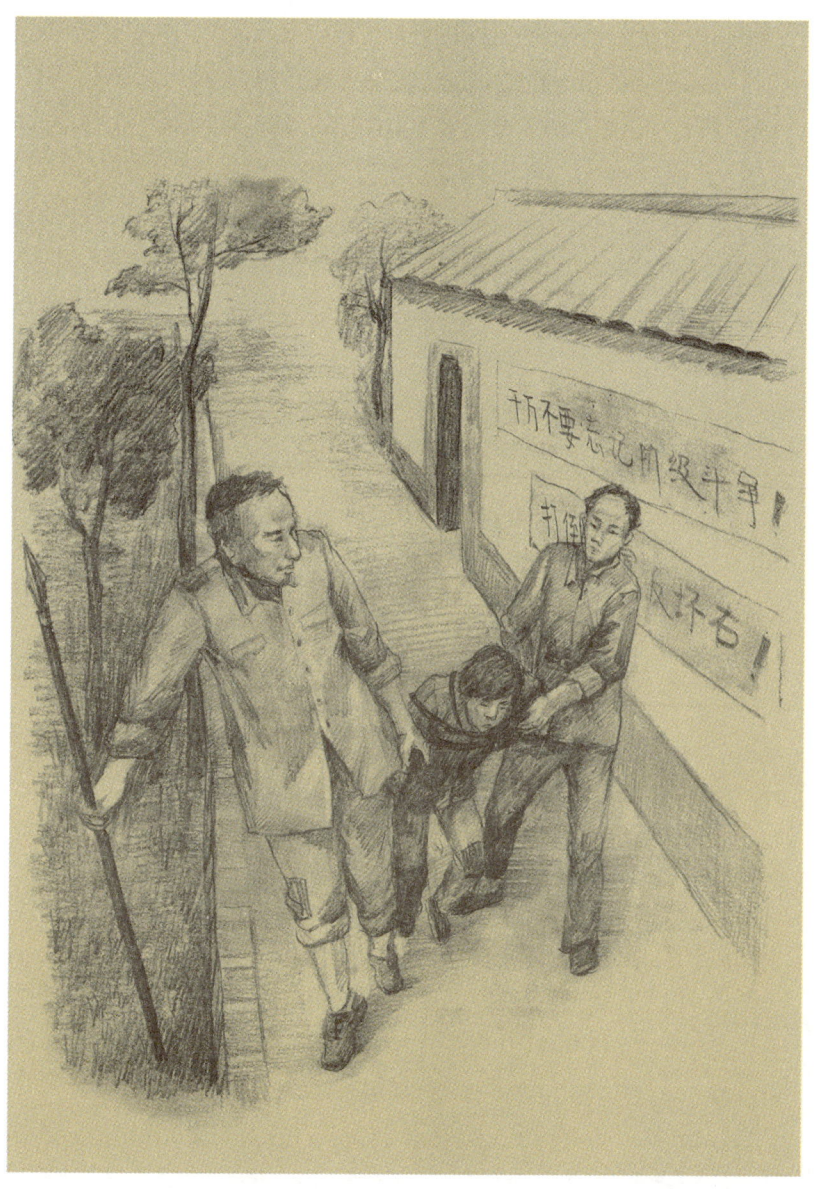

Wang Zeng was doomed as the son of Wang the Sixth, who, by the social classification of the time, belonged to one the "four types of bad elements."

compositions in class as models. But his fate took a downhill turn as soon as the Cultural Revolution started.

On that fateful day Wang Laoman, director of the village revolutionary committee, came to our school to give a speech.

"Our school is a socialist school," he said. "It's a school for the children of the poor and lower-middle peasants. It can't be used to bring up successors of the 'four types of bad elements'."

Pursued by shouts of "Down with the brats of landlords, rich peasants, reactionaries, bad elements and rightists!" Wang Zeng left school with his books under his arm, his bench on his shoulder, and tears glistening in his eyes. Thereafter he was seen either collecting scraps with a basket on his arm or helping his father sweep the streets.

On my way to school one morning I saw a small figure ahead of Wang the Sixth sweeping up the fallen leaves with a short broom, his face shrouded with a piece of rag. It was Wang Zeng.

It served him right, I thought, since he was the son of a Yiguandao adherent. If his father were a poor peasant, with his grades he could have been enrolled by Number One High in the county town.

One late autumn night I was sound asleep, when the clanking of buckets awakened me. I opened my eyes to see my father dashing out with a bucket in each hand.

"Damn! Someone's house has caught fire." I heard him yell to my mother.

I hurried out into the yard, and saw the sky to the northeast was glowing red, and I could catch distant shouts of "Fire! Fire!"

I grabbed a basin and ran toward the sound.

I found that it was the house of the director of the village revolutionary committee Wang Laoman. Somebody had stacked a bundle of corn stalks at his gate, and the red tongues of fire were licking at the eaves. Silhouetted against the flames, people saw a small figure beating the fire with a three-pronged iron fork.

"Get out of there! Get out immediately!" people shouted.

But the figure seemed not to hear and kept beating at the fire like mad.

It was only when the fire was quenched that people found the small figure was none other than Wang Zeng. His hair and eyebrows were all seared, and his face was blistered. Blue smoke rose from his soaked clothes as he lay on the ground screaming, half deliriously, "Uncle Man's house is on fire! Save Uncle Man's house!"

People said that it was he who first detected the fire and raised the alarm. If it were not for him, Wang Laoman's entire family would have been burned to death.

The Wang family crowded around him, shaken and touched. Laoman's mother, over 80 then, tottered over on a stick and asked, "Whose child is this? He saved my whole family."

"He's Wang the Sixth's son," someone told her.

"Wang the Sixth? The one my son so often denounces at meetings? Is this boy the son of one of the 'four types of bad elements'?"

Even when this was confirmed, she still found it hard to believe. She tapped her stick on the ground, and raised her eyes to Heaven.

"See this?" she said passionately. "Who said the offspring of the 'four types of bad elements' are all bad?"

It looked as if she were questioning Heaven and Earth.

"My little savior, why did you try to save us?" she looked down and asked the small figure on the ground.

"I ... I hope Uncle Man will let me go back to school," the boy said faintly.

"I promise you. I'll tell my son right way. If such a good boy cannot go to school, Heaven will not be pleased." She staggered away to look for her son.

Wang Zeng became a hero overnight, but before the week was over the 15-year-old boy was arrested by the county security bureau. According to the police, it was he who had started the fire.

On the day of the arrest a public meeting was held in the village. Wang the Sixth and the other members of the "four types of bad elements" were lined up on the platform with Wang Zeng in front, his hands tied behind him, his back so bent his head nearly touched he floor. Slogans were shouted.

"Down with the landlords, rich peasants, reactionaries, bad elements and rightists!"

"Never forget class struggle!"

"Wang Zeng, why did you set fire to Director Wang's house?" a policeman asked.

"I hoped Uncle Man would let me go back to school."

"Bullshit!" Wang Laoman sprang to his feet, and pointed a finger at Wang Zeng. "Who's your uncle? Comrades, now you can see with your own eyes how complex class struggle is. At this young age he has the nerve to set a house on fire. It's not difficult to imagine that when he grows older he'll take up a gun to fight us. We must always bear in mind Chairman Mao's teaching: 'Never forget class struggle.' We must criticize and denounce the landlords, rich peasants, reactionaries, bad elements and rightists, and put a foot firmly on them so they'll never be able to get up again!"

It started to drizzle when the meeting was over. Wang Laoman gave the two policemen each a straw hat as they escorted Wang Zeng out of the village. As he passed by, I could clearly see rain dripping from his hair and tears rolling down his cheeks.

Three years later he was released from jail, only to be put under public surveillance like his father. The village revolutionary committee also assigned him a street to sweep. Since then, his broom added to the swishing sound in the morning.

About ten days later he was found dead in Wang Laoman's sheep fold. He had left a penciled note before he hanged himself. It read, "Uncle Man, in my next life I want to be *your* son. Please let me go to school."

Ding Mao,
an Urban Youth Back in the Village

Ding Mao did not grow up in my village. His grandfather left with his family in the great famine of 1943, and finally settled in the city of Xi'an. During the movement of "educated urban youth to settle down in the countryside and mountain areas" in the Cultural Revolution, Ding Mao, for reasons unstated, returned to the village where he had never spent a day before.

He was of average height, had a narrow face, and would break into a smile when he met people, revealing two front teeth crowned with gold. But a second look would tell you the smile was no more than a jerk of his facial muscles, for there was no glint in the eye – a skin-deep smile, as people used to call it.

His initial arrival in the village was accompanied with guessing and suspicion. And the reason for returning to his ancestral village was first leaked by his relatives, who said that he didn't have any decent occupation in Xi'an, but was engaged in pilfering and burglary. His father had exhausted his means to control his unruly son, who had ended up in prison for stealing precious metals from the Xi'an Airplane Factory.

Unable to stand the harshness of jail life, he plotted a jailbreak with a handful of inmates. They took advantage of the relative laxity of prison management at the beginning of the Cultural Revolution, and put their plan into action one stormy night.

"You go first. I'll bring up the rear," he said as the others started to escape.

That made his buddies believe he was a friend who would sacrifice himself for others. But before they had gone far, he suddenly blared out, "Convicts are escaping! Catch them!"

The guards and security forces quickly rounded up the slow runners. And because he had alerted the guards, he was released before his sentence expired.

Those who were recaptured because of his betrayal hated him to the marrow. They swore to kill him once they got out of jail, and he certainly knew they were serious. So he availed himself of the movement of going to settle down in the countryside and returned to his native place in Henan Province in the guise of an "educated urban youth."

It didn't take long for the villagers to realize that he was rather sly, and certainly not the reliable type.

One winter evening at their usual gathering to chew the fat around the coal fire in the crowded barn, Li Ergou entertained the group of village youth with sensual stories of his private life. He boasted that no matter how late he went home his wife never needed to get out of bed to open the door for him, for he had designed a clever mechanism. It was simple. A nail was fixed to the door bolt and he had stretched a string from the nail all the way to the head of the bed. So he only needed to tap four times on the window lattice and his wife would know he was back. She would then give the string a pull, and the bolt would slide back. He could enter the house without any noise.

The youths cheered and complimented him on his resourcefulness as well as his thoughtfulness for his wife. She could save herself getting out of the warm bed on a cold night.

As stories like that were swapped around, it was suddenly noticed that Ding Mao was no longer in the barn.

"Ergou, look out," someone joked. "Ding Mao might have gone to knock on your window."

"I dare him to!" Ergou snapped back, but at heart he was not that confident. Ding Mao came from a big city – no doubt a man of the world – and he had been in jail. What would not a man like that do?

On ordinary nights Ergou was among the last to leave the barn, but that night, after lingering a little bit longer, he made an excuse and hastened home.

The joke turned out to be a good guess. Ergou's revelation had kindled an evil spark in Ding Mao's mind. He had sneaked out and gone to Ergou's place, where he gave four taps on the lattice just as Ergou had described and heard the click of the bolt sliding back.

He pushed open the door and without uttering a sound fumbled his way to the bed. He slid into bed with Ergou's wife and ran his hands all over her naked body. Still drowsy in her sleep, she thought Ergou was drunk again and allowed him to have his way. She didn't fully wake up till it was all over, and only then did it occur to her that the body odor and playful ways were unlike her husband's. She struck a match and screamed like a pig under the butcher's knife when she saw Ding Mao's face in the light. Just then, Ergou reached home and the couple gave Ding Mao a sound beating.

The next morning when people noticed the black and blue patches on Ding Mao's face, they asked, "What happened to your face?"

"I bumped my head on something last night in the dark."

"How could you got so many bumps?"

"Get lost! Don't be so fucking nosy!"

That raised a laugh among the villagers.

Toward the end of the 1960s a power line was extended to my village, and people were able to use electric lamps for the first time. The village revolutionary committee decided to pay for the installment and wire, but the villagers had to buy their own light bulbs. At that time the price of a 10-watt bulb was 20 to 30 *fen*, but for the poorer families it was still beyond their means.

Then one day, Ding Mao brought back from Xi'an some recycled light bulbs, that is, the tungsten filaments of the burnt bulbs had been replaced and the bulbs re-vacuumed. As a result of the sealing, such bulbs had a one-centimeter-long glass taper joint sticking out at the bottom. The price of such a bulb was ten *fen*, but Ding Mao had probably bought them wholesale at the Xi'an market for half the price. Anyway, he became a benefactor of the villagers, and family after family went to his place to buy recycled bulbs, and were never disappointed. Soon the recycled bulbs were lighting up many homes. In the evenings when someone dropped in at another family he or she would point at the bulb and ask, "That's a bulb from Ding Mao, right?" or "You bought it from Ding Mao?"

Since Ding Mao brought benefits to the whole village, people gradually pardoned his skin-deep smiles, his sneaking into the bed of Ergou's wife, and all the rumors that followed him from Xi'an.

It happened that the higher authorities were looking for models of educated urban youth in the countryside for propaganda purposes. The village revolutionary committee then penned a long report on Ding Mao's meritorious deeds and sent it to the people's commune, which in turn passed it on to the county authorities.

It also happened that the county was organizing a report on how the educated urban youths studied and applied Chairman Mao's works in a creative way, and Ding Mao was selected to give speeches at the people's communes in the county. Ding Mao was very modest in his speeches. Rather than bragging about his achievements, he focused on how the poor and lower-middle peasants cared for him and helped him. Whatever good he had done was only to repay the kindness of such folks. He swore that he would forever follow Chairman Mao's teachings and "be modest and prudent, and guard against arrogance and impetuosity" and he would "make new contributions rather than rest on his laurels."

Since Ding Mao brought benefits to the whole village, people gradually pardoned his skin-deep smiles, his sneaking into the bed of Ergou's wife, and all the rumors that followed him from Xi'an.

Thus he became a well-known figure in the county. Later on, his exemplary deeds were even published in the provincial newspaper under the title of "Ding Mao – a model of the educated urban youth who returned to work in his home village." His name soon spread across the province. Consequently, he was elected to the leading body of the people's commune and became a leading member.

One day, he brought back from Xi'an some fist-sized adaptors and grape-sized light bulbs.

"These are the latest money-savers," he told the villagers. "This small adaptor can change the 220-volt power to three or five volts. And these bulbs are only three or five watts. Though they need very little power they are fairly bright and can save money. Your monthly electricity bill will not exceed one *yuan*. They are specially designed for the rural areas."

Money-saving news was always welcome to country folks. Ding Mao installed an adaptor and bulbs in his own house. People swarmed over to take a look, and were strongly impressed.

"Ding Mao is a nice guy," they remarked. "He always has the interest of us poor and lower-middle peasants at heart. He's an educated urban youth armed with Chairman Mao's thought."

All of a sudden someone asked, "Ding Mao, how much would it cost to have this thing installed?"

The excited crowd fell quiet at the mention of cost. Their eyes concentrated on his face, because no matter how wonderful the device was, its price was always the decisive concern.

His facial muscle jerked and the golden teeth flashed.

"Do you think I'm so mean as to make money out of you? The production price of the adaptor is 25 *yuan*. Now I'm asking only 20 without even counting the trouble of carrying them all the way from Xi'an right to your door. The bulbs are eight *fen* each, but I'll take only five *fen*. What do you say to that?"

There was no immediate response, for people were all doing silent calculations. Twenty *yuan* for such an adaptor? At that time the day's work of an able-bodied man brought only five *fen*. That would mean that he would have to sweat and toil for more than one full year to buy an adaptor, and on condition that he did not eat or spend one *fen* on clothing.

"If you think this is too expensive," Ding Mao continued, "I can sell them to other villages. Several villages have already contacted me to buy them."

"Ding Mao, you son of a bitch," a voice burst out from the crowd, "remember that our village was the birthplace of your father, grandfather and great-grandfathers. What do you say if we first pay ten *yuan* and pay the remaining ten *yuan* next year?"

"I have no objection, but I'm afraid the manufacturer won't agree," he replied with a face of innocent helplessness. "Well, how about I give you another discount of two *yuan*, and you borrow some money from friends or relatives? In that way, our village will be taking the lead in marching toward the revolutionary new countryside. Let the other villages envy us!"

Without further argument the villagers quietly sidled out of the room.

The next day, several families placed money in his hand, and he immediately installed the light bulbs for them. And in a few days the dozen sets he had brought back from Xi'an were all sold out. Looking at the bright money-saving lights of the lucky families, those who hadn't been able to buy an adaptor regretted that they did not go all out to raise the money. So they tried by all means to borrow money from their friends and relatives in other villages, and begged Ding Mao to make another trip to Xi'an to purchase a new batch, which he gamely agreed to do.

A few days afterward, he set out with the more than two thousand *yuan* entrusted to him by over a hundred families of the village and even other villages.

Ten days passed. Then 20 days. But he neither returned nor sent word back. People started to worry. At first they knocked on his door. Then they kicked the door. The kicking became stone throwing. Finally the angry mob knocked down the door, only to find that the rooms were stark empty. Nobody knew when he had moved his things away, but they knew they had been cheated.

The village revolutionary committee lost no time in reporting the case to the people's commune and the county security authorities. The county authorities replied that Ding Mao was an advanced model of the educated urban youth returning to work in his home village. Both the county authorities and the provincial newspaper had propagated his meritorious deeds, and he was a well-known model in the county and even in the province. It was unlikely for such a person to do such a thing. Even if he did, it should be hushed up, for it would certainly discredit the county revolutionary committee.

Someone took his anger out on Ding Mao's house, burning it down.

Ding Mao never again returned to the village, and no one has heard of him since.

Jiang Yue, a Revolutionary Veteran

Jiang Yue was a music teacher at Number One High School in the county town. He was a thickset man of average height. He wore a pair of thick glasses and walked in an unhurried way as if he were beating time with his steps. He spoke slowly as if he were immersed in deep thought. You could tell at first sight that he was a learned man and had seen the world, and he really had, for from time to time he would come up with something unimaginable.

It was said that he was a revolutionary veteran, and rather talented. He once studied at the Lu Xun Academy of Arts in Yan'an and was the composer of quite a number of anti-Japanese songs popular during the War of Resistance Against Japanese Aggression. After liberation he worked in Beijing. In 1957 he was branded a rightist, and was demoted and transferred to the Henan provincial government to work.

However, he showed no repentance after coming to work in the provincial government, and continued to articulate inappropriate opinions. As a result, he was further demoted and

You could tell at first sight that he was a learned man and had seen the world, and he really had, for from time to time he would come up with something unimaginable.

transferred to Number One High in my county.

At approximately the same time a Mr Yuan was also demoted and transferred from Beijing to the Henan provincial capital, and finally to Number One High, but the latter was a native of Wen County. Though they had never met before they were dumped in the same school, their similar ups and downs made them sympathetic to each other and they became friends.

Having drunk a bit too much on the eve of one Spring Festival, the emotionally worked up Jiang Yue wielded his brush pen, and wrote one New Year couplet for Mr Yuan, which read:

From Beijing to Wen County we came in step;
Though twice demoted I remain myself.

And a horizontal scroll, which read: *Joined by Fate.*

As Mr Yuan declined the gift after weighing the consequences, Jiang Yue hung the scrolls up on the door frame of the music teacher's office. The couplet soon became the gossip of the school and the town.

Jiang Yue was somewhat eccentric, to the extent that it sometimes was hard to tell whether he was ignorant or arrogant, for once he copied out a poem he had composed to the tune of *Ode to the Plum Blossom* in large brush pen characters, and made a copy of Chairman Mao's poem to the same tune, and hung them side by side on the wall of his office. When two colleagues happened to drop by, he asked them right to their faces: "Gentlemen, which poem do you think is better? I mean which imparts a bolder vision?"

His two colleagues took a look at the poems and eyed each other in stunned speechlessness.

He laughed and pointed at the one he had composed. "I think mine is better, for it imparts a bolder vision."

So, as soon as the Cultural Revolution was launched, he was among the first to be marked out as a major target of criticism. His couplet became evidence of the undying hatred of a rightist against the Communist Party, and his poem was even more telling proof of a malicious attack on the great leader Chairman Mao. The Red Guard organizations took turns criticizing and denouncing him.

At one gathering of the Red Guards in the auditorium of Number One High, the condemned teachers, Jiang Yue among them, were led onto the stage amidst deafening shouts of revolutionary slogans. He had a peaked hat made from rolled-up newspaper clapped on his head, a wooden board hanging from his neck inscribed with the words, "Down with rightist Jiang Yue!" and his hands tied behind his back. A complication of feelings seemed to flicker through his thick glasses.

The head of the Red Guard then was a student called Li Dongyuan. He clutched Jiang Yue by the neck, pushed him to the front of the stage, and gave him a kick in the hollow of the knee to make him kneel on the floor.

"Jiang Yue," he roared, "now you must confess your crime of viciously attacking the Communist Party and our great leader Chairman Mao."

"I have followed Chairman Mao and the Party to make revolution since my days in Yan'an," Jiang Yue replied calmly and thoughtfully. His voice was low but clear enough for everyone to hear. "I never attacked Chairman Mao or the Party."

"Bullshit! Then how dare you say your poem *Ode to the Plum Blossom* is better than Chairman Mao's?"

"Chairman Mao teaches us that we should let a hundred flowers blossom and a hundred schools of thought contend. Mine is just one school of thought."

His answer enraged the Red Guards. Shouts of "Down with the mad dog Jiang Yue!" "If Jiang Yue does not surrender, he shall be doomed!" rocked the hall.

Several Red Guards jumped onto the stage. They kicked him, punched him, slapped his face, and finally resorted to rods and clubs. After the beating they forced him into a kneeling position again.

Now his face was smeared with dust, his hair disheveled, his spectacles gone, and blood was trickling down his forehead. His eyes were shut and no matter what Li Dongyuan or others asked, he made no reply.

Worried that a prolonged stalemate like that might dampen the mood of the Red Guards, Li Dongyuan ordered him to be taken into a small backstage room for individual interrogation.

Li was the head of the Red Guard organization "December the Ninth." He was a renowned figure in the county, for he was among the first to make revolution, and took part in all kinds of beating, smashing and looting. His favorite attire was an army uniform, complete with an army cap, a belt, and a Mauser pistol slung across his chest, which had been stolen from the county's armed forces department. When he walked, he looked straight ahead; when he talked, he spoke with the dignity of an army general issuing orders. But faced with this die-hard element who would not "soften down by either steaming or boiling," he felt he was losing face in front of his Red Guard comrades, and he was burning with fury. He came to the backstage room and pulled out his pistol.

"Jiang Yue, do you know what this is?" he asked as he laid the pistol on the table in front of Jiang Yue as a threat.

"Dongyuan," Jiang Yue said impassively, "I played with things like this as far back as my Yan'an days. At that time you probably were not put in your mother's womb yet."

This answer further enraged Li Dongyuan. He grabbed the pistol, clicked open the safety catch and loaded the gun. As he slapped the gun down on the table, he wasn't skilled enough to slip out his forefinger in time, and pulled the trigger. At the report of the gun the Red Guards swarmed into the room only to find Jiang Yue as calm as if nothing had happened, while Li Dongyuan was scared white and transfixed with horror, for he had never before fired a real gun.

Since no one in the room was wounded, the buzzing crowd realized that it was only an accidental discharge. Just as the room was quietening down, a shout came from outside, "Wang Maolü has been shot dead!"

The Red Guards flocked out of the auditorium, to find a fellow student lying on the ground about 20 meters away at a classroom door. His eyes were closed and blood was gushing from his chest and staining his clothes red. In a moment he stopped breathing.

What had happened was that when the gun went off the bullet shot through the thin door of the backstage room and hit Wang Maolü who just happened to be passing by.

Wang belonged to another Red Guard faction, and his death ignited a sharp conflict between the two. The other faction demanded that Li Dongyuan pay with his life, while Li Dongyuan's faction blamed Jiang Yue for the accident, claiming that the gun was fired only because Jiang was trying to snatch it from Li's hand. After negotiating the two groups acknowledged that they were both Chairman Mao's Red Guards and should be one family, and therefore agreed to pin the blame on Jiang Yue alone. With homicide added to his other crimes, Jiang Yue was more relentlessly criticized and beaten.

The winter day of Wang's funeral was very cold, so cold that water drops immediately turned to ice. While Jiang Yue was forced to kneel before Wang's portrait, Li Dongyuan came up from behind and poured a bucket of water over his head. Though soaked to the skin, Jiang Yue kept his eyes closed and his mouth shut.

After the Cultural Revolution, Li Dongyuan was sentenced to imprisonment for beating, smashing, looting and murder. Jiang Yue was exonerated from all accusations and transferred to the provincial capital to take up a new job.

Blackie's Ma

Blackie's Ma was of average height. She was a capable woman and friendly to others, but she could be very stubborn sometimes, for she would stick to her own view and be deaf to exhortation or coercion. In the end she suffered the consequence of this temperament of hers.

In the late 1950s the "boasting" trend prevailed throughout Henan Province. As I was at an innocent age, I can't remember exactly when it started, but its connection with Blackie's Ma lives in my memory till this day. I can clearly recall how she was labeled a "sluggard" or backward person, and how she was criticized and paraded through the village streets.

My memory goes back to one noontime. Coming home from school for lunch I saw my mother stuffing straw into two big vats and using her hands to press it firm till it nearly reached the brim. Then she spread an old bed sheet over the straw, on which she laid two layers of newspaper. At last she poured the grain on it. A vat that could have held six or seven bushels of grain was now filled to overflowing with a little more than one.

"Ma, why are you putting straw under the grain?" I asked out of curiosity.

"You're too young to understand," she whispered wearily. "The leaders told us to do this at the production brigade meeting. If we don't, we'll become sluggards like Blackie's Ma. And we'll be criticized and paraded through the streets in shame."

And indeed, that very afternoon all the pupils of the elementary school were summoned to a village meeting to criticize the sluggard – Blackie's Ma.

The meeting was held beside an earth mound and the commune members were sitting in the open space in front of it. When we filed in and sat down, Tie An, the production brigade's Communist Party secretary declared the meeting open.

"Bring forth Blackie's Ma, the sluggard!" he commanded solemnly.

Two members of the Youth Shock Team pushed Blackie's Ma from behind the mound.

"Blackie's Ma," Tie'an pointed at her with the long stem of his pipe, "all families in the village were able to carry out the production brigade's call to fill their vats and bins to the brim. Some even can't find enough containers. Why is it your family has only half a vat of grain? Are you trying to blacken socialism? You may name your son Blackie, but you're not allowed to paint socialism black!"

"Goudan's Dad," she replied, "you're the Party secretary. You know that's all the grain my family has. What else can I do?"

"What can you do? Every family has enough grain to fill their

"That's because the womenfolk stuffed the vats with straw and the bins with old cotton wadding. My vat is for grain only. No straw in my grain vat!"

vats and bins. You're certainly not the poorest, are you?"

"That's because the womenfolk stuffed the vats with straw and the bins with old cotton wadding. My vat is for grain only. No straw in my grain vat!" she emphasized stubbornly.

All at once the woman team leader Wang Xiying sprang up the mound and gave her two loud slaps on the face.

"Don't throw mud at all the womenfolk of this village!" she hissed angrily. "Don't you know what you're doing is pulling out the socialist red flag?"

"I'm not throwing mud at anyone. You came personally door to door to teach us how to do it. You also threatened to criticize me if I refused to do it your way. You want to beat me? Beat me then!"

As she said that, she rammed her head against the woman team leader. Her hair bun had got loose and her hair fanned out, like the mane of an enraged animal. The team leader leapt off the mound in panic. Except for a few frightened whimpers from the younger pupils, the gathering watched in silence.

With a grim face Tie'an ordered the two Shock Team members to whisk Blackie's Ma down the mound. Then he warned the villagers that they should go home to further spruce up their grain vats and bins. No one was allowed to blacken the reputation of the village and socialism.

Blackie's Ma was then paraded through the streets. Blackie and his two younger brothers were absent from school for several days.

The "boasting" trend led to the establishment of the collective kitchen. There were altogether nine production teams in my village, and each team was to have *one* kitchen. Families were told to smash their woks and send the scrap to the village's smelting furnace to produce iron, and their entire grain store should be handed over to the collective kitchen. The policy slogan at that time was:

> *No household may keep a store of grain;*
> *No family may have kitchen smoke.*

Before long, sacks of grain, smashed woks, tables and benches were all stacked at the gates on both sides of the streets. Team leaders with the Shock Team members would come to check each and every family. They not only took away what was stacked at the gate, but also entered the yards and houses to poke around with iron rods three or four feet long. If the earth seemed to have been moved, they would dig down to find the buried grain or other objects which should have been turned over to the team. They would descend into sweet potato cellars, climb up to search the ceilings, and even poke around in the outhouse. In a word, they literally left no stone unturned.

After Blackie's Ma gave birth to her sixth child, her husband passed away. Blackie was her eldest son. He was about 12 years old at the time and had five younger brothers and sisters. As there was no able-bodied man in the family, they were unable to earn much, and certainly did not have much grain to hand in. The half bag of grain she placed at the gate was the smallest in the whole village.

What was unexplainable was that the production team did not criticize her for the small amount she surrendered, not even mentioning her name at meetings. The search for grain ended peacefully, and the collective kitchen opened up without trouble. At meal time every day, the cooks of each production team would blare through a self-made tinplate trumpet along the streets, "Good folks, meal time! Bring your bowls and chopsticks with you."

At the announcement, the commune members and their families would put down their work and go to the kitchen with a basket of bowls and chopsticks on their arms and a small pail in their hands.

At first, food at the collective kitchen was pretty satisfactory. There were wheat-flour steamed buns and porridge at every meal, and everyone could eat his or her fill. But such good days didn't last long. The buns shrank in size and wheat-flour was soon replaced by corn-flour. The porridge got thinner and thinner till it wasn't much different from boiled water. And then rationing was introduced – three ounces a day for an adult and two ounces for a child. The starving people started to eat tree leaves and wild herbs. It was only then that people came to regret that they had handed in all their stored grain. They should have kept some to tide over the difficult times.

Then they perceived that Blackie's Ma and her children did not seem to be very hungry, for they never cried with hunger like other families. The faces of her children even looked ruddy when those of the other kids were sallow. How did she manage that?

As you might have guessed, her secret was soon revealed – by the woman team leader Wang Xiying, who after turning the matter over and over in her head and spying on her, noticed that as soon as it grew dark Blackie's Ma would bolt her yard gate and lock the door to her house from inside. Not a streak of light came out of the house, neither was there a sound. Wang Xiying was unable to get a clue as to what was going on inside until one day she came upon the crap Blackie's Ma had left in the field. She lay on her stomach to examine the excrement, in which she discovered undigested wheat grains – and an explanation for the mystery.

That very night she led the Shock Team to Blackie's Ma's place. They quietly climbed over the yard wall and burst open the door to the house. Lighting an oil lamp, they saw Blackie's Ma and her six children chewing raw wheat grains that had been soaked and softened in water. They searched the rooms and found there was a covert cellar beneath the bed of Blackie's Ma and in it were hidden two or three bushels of wheat.

A grin of triumph flashed across the team leader's face. She made an immediate report to the leaders of the production brigade, who in turn reported to the people's commune and the county authorities. In no time Blackie's Ma was cited as an infamous example of sabotaging the socialist collective kitchen. A special workgroup was promptly organized by the county authorities to further investigate the case, but the night the workgroup arrived at the village Blackie's Ma hanged herself on the persimmon tree at the gate of the collective kitchen.

Blackie was about 12 years old when his mother died, and his youngest sister was only one. The villagers mourned her death with silent tears. After her burial, Blackie and his siblings were taken away by his mother's brother. Their house remained vacant after that.

Many years later, under the new policy of reform and opening-up, Blackie and his brother founded a grain processing and trading company in the provincial capital, Zhengzhou City. It became a very successful business and they made a fortune. Learning of this, the village leaders paid Blackie a visit to solicit his support for the village's grain processing, but their request was flatly turned down. Blackie said he had no relation whatever with the village and he had never even heard of its existence.

Maiduo, Chairman of the Peasant Association

Thick snowflakes drifted all night, and turned the village and fields into a silvery world. Maiduo had to probe the snow-covered ground with a stick to find the road. He walked slowly out of the village, his feet sometimes sinking deep into the snow.

The hills and villages in the distance, as well as the road and fields beneath his feet, were all blurry white. He marched straight ahead, undaunted, because he had an appointment with a matchmaker to find a possible wife for his son. He was determined not to miss the appointment even if he should fall into a ditch or drop into a well. Snow, he thought as he trudged forward, is a really good thing. Be it a grand brick house or a humble mud hut, a neat sports ground or a mucky manure pile, a smooth paved road or a bumpy dirt path, an evergreen pine or a bare-branched elm – now they all look the same. Snow changes the world. With all the differences gone, it's so unlike the mortal world, where human beings are worried about this or that.

He thought of his sons. The eldest was over 20 and the second was already 18, time to find a wife and beget children. But so far, neither of them had the slightest prospect of even getting engaged. Considering his family situation, Maiduo thought with satisfaction that he was not particularly poor. Peasants are more or less in the same condition these days, he reflected. As long as you don't have to worry about your next meal, life is good. As for his class status, he belonged to the poor-peasant class, the mainstay of the revolution, and he was the chairman of the peasant association during the land reform movement. The only setback was that he had married the ex-wife of a former landlord. It always happened that the family of a girl who was a likely prospect for one of his sons were happy to learn that the proposed groom was from a poor-peasant family, but as soon as they learned that his mother had been the ex-wife of a landlord, they would walk away. ... Seeing his two grown-ups, Maiduo couldn't help feeling annoyed and worried.

As he trudged on he suddenly tripped over something buried in the snow, and fell flat on his face. He sat up. It took him a minute to collect his wits again. Then he swept away the snow with his stick, and saw half of a broken gravestone. As he wiped off the snow with his sleeve and saw the words carved on it he couldn't help cursing out loud, "Fuck it! Isn't this the grave of Wang Laogen? How could I have wandered all the way here?"

Wang Laogen had been one of the village landlords. He had been killed more than two decades previously. The gravestone had been smashed by the Red Guards at the beginning of the Cultural Revolution.

As Maiduo sat on the snowy ground and gazed at the broken

stele, the past arose before his eyes. He was born into poverty. His parents had died early, and he had made a living by begging and doing bits and pieces for others. In 1946 the Eighth Route Army made a thrust from the southern tip of the Taihang Mountains and liberated the northwestern part of Henan Province. He followed the lead of Old Jiao, the head of the Fourth Military Sub-area, in suppressing bandits and denouncing local despots, and was made the chairman of the peasant association.

Wang Laogen then had about seven acres of land and six houses in two compounds, as well as two wives. To be fair, he was not very rich and he was not a particularly bad man. But in such a small village with so many people living in stark poverty, he could not but become the target of revolution.

His public accusation was held in the evening. For fear that people of the same village might have personal concerns, the workgroup had summoned from other villages seven or eight young enthusiasts to denounce him. After midnight they beefed up their beating, and rods and clubs were used. At first he howled and writhed in pain, but he soon lay quiet. Maiduo elbowed his way through the crowd, crouched beside the limp body and placed a hand in front of the landlord's nose.

"He's dead," he announced. "Carry him out of here."

Several young men carried the body out and dumped it in the graveyard about a hundred yards away. The meeting went on to denounce Tiger Zhi, a despot from a neighboring village.

In fact Wang Laogen wasn't really dead. He had only gone into a coma, and Maiduo had lied to save his life. But the cold wind revived him, and his moaning drew attention. Old Jiao walked over, pulled out his pistol, and fired two shots into his chest. Wang Laogen's legs jerked a couple of times before his grunting ceased.

Maiduo cursed to himself. Why couldn't he have borne the pain a little bit longer and kept quiet? Now it's too late, he thought. Old Jiao is too merciless, he told himself. A life is a life. Why did you have to take away his life?

Wang Laogen's property was divided up after his death. As chairman of the peasant association, Maiduo was given one of the compounds. Though he moved out of his old mud hut into the grand brick house, he didn't feel happy at all. Late at night when he lay alone on the wide, solid mahogany bed, he often felt he could see Wang Laogen sitting in the wicker armchair in the main hall smoking a water pipe, while his first wife, Emerald, squatted in front of him washing his feet and his second wife, Lotus, stood behind him massaging his back. Wang Laogen never had servant girls in his house, for, in his opinion, two wives were enough. They could do all the housework during the day and share the bed at night. There was no use wasting money on maids.

Now Wang Laogen is dead and he, Maiduo, is living in his house, sleeping on his bed, and breathing the air he once breathed. Everything seems unchanged except that Emerald and Lotus are not in the scene. A nameless loneliness and sorrow floated up in his mind. Was it for Wang Laogen? For himself? Or for Emerald and Lotus?

Just then he heard a knock on the door. He slid out of bed, and grabbed his rifle.

"Who is it?" he asked in a low, stern voice.

"Me."

"Who?"

"Lotus."

Good God! You think of someone and here she comes! Or is it her ghost? Despite his caution, he opened the door and Lotus threw herself into his arms. "Brother Maiduo," she begged, sobbing, "I'm done for. Please marry me and protect me!"

He was stunned by this unexpected bliss.

Who was Lotus? She was a most beautiful flower, exquisite as if carved out of jade. Wang Laogen had bought her for a fabulous price in Kaifeng City. She was the dream of any young man who saw her.

Then who was Maiduo? He was a pauper who didn't have a plot of land or a roof above his head. In the past, marrying such a beauty had been beyond his wildest dreams. But now, having lived through the revolution, liberation, land reform and the death of Wang Laogen, he was now the chairman of the peasant association. Lotus being driven away, her reemergence, her teary pleading – what could he do but marry her?

His decision shocked the whole village. Even Old Jiao could not believe his ears. The chairman of the peasant association marrying the ex-wife of an executed landlord? What kind of marriage was that? He had several heart-to-heart talks with Maiduo, hoping to dissuade him.

"Love or hate, class status dictates," he quoted. "You are from a poor-peasant family. What happened to your class stand?"

"Love or hate, marriage dictates," Maiduo retorted. "If a man marries a woman, that'll be love. In the past I was poor and now she is poor. Why can't two poor people marry?"

Old Jiao was speechless. All he could do was discharge Maiduo from the position of chairman of the peasant association. Maiduo, however, couldn't have cared less. So he lived guiltlessly in Wang Laogen's house, slept on Wang Laogen's bed, and held Wang Laogen's ex-wife in his arms. Isn't the goal of revolution to let the poor have a house to live in, have food to eat and have a wife to sleep with?

However, the situation was reversed in just half a year. The Eighth Route Army made a strategic shift, and withdrew into the Taihang Mountains. The 117th Brigade of the National Army's 38th Division reoccupied the region, and the "landlords' restitution corps" under the lead of Zhang Qiang returned to the village. They killed the new chairman of the peasant association and the land reform enthusiasts in retaliation. Unable to escape in time, Old Jiao, the head of the Fourth Military Sub-area, was captured and murdered in a deserted temple. Under the "white terror," no one in the village dared to retrieve and bury his corpse. Only Maiduo volunteered to go.

"Old Jiao was a communist chief," Lotus reminded him. "Aren't you afraid the Kuomintang army will kill you for that?"

"What has it got to do with the Communist Party or the Kuomintang Party? Once a man is dead, he's just a human being."

So one night he laid Old Jiao's corpse in a plain coffin and hired a cart to send his remains back to his native place in Yuncheng, Shanxi Province.

In 1947 the Eighth Route Army struck south again, and the northwestern region of Henan Province was liberated a second time. Though Maiduo had married the ex-wife of a landlord, the workgroup and villagers didn't trouble him, because he was of poor-peasant origin, had been the chairman of the peasant association, and – most of all – had taken proper care of Old Jiao's remains.

So, just as the sun rises every day, life continues month after month. He still lived in Wang Laogen's house, slept on Wang Laogen's mahogany bed, and held Wang Laogen's ex-wife in his arms. During those years, Lotus gave birth to four sons and brought vigor and laughter to the compound.

In 1966 the Cultural Revolution was launched. Having learned of the history of Lotus, the village Red Guards claimed that she was a member of the landlord class who had slipped through the land reform movement unpunished. They caught hold of her, shaved her head, and made her stand bent over on a table with a tall peaked hat on her head. All the while Maiduo sat quietly among the audience and smoked one pipe after another, showing no emotion whatsoever.

"Zhang Maiduo," a Red Guard suddenly pointed at him, "love or hate, class status dictates. You are of poor-peasant origin. Why did you choose to marry the former wife of a landlord? Why not divorce her and make a clear-cut class alignment?"

Maiduo stood up, remarkably composed. Since he was of poor-peasant origin, what was there to be afraid of? And since the poor peasants were the mainstay of revolution, what could they do to him? He strode purposefully to the table, and helped Lotus down.

"Lotus was married to Wang Laogen for only two years and didn't beget a child for him," he said to the Red Guards, "but she has been married to me for more than 20 years and gave birth to my four sons. Why is she still considered Wang Laogen's wife? Tell me whether she is the wife of the poor peasant Zhang Maiduo or the landlord Wang Laogen? Look at my four sons. They're tall and straight. They're honest and candid. Why should they feel humble and low? Two of them have attained marriageable age, but they can't find a wife. Why? Because some people still think their mother is a landlord's wife. Bullshit! For generations my family have been poor peasants. Who in this village doesn't know this? Who dare say my sons are not the sons of the poor peasant Zhang Maiduo? Lotus, let's go home. You're the wife of the poor peasant Zhang Maiduo. Anyone like to quibble about that?"

No one raised any objection.

As he thought of that, a smile broke out on his face.

He looked up at the sky. The snow had stopped, and the clouds were thinner, though the sun had not yet broken through. He saw that it was going to be a bright, sunny day. He stood up and flipped off the snow from his clothes. Then he walked firmly ahead with the help of the stick.

In about two hours the village he was heading for finally came into sight. Facing him on the wall was a slogan painted in bright red: "Love or hate, class status dictates."

The sight of the slogan caused his head to reel. He looked around and saw no one.

"Fuck that bullshit slogan!" he muttered. "Love or hate, marriage dictates!"

Wang Laobiao, Village Calligrapher

Wang Laobiao had been to a traditional private school when he was young and learned to use a writing brush. As few people in the countryside were good at calligraphy in the 1950s and 1960s he became a kind of rarity in the village and had plenty of opportunities to display his skills in the successive political movements, such as the movement against the evils of corruption, waste and bureaucracy within the Party, government and mass organizations in 1951 and 1952; the movement against the Five Evils of bribery, tax evasion, theft of state property, cheating on government contracts and stealing of economic information as practiced by owners of private industrial and commercial enterprises, which started in 1952; the Anti-Rightist Campaign of 1957; the Great Leap Forward and the establishment of the people's communes in 1958; and the Four Clean-ups movement of 1963-1966. Almost all the slogans in the village, whether they were in big characters or small characters, were done by him. So, when the Cultural Revolution began he was already an expert in slogan writing.

He was then in his 50s. In the mornings he would carry a bucket of paint made out of red soil mixed with dye and water, and the stub of a broom to write slogans on the walls along the main streets of the village. The characters were about two square feet each and blood-red. For example, there were such slogans as: "Long live our great teacher, great leader, great commander and great helmsman Chairman Mao!" "We vow to carry the proletarian Cultural Revolution through to the end!" "Down with evil people of all description!" "Destroy the four olds and establish the four new ones!"

When that was done, he would cut colored paper into long strips and write the slogans on them with his writing brush and ink, and then paste them on the walls beside lanes, and around the yard and in the rooms of the production brigade office. The omnipresence of slogans created an atmosphere of excitement – an anticipation of what Ma Xi called the approaching storm of a new revolution. Ma Xi himself acted in good time to organize the "Prairie Fire Combat Unit" to rebel against the production team leader, Old Pao.

One day Ma Xi summoned Wang Laobiao to the production team office and said, "Laobiao, here I have some materials listing Old Pao's crime in taking the capitalist road. You turn it into a big-character poster and paste it up on the wall right by the gate of the production brigade office."

Old Pao was in fact Wang Laobiao's elder half-brother on the paternal side and they were on good terms. How could he put up a poster to denounce his elder brother? Caught in a dilemma, he made no reply.

"Hey!" Ma Xi said. "Are you hesitating because he's your elder brother? Chairman Mao says, 'Love or hate, class status dictates.' Since he takes the capitalist road, he's no longer in the same class as we are. If you don't write a slogan like I tell you, you'll surely regret it, for I'm going to give you ten workpoints for one day's work."

"No kidding?" Wang Laobiao asked in all seriousness. In those days it took an able-bodied man to do a whole day's heavy work just to earn ten workpoints.

"No kidding. I'm the leader of the combat unit. What I say goes." Ma Xi replied firmly.

Well, then! If I can stay indoors and earn ten workpoints without working all day in the fields rain or shine, why not? Can there be anything better? As this thought struck him, he accepted Ma Xi's proposal with alacrity.

So he started his day's work with spreading out large sheets of paper on the ping-pong table in the production brigade office and wielding his writing brush to produce big-character posters exposing Old Pao's crime. At the end of each denunciation he would add a few slogans in different calligraphic styles; for example, "All poor and lower-middle peasants unite to overthrow Liu Shaoqi's loyal progeny Old Pao!" "If Old Pao does not surrender, he shall be doomed!"

The posters he wrote were very artistically done, and they attracted a daily gathering of readers.

Not long afterward, another revolutionary unit was organized.

Its leader was Wang Dapen, who was of the same Wang clan as Old Pao and a staunch defender of his. They named their organization "The Paupers Combat Unit," because as a great admirer of "the pauper spirit" eulogized by Chairman Mao, Old Pao was once commended by the county Communist Party committee for his active role in the establishment of the mutual aid group and the co-op.

The "Paupers Combat Unit" also wanted to put up big-character posters, but this was in order to expose the production team accountant Li Dashuan, who was on Ma Xi's side. However, they simply couldn't find a writer as good as Wang Laobiao – a comforting piece of news to Ma Xi and his team.

But surprisingly, a few days later the "Paupers Combat Unit" was suddenly able to put out many essays exposing Li Dashuan. The posters filled two full walls on the eastern side of the village, where the Fifth Production Team was located. There were such denunciations as "Li Dashuan made false reports of the grain yield and squirreled away the hidden output!" "Li Dashuan has committed countless crimes and cannot be pardoned!" "Li Dashuan's illicit sexual relations are beyond denial!" "Down with Li Dashuan! Deep fry Li Dashuan!" The titles were eye-catching, the language was fluent, and the revelations were shocking.

"How on earth could the writing be so much like Wang Laobiao's?" Ma Xi wondered as he went over to read the posters. Angry, he sent for Wang Laobiao, and, just as he had guessed, it was indeed the work of the latter.

"Dapen agreed to give me ten workpoints for every evening

I write for him," Wang Laobiao admitted frankly. "So I write for you during the day and write for him in the evening. What's wrong with more workpoints?"

"What? Are workpoints the only thing you care about? Chairman Mao is leading the whole country in making revolution. Did he ever ask for even one workpoint?"

After the scolding, Ma Xi ordered his team to lock Wang Laobiao in the courtyard of the production brigade day and night, not even letting him out for meals. Ma Xi figured that would prevent him writing posters for other organizations.

Wang Dapen was annoyed to learn that Wang Laobiao had been locked up. He called together a handful of close friends to find a solution, and they rescued Wang Laobiao under the cover of night. Then they hid him in a deserted yard in the Wang neighborhood, and also provided him with three meals a day so he could concentrate on writing posters to expose Li Dashuan.

It didn't take long for Ma Xi to find out where the calligrapher was hidden, and a group was dispatched to bring him back by talk or by force.

The two sides started to fight for Wang Laobiao. Some grabbed his legs, some pulled his arms, some held him by the waist and some clutched him by the hair. Those who could not lay their hands on him laid their hand on others. Among the fighting and cursing, Wang Laobiao hollered in pain, "Fuck the lot of you! What if I write for neither of you?"

"No! You have to write for us!" Ma Xi's team said.

"No! You have to write for us!" Wang Dapen's team said.

As the brawl went on, more and more people gathered around to watch, and Wang Laobiao's voice grew weaker and weaker.

"Stop pulling him like that," someone objected. "If you pull him to pieces, he won't be able to write for either of you."

When the two groups finally stopped grappling, Wang Laobiao looked no better than a street beggar, his clothes torn to rags, his legs bared to the thighs, his belly and back exposed, his hair disheveled and his face bloodlessly pale. By that time, he didn't even have the strength to speak.

A negotiation brought the two sides to an agreement that no unit would ask him to write big-character posters any more. If they wanted to put up posters, they would have to find a writer from among their own ranks. But at the same time they agreed that Wang Laobiao's talent shouldn't be wasted, and eventually made him responsible for writing quotations from Chairman Mao.

There was an art to this. The selection of the place was the first consideration. The rammed-earth walls that lined the main streets and lanes, and the sheltered walls under the eaves of houses were good places. Then came the technical part. He would first splash the selected wall with fresh water and then spread an inch-thick plaster of mud over the area. When the plaster was dry, a coat of whitewash was applied. It was only when the whitewash was thoroughly dry that he could write on it with a brush in red paint. The contents of the quotations covered a spectrum of topics, from encouraging revolution to "grasping revolution and promoting production," and to supporting world revolution –

anything as long as it was a quotation from Chairman Mao. In the larger spaces he would choose longer quotes, and in the smaller spaces he would choose shorter ones. Soon, the whole village, from the main streets to the narrow lanes, inside and outside courtyards, the fronts and backs of houses, was filled with Chairman Mao's quotations wherever the eye alighted.

Writing the quotations not only brought him workpoints, it also gave him an opportunity to remodel his old mud house, which stood by itself on the edge of the reed pond south of the main street, so old that no one could remember when it was built. Eroded by weather and years, it was in a dilapidated state. Taking advantage of his new job, Wang Laobioa plastered the outside of all the four walls with a thick layer of mud and then gave the lot a fresh coat of whitewash. On it he copied Chairman Mao's five most famous essays in small, dense characters. Looking at it from afar, one would mistakenly think the whole house had a coat of red paint.

"I love reading Chairman Mao's works," he used to say to people. "I love every word of them. If you have spare time you're welcome to drop by and study Chairman Mao's works."

After he finished the outside, he went on to plaster the inside walls and fill all the spaces with Chairman Mao's quotations. As a result, his house became entirely new, inside out.

"The villain!" Ma Xi's team clamored indignantly. "He's trying to benefit from Chairman Mao's quotations."

"So what?" Wang Dapen's team counterattacked. "Are you against that? The people of our whole country, even the whole world are benefiting from Chairman Mao. Who isn't?"

The argument between the two factions was all to Wang Laobiao's benefit, and he lived unmolested through the rest of the Cultural Revolution.

I asked about Wang Laobiao when I returned to the village in the mid-1980s. The villagers told me that after the Cultural Revolution he was no longer able to earn workpoints by writing big-character posters, and his expertise was limited to writing couplets for people at festivals. Following the introduction of the policy of reform and opening-up, he went to the county town and set up a roadside seal-engraving stall. In order to earn more money he went so far to forge seals and business for fake companies, and was sentenced to several years in prison.

After his release and until his death he never again wrote a character or engraved a seal.

Grandpa Wang, a Daring Fellow

Grandpa Wang was a clansman of mine. His full name was Feng Wang, but I respectfully addressed him as Grandpa Wang, for he was of my grandfather's generation, though of the same age as my father.

I met him again last year when I went home to commemorate the third anniversary of my father's decease. Although he was in his 70s, his back was still straight and his voice sonorous.

"Look how healthy your Grandpa Wang is," my mother kept saying admiringly. "He was born in the same year as your father, but he really knows how to take care of himself. He's raising a nanny goat and drinks its milk every day."

I remembered that Grandpa Wang was a daring fellow when he was young, certainly not the type of person who is always content with his lot. One day in 1960, a year in the middle of the three successive years of natural disasters when many people died of hunger in Henan Province, I saw a huddle of neighbors talking to two people in police uniform, who had Grandpa Wang sandwiched between them. It turned out that on the previous night he had entered the production team's mill by climbing over the wall to avail himself of a few handfuls of wheat flour, and had been discovered.

I was only six then. I found my father and neighbors nervously begging the two security people to forgive Grandpa Wang, who, on the other hand, showed no sign of fear at all.

"Is it a big deal to eat a few handfuls of flour?" I heard him say defiantly. "One can't see himself starving to death without doing something. Even if you throw me in jail, you'll have to feed me with bran buns and rotten vegetable leaves!"

In the end he wasn't arrested.

In those years every inch of land belonged to the production team. Families were not allowed to keep a private plot, and couldn't grow anything in their own courtyards, which was condemned as the remaining tail of capitalism that had to be annihilated. But Grandpa Wang ignored the rules. Not only did he rig up bean trellises and plant vegetables in his own yard, he also opened up small plots of wasteland on ditch sides and river banks, where he planted corn and sorghum. He invited my father to join him, but my father declined out of fear.

"What is there to be afraid of?" Grandpa Wang asked. "The worst is that they won't let you harvest it, but no one can prevent us from stealing what we've planted. One can't see himself starving to death without doing something!"

My childhood was mostly spent in the Great Leap Forward movement and then the three years of natural disasters, and his catchphrase "One can't see himself starving to death without doing something" left a very deep impression on my mind. If adult gossip is reliable, during that period he'd stolen quite a lot of edible things from the production team, from sweet potatoes and corn ears to turnips.

However, that doesn't mean he knew no fear. In the early days of the Cultural Revolution the village revolutionary organization asked every family to make a straw man, put the name of "Liu Shaoqi" on it, and stand it at their gate as a target of criticism against Liu's policies of "more plots for private use, more free markets, more enterprises with sole responsibility for their own profit or loss, and fixing output quotas on a household basis" and "the freedom to loan money, rent out land, hire labor and trade."

At first Grandpa Wang refused to do it. He said, "If it were not for Liu Shaoqi's policy of allowing each family a private plot, many more people would have starved to death. What's there to criticize?"

"Feng Wang, what did you say?" a Red Guard shouted at him. "Do you want to be an active counter-reactionary and be paraded through the streets with a dunce's cap on your head?"

That gave Grandpa Wang a real start. "I was wrong. I was wrong," he conceded immediately. "Liu Shaoqi should be criticized, should be criticized."

As soon as he was back home, he made a straw man and stood it at his gate, but he didn't put Liu Shaoqi's name on it. His excuse was that since he was of poor-peasant origin and never went to school, he could neither read nor write.

One day I saw him standing beside my father, one hand pointing at the straw man and the other patting his chest. All the while his eyes roved around with a frightened look and his face displayed a mixture of expressions, though he didn't say a word. When I look back on the scene many years later, I'm now in a better position to understand his dilemma: At heart he couldn't bring himself to criticize Liu Shaoqi, but outwardly he had to make Liu a target.

I also remember that in his youth Grandpa Wang was fond of hunting hares. In autumn and winter he would often go out with his home-made hunting gun on his shoulder and return with a blood-dripping hare or two hanging from the barrel.

One snowy winter day, he took me and his eldest son with him on a hunting trip. We boys each carried a stick, and were told to beat the bushes and grass clumps and poke into the holes in ancient tombs as we walked. Suddenly a frightened hare sprang out from the grass and skipped away over the snow, but it wasn't able to run far before it was caught.

As we walked on we came upon a line of hare footprints.

"You two wait here," Grandpa Wang said. "I'll follow the track and the hare will return in a minute."

Before long we heard him call out to us: "The hare's coming toward you. Get ready!"

And sure enough, a hare tumbled toward us like a ball of snow with Grandpa Wang at its heels. It was easy enough to surround and catch the exhausted animal.

When he was young, Grandpa Wang had had another hobby – training eagles to catch hares, a hobby he was well-known for in the surrounding villages.

The first step was to catch the eagle. Four nets were set up in an open space and a few starved young roosters placed in the square. The square would then be covered with another net. This covering net would be nearly invisible to a swooping eagle intent on its prey. While the hungry roosters cackled and fought each other, Grandpa Wang would sit nearby under a big tree drinking tea and watching the sky. Once he saw an eagle circling above he'd immediately put down his teacup and put on a pair of thick gloves. At almost the same time, the eagle would come swooping down to snatch the roosters but would strike headlong into the net and bring the whole structure down. It was then easy enough to get hold of the entangled bird.

The next step was to train the eagle. A yard-long leather strap was tied to one leg of the captured eagle and the other end to a copper ring. Then a 20-to-30-yard-long iron wire attached to the ring. Grandpa Wang would stand at one end of the wire with the eagle perched on his shoulder and his helper would sit at the other end and wave a dead hare while making an "ah … ah" sound to attract the eagle's attention. Once the eagle detected the hare, it would swish toward the prey. The copper ring scraping along the iron wire would flash like a bolt of lightning. But the helper would already have the hare hidden behind his back, and the frustrated eagle could only roll its eyes in rage. At that moment, Grandpa Wang would call to it, "Come back! Come back!" And the disappointed eagle would return to his shoulder.

It usually took two or three weeks before the eagle had learned to take off and return at Grandpa Wang's command, and then

In fact, I didn't have many opportunities to associate with Grandpa Wang when I was young, because my mother was afraid that I might learn his daring ways.

the wire could be discarded.

The last step was endurance training. For days the eagle would be tied to a suspended horizontal bar and not given any food or allowed to sleep. Finally, Grandpa Wang would take the hungry and sleepy bird to an open field and let it fly. It would soar up and make circles in the sky. Once it detected a hare it would swoop down and, with a quick snatch, bring the prey back to Grandpa Wang's shoulder.

Grandpa Wang would take out a sharp knife and cut off a warm piece of blood-dripping meat and put it in the eagle's beak, which it would swallow with a mere stretch of the neck.

In fact, I didn't have many opportunities to associate with Grandpa Wang when I was young, because my mother was afraid that I might learn his daring ways. But now that I myself am getting on in years and recall my childhood days, Grandpa Wang often recurs to my memory.

Son

Son was the name of a person living on the south street of my village. He was five or six years older than I. Since the residents on that street were composed of miscellaneous clans, I have no way of telling what his family name really was.

It is said that his father died before he came into this world and his mother died soon after. He was raised by his grandmother, who carried him in her arms from door to door, begging for milk and food. She never bothered to give him a name even when he was able to walk steadily and run around. One day someone accidentally remarked that he was the son of the whole village. From then on people, old and young, started to call him Son, and so Son became his name.

When he reached school age he had to stay at home because he was too poor to pay for the fees and textbooks. His grandmother grew anxious when children much younger than he were starting school. She went to the village Party branch secretary to seek help.

"Elder sister, don't worry," the Party secretary assured her. "Since he's the son of the village, we must send him to school.

Let's do it this way: Every household will chip in five *fen* for his fees."

So, with the help of the whole village Son was able to go to school.

His grandmother died in the three years of natural disasters, and he was left alone in the world.

"Now you take care of Son," the Party secretary said to Liu Quan, the leader of the Eighth Production Team. "Your production team must provide for him."

"We have nothing ourselves," Liu Quan answered. "How can we provide for him?"

"Doesn't your team have a storehouse? Put him in there. On the one hand he can keep an eye on the place, on the other he won't starve to death. As for clothes, see which family has children of his size and beg for a piece or two. As long as he has a loincloth or something in summer and won't freeze to death in winter, it will be good enough. As for school, the whole village will continue to share the fees."

So Son had a place to live, clothes to wear and a school to attend. If he were hungry in the evenings, he could munch on the corn, wheat or beans in the storehouse. While everyone else was famished and sallow, he alone looked ruddy and robust. No one ever heard him say he was hungry.

What Liu Quan was most afraid of was the school vacations, because during vacation time the school no longer provided meals. Then what about Son? He put the question to the Party secretary.

He was five or six years older than I. Since the residents on that street were composed of miscellaneous clans, I have no way of telling what his family name really was.

"Are you dumb?" the Party secretary replied. "Treat him as we treat the workgroup – one household provides one day's meals."

"But the workgroup member pays 15 *fen* after the meal. Where will Son get the money? Eat without paying?"

"Do you have any better idea?"

The Party secretary also made that point at the village meeting. "During school vacation," he said categorically, "Son will eat at each household in turn, like the workgroup, and he's not going to pay. Any objections?"

Nobody said anything, either in support or disagreement. It was a difficult time for everyone – even wild herbs and tree barks were consumed. Who could afford to feed one more mouth? But everyone took pity on the homeless child. If they didn't help him, who would?

Finding no objection, the Party secretary announced, "So this is settled. Look out if you mistreat the child. I'll have you publicly criticized."

Since then, Son never had to worry about food or clothing. On school days he ate at school, during vacation time he ate with one family or another. He was the most envied person in the village.

When the Cultural Revolution started he was a junior student at Number One High in the county town. He collected a group of students to plunder the warehouse of the county's armed forces department, and each of them got an army uniform, which they wore with a leather belt and a red armband with the words "December Ninth Rebellion Corps" printed on it. Son became the associate director of the corps. They started to make revolution at the school by criticizing the teachers. Then they went to the compounds of the county government and Communist Party committee to beat, smash, loot and criticize Li Changlin, the head of the county government and Li Shulin, the chief secretary of the county Communist Party committee. Both were revolutionary veterans. Son made them wear dunce's caps and paraded them through the streets of the town. With a bullhorn in one hand he waved his fist in elation as he led the procession in slogan shouting. There were fluttering banners and colorful posters everywhere. Shouts of "Down with Li Changlin!" and "Deep-fry Li Shulin!" filled the air, and people filled the streets to watch.

It happened that the village Party secretary and Liu Quan were in town taking a calf to a vet. When they saw Son making revolution, they pulled him aside and whispered, "Son, these guys are what we used to call county magistrates. You can't insult them. You really shouldn't."

"Chairman Mao teaches us, 'He who is not afraid of death by a thousand cuts dares to unhorse the emperor.' So what if they were county magistrates?" Son replied defiantly.

"Son, don't fool around," the village Party secretary warned.

Son's face fell immediately. "What do you mean by 'fooling around?'" he roared. "I'm answering Chairman Mao's call, and you call that 'fooling around?' Are you two on their side?" Son turned and ran to catch up with the procession.

The village Party secretary and Liu Quan were struck dumb. They looked at each other and did not know what to say. After a long while, Liu Quan tugged at the secretary's arm and said, "What on earth's happened to that child? Brother, let's go. He's old enough to take care of himself."

The Party secretary returned to the village without saying another word, but that night he was unable to sleep.

In fact, Son's seemingly sudden change of face had a more deep-rooted reason, especially when the phrase "fool around" was mentioned. From babyhood to his teenage years he had heard it too many times, for it was a ready phrase on the Party secretary's lips when lecturing him.

When he had a fight in elementary school, the Party secretary would say, "Son, don't fool around. It's illegal to hit others."

When he was caught stealing, the Party secretary would say, "Son, don't fool around. Thieves used to have their fingers chopped off."

Or when the Party secretary learned he'd played truant from school, he would say, "Son, don't fool around. If you don't study hard, you'll be working in the fields with muddy legs all your life."

But most of all it was because of the Party secretary's youngest daughter, Rong, who was the same age as he was. She was quite pretty, and after graduating from a drama school she was assigned to the county's Henan Opera Troupe as an actress. She was gifted and had a beautiful voice. Her acting could always bring the role alive. When she played the young widow in the opera *The Young Widow Visiting the Grave*, the audience couldn't help shedding tears of sympathy. When she played Mu Guiying in *Mu Guiying Takes Command*, every young woman in the audience was eager to join the army. In less than two years she became the star actress of the county troupe.

Son could not be described as handsome, but that did not prevent him from thinking of marrying Rong. At first he sent her love letters. Then he knocked on her window at midnight, and eventually he would intercept her on her way home after a performance. When Rong told her parents about his behavior, the Party secretary gave him a serious dressing down, warning him, "Rong is your elder sister. Don't fool around with her. You're young. At your age you should devote yourself to your studies."

Though Son apologized and promised to be good, he held a grudge in his heart.

As the parade procession passed the gate of the county troupe, he saw a slogan on the wall, which read: "Down with the lecherous Director Li!" Rong works here, he thought. Could she be having an affair with the director?

The next morning he led a group of Red Guards to the troupe and learned that his guess was correct. The rebel factions of the troupe told him that the director was locked up in the props' room and Rong had fled home.

"Let's go catch her!" Son said with a wave of his arm. "Follow me. She lives in my village."

So the rebel factions of the troupe joined those of Number One High and they marched off led by Son.

On his way Son was seething with anger. He hated Rong. What's so good about the director? Except for singing a few tunes, what else does he know? I'm also a director. Ain't I better than that guy? Your father always tells me "Don't fool around." How is it you're fooling around with such an old goat? The more he thought about it, the angrier he became.

Reaching the village, he went straight to the Party secretary's place and pounded on the gate. Rong's mother answered the door.

"Son, what's up?" she asked in surprise.

"Where's Yang Rong? I hear she's hiding at home."

"Your sister Rong is not at home," she said as she tried to push the gate closed.

"Whose sister is she?! She's an actress! She's a tramp!" he bellowed.

"Bullshit!" the mother scolded back. "Isn't she your sister? When you were babies, Rong sucked one of my breasts and you sucked the other. If not your sister, what do you call her then? If we'd known you'd turn out this way, we should have let you die of hunger!"

Son was unable to think of a retort, for he knew she was right.

Just then someone yelled, "Yang Rong has escaped through the back door!"

Like a horde of locusts, the Red Guards swarmed toward the back door, leaving Son standing at the gate feeling foolish.

"Where did this son of a bitch come from? Does he think he can run amok in our village?" he heard people say.

"Who does the little bastard think he is?"

"We should have let him starve to death."

Suddenly he felt a slap on his butt. Then he heard, "He you! Get lost! Don't fool around here."

He turned around and saw Liu Quan, behind whom stood the Party secretary, who was smoking a pipe contemplatively and staring coldly at him with a frown on his face.

Without knowing why, Son felt deflated and his head empty. There was a twinge in his nose and he felt like crying.

Heaven Kills "Heavenly Law"

Tianfa was my classmate at elementary school. He was five or six years older than I, and the oldest one in my class. He was from a neighboring village. His family name was Tian and his first name Tianfa, which literally means "Heavenly law."

His family was quite poor. There were four boys in the family, but they only had a two-room thatched hut. That probably contributed to his unruly character. He was often engaged in stealing hens and dogs, in quarrels and brawls. People shook their heads in disapproval when they talked about him.

One winter day it snowed, and by the time school let out the snow was already three or four inches deep. Since few of my classmates had cotton-padded jackets, we stood shivering at the door wondering how to get home.

"Give me a pancake and I'll go home in my underpants only," Tianfa said.

"Are you serious?" another classmate took up the challenge.

"If I break my word I'll call you Grandpa!"

"Here's a pancake. Eat it and go!"

Then he flung off his coat, slipped out of his pants and bent down to take off his shoes. With nothing but his underpants on, he raced out of the classroom and ran barefoot across the snow.

"Hurray!" the whole class cheered. "If you go back on your word, you have to call us all Grandpa!"

The classmate handed him a corn-flour pancake, which he gulped down in a couple of mouthfuls. Then he flung off his coat, slipped out of his pants and bent down to take off his shoes. With nothing but his underpants on, he raced out of the classroom and ran barefoot across the snow. No one in the class made another complaint about the cold.

Tianfa was quite clever, but his schoolwork was poor. In fact, in Chinese and maths he was always bottom of the class. The most remarkable was his compositions, which were usually no more than a few sentences strung together. It seemed he had difficulties in mastering the more complicated characters, for he tended to use characters with fewer strokes. In one composition that didn't fill half a page, he put down more than a dozen "*了*'s" (an auxiliary word to indicate a past action). The teacher's remark was rather humorous. He commented in red ink: "You've used far too many *了*'s in this piece. Please save a few for future use." That became a standing joke in the class.

Tianfa was about 18 when the Cultural Revolution began. Probably in revenge for his poor marks, he took the lead in setting up a revolutionary organization at the school, called "The Prairie Fire Spark Combat Unit."

One day, he called a meeting to criticize and denounce the schoolmaster. Standing barefoot on a desk, he waved his arm, and shouted, "Revolutionary comrades, we must answer our great leader Chairman Mao's call to smash the old education system.

We shall no longer be the victims of the 'submissive lambs with good marks' policy. We must overthrow the reactionary gang headed by the schoolmaster. We must criticize and denounce them till they smell like hogs!"

While he was making his speech he felt two heavy spanks on his buttocks, but in his elation he didn't even deign to turn and look.

Then he cursed with his hands over his behind. "Who the hell dares to beat a young revolutionary? Have you got the guts of a dog?"

The person didn't answer but gave him two more loud slaps with the sole of a shoe.

This time he turned around, and saw it was none other than his father, who, with a shoe in one hand, was glaring at him ferociously. The old man didn't say anything but raised the shoe again.

Tianfa jumped off the desk and hopped away with his hands over his behind. "You're sabotaging the Cultural Revolution!" he yelled as he ran. "Chairman Mao says, 'Love or hate, class status dictates.' From now on you're no longer my father!"

The crowd burst out laughing. Still without a word, his father threw the shoe on the ground, put his foot in it and shuffled away.

As the Cultural Revolution went on, the slogan "To rebel is justified" became Tianfa's pet phrase. He led his combat unit from one household to another to "destroy the four olds and establish the four new ones." They smashed incense burners and memorial tablets, and burned ancient books and paintings.

One day he might be criticizing teachers, another day he could be denouncing Party secretaries, and the following day he would be supporting revolution in neighboring villages. If someone was offensive in his eyes, he would summon his combat unit to beat and criticize the person, then have him paraded through the streets wearing a dunce's cap. All at once, he became a herald of evil in the villages.

People were scared at the sight of him. If they saw him approach when they were having lunch, they would stop eating and ask, with their bowls held respectfully in both hands: "Tianfa, would you like to have something to eat?"

If they saw him approach when they were working in the fields, they would stop their work and ask respectfully: "Tianfa, would you mind sitting here and taking a rest?"

If they saw him approach when they were chatting, they would immediately fall silent and ask respectfully: "Tianfa, would you like to have a smoke?"

And yet, Tianfa never responded to those greetings. He just strutted past with a face as grim as his father's at the shoe-sole spanking.

Behind his back people started to call him "Tiansha," which literally means "Heaven kills."

And as if it were a prediction of fate, in the fall of 1967 when a group of rebel factions from the provincial capital Zhengzhou came to my county to seize weapons, he was hit during an armed clash by a stray bullet, and dropped dead without a sound.

After that, no one in the village mentioned him again.

Chang Gen,
a Crippled Fan of an Actress

The recent rise of groupies in China reminds me of a super fan in my village as far back as the 1960s. His name was Chang Gen, but he was later called Lame Gen, for he became crippled in a chase after "The Actress."

"The Actress" was the pet name of an actress of the county's Henan Opera Troupe. She was a native of Yangwa Village, good-looking and had a beautiful voice. Though quite young, she was already a household name and the star actress of the troupe.

Chang Gen first learned of her name from hearsay, for he never had the spare money for theater tickets. When Old Pao, Son, Gouwang or others talked about her at lunch gatherings, saliva spluttered from their greasy mouths, their faces flushed with excitement, and their eyes shone like those of hungry wolves at the sight of meat which they could smell but could not reach. Sometimes they extolled her gorgeous looks, sometimes they satirized her for being a flirt, sometimes they imitated her coquettish way of singing, and they often bragged about their close relations with her. Gouwang said she was a classmate of a sister of his aunt's daughter-in-law; Son said his grandma's brother-in-law and The Actress' aunt were in-laws; Old Pao said he had seen her photograph at his elementary school best friend's place. He certainly wasn't so rude as to ask his friend about their relations, but they were no doubt intimate. Well, whenever the gossip drifted to this topic, Chang Gen was always silent, but inwardly he was cursing: What the fuck is the use of bragging about this? However, he was sure about one thing – she was not only a good actress, but had the most attractive looks.

In order to hear her coquettish voice or catch a glimpse of her beauty, he racked his brains day after day. When he learned that actors and actresses had a habit of going into the suburbs to train their voices on hilltops, in ravines or by riverbanks in the early mornings even during the winter, for several nights in succession he gave up sleep to search for them in such places. With a flashlight in his hand he walked miles upon miles braving the chilling winds. But to his great disappointment, all he found was a group of young apprentices of the troupe howling against the wind. The Actress was not among them.

Another day he heard that the troupe was staging *The Daughter of the Head of the People's Commune* in town, with The Actress starring as the daughter. He wanted very much to watch the performance but he couldn't afford the ticket. After turning the matter over and over in his head, he decided to scale the back wall of the theater after dark. This wall was no less than 20 feet high. What he didn't know was that the troupe had spread a layer of human waste at the foot of the wall. So when he lowered himself to the ground, he slipped and rolled over in the stink. Worse still, he fractured his shinbone. Being poor though, he didn't go to a doctor, and was left crippled. That was when people started to call him Lame Gen.

Although he was crippled, he didn't give up the hope of seeing The Actress. Then the Cultural Revolution began. The revolutionary organizations in the county town made the opera troupe a major target. As The Actress was the star and had acted the main roles in such traditional plays as *Mu Guiying Takes Command*, *Yang's Fourth Son Visits His Mother* and *Judge Bao*, she was cited as an infamous example of propagating the feudal ideology of hero-and-beauty.

At the same time, Lame Gen was also making revolution in the village. With a green army cap on his head, a red armband around his left sleeve, an old leather belt round his waist, and a walking stick in his hand, he limped around the village to destroy the four olds.

One day he caught news that the Red Guards of Number One High in the county town was going to criticize The Actress at a public meeting the next day. The mere thought that she was going to be paraded through the streets with a dunce's cap on her head and a blackboard hanging from her neck was too exciting for him to go to sleep. Early next morning, without even having breakfast, he limped eagerly to town. At the gate of the troupe's compound, he saw a host of Red Guards waving a sea of red banners and shouting deafening slogans, but, believe it or not, the main target of criticism was absent. Amidst the din he heard a whisper that The Actress had slipped away the previous night back to her parents' home about seven miles from town. The crowd then swarmed toward her home village. He tried to keep up with the procession but the Red Guards with good legs and high spirits were soon out of sight.

Leaning on his stick, he pushed on as fast as his crippled leg could carry him, while stopping from time to time to ask the way. The July sun was like a ball of fire scorching the ground. On the dusty and empty road his lone figure hurried along. Sweat poured off him, but his spirit remained as high as ever.

By the time he finally reached Yangwa Village, he was surprised to see the Red Guards already returning. Some looked dejected, some were foaming with obscenities, and some had faces dark with rage. He learned that they had failed to find The Actress at her parents'. It was a piece of false information.

How could it be so difficult just to have a peep at The Actress? The day was hot, the journey had been long, and he was hungry and thirsty. But since he was already there, why not take a look at her place of birth? That would be certainly better than having traveled so far for nothing.

So he found his way to her parents' house, and sat down in the courtyard. As he watched the desolate aftermath of the Red Guards' smashing, looting and burning, he felt both angry and happy. He was angry because he had failed once again to see her, and yet he was happy to see that she could also come to such a pass. Her parents were nowhere in sight, probably scared away. And in the empty yard there was only him sitting there alone.

Just then he heard a rustling in the straw stack in one corner of the yard. He went over and as he brushed aside the loose straw with his stick, a woman's face emerged – a pretty face. The straw and leaves tangled in her hair and the terror in her eyes couldn't hide the loveliness of that young face.

"Are you The Actress? Come out of there!" he shouted.

The woman shuddered, unable to speak or move. She must be The Actress, he thought, and he felt the blood rushing to his head. He dropped the stick and stretched out his quivering arms to the woman. He was going to help her out from the straw stack so that he could look the woman in the eye and face to face, a face he'd been dreaming of for days and nights. It was a dream come true! But before his hands reached her and even before he could get well focused on the face, he felt something hit him on the head from behind, and he lost consciousness.

When he came to, he found he was lying on the ground, encircled by the Red Guards of Yangwa Village. Some were kicking him, some were spitting at him, and some were calling him a lecher. He was angry. He wanted no more than to take a good look at her. Would you call that lechery? He struggled to his feet. He was going to say that he had been her admirer for years. Although he too was a Red Guard, he wasn't going to treat her like those from town. He had no bad intentions. Only a look, a look at that pretty face. But he was quick to catch himself, for he could see those standing in front of him were also Red Guards. If he said he had a liking for the hero-and-beauty, they might criticize him for blurring class alignment. As he thought of that, he said aloud, "Tell me, comrades-in-arms of Yangwa Village, was that woman The Actress?"

"What do you mean by 'comrades-in-arms?' " the Red Guards asked him. "And who are you?"

"We're all Chairman Mao's Red Guards and we're comrades-in-arms fighting in the same trench. We can't let the 'heroes-and-beauties' go unpunished. I'm going to take her to town and have her paraded through the streets."

"Who are you going to parade through the streets, you smelly lecher? Beat him!" Fists and kicks landed on Lame Gen with the curses.

"Revolution is already underway and you're still protecting The Actress!" he wailed in pain. "Are you Chairman Mao's Red Guards?"

"Who did you say is The Actress?" one of the Red Guards asked matter-of-factly.

"Wasn't the woman hiding in the straw stack just now The Actress? Are you treating me this way because you want to protect her? What happened to your class stand?"

"The Actress didn't come back here," the Red Guard said. "The girl just now is a neighbor. She was scared by the Red Guards from town and was hiding there. We caught you trying to rape her!"

Lame Gen was struck dumb, and failed to come up with a word of defense.

At last with the intervention of some onlookers, the Yangwa Red Guards let him off.

... for he couldn't bring himself to hear somebody mention the two words. They were too much for him to bear. It wasn't until many years later that he learned that the woman hiding in the straw stack was in fact none other than The Actress.

With his body covered in bruises, an empty stomach, a dry throat, and a chest full of pent-up anger, he limped home under the blazing sun.

"Revolution is underway and people are rebelling against old things," he wondered as he limped. "How could they beat me up for wishing to have a look at a damned actress? And why on earth is it so difficult even to catch a glimpse of her?"

From then on, whenever Old Pao, Son, Gouwang or others spoke of "The Actress" at lunch gatherings, he would just walk away, for he couldn't bring himself to hear somebody mention the two words. They were too much for him to bear.

It wasn't until many years later that he learned that the woman hiding in the straw stack was in fact none other than The Actress. The Red Guards of Yangwa Village had lied to protect her.

Great Leap Forward Nights

In the late 1950s the Great Leap Forward movement spread into the rural areas. Workgroups were dispatched from the county government and the people's communes to the villages, and the leader of the group overrode the power of the village Communist Party branch. He ordered people about and was the de facto supreme leader of the village. As far as I can remember, the Great Leap Forward movement in my village was directly guided by the workgroup.

The leader of the workgroup stationed in my village was a Mr Jin. He was a native of Shanxi Province and had come south with the People's Liberation Army to carry out administrative work. He was of medium height and not very talkative, but once he spoke his words were harsh and authoritative. Not only were the village leaders and ordinary commune members afraid of him, the children were also afraid of him. The former were afraid of being criticized; the latter were afraid of being debarred from the kitchen. At that time, people had their meals at the collective kitchen. Their woks were smashed and their grain store was confiscated. Families were not allowed to cook. The daily rationing was three ounces of grain for an adult and two ounces for a child. If one was debarred from the kitchen, it meant starving to death. Therefore those two punishments were the most powerful weapons of Old Jin and his workgroup, which consisted of half a dozen people also dispatched to the village from above.

There were two recognizable characteristics that distinguished them from ordinary peasants. One was that they didn't wear their jackets properly but draped them over their shoulders. The other was that they had the habit of sticking their hands in their pants' pockets. When they walked, they looked straight ahead, with an air of importance. They walked quickly, their arms slightly bent, so that their jackets puffed up like the cloak of Astro Boy in the Japanese TV series decades later.

Bragging and making headlines were the hallmark of the Great Leap Forward movement. According to Old Jin's arrangement, some events were to be put on in the daytime, while some were to be staged in the evening. For instance, the cart-pulling contest was a daytime show to prove that a human being is more powerful than a draft animal. For that purpose a sinewy young man was selected. He stripped himself to the waist, drew a red sun on his belly, put on a horse-head mask with a large firecracker suspended from each ear, grabbed the shafts in his hands and pulled the cart along the street.

Another daytime show was iron smelting. Along the main street of the village a small furnace made of sun-dried mud bricks was built every dozen yards with firewood at the bottom and the smashed woks, old iron pails, door knockers and all sorts of iron scraps above. Once the fire was lit the whole village would be blanketed in smoke so dense that one couldn't see the person in front. When leaders from the county or people's commune came on inspection tours, their way of gauging the achievement of iron production was simply judging the density of each village's smoke. Once when Old Jin learned the inspection team was on its way to the village, he immediately sent out the workgroup members to the production teams to tell the commune members to light the furnace, not only the fires in the chambers of the furnaces but also firewood piled beside the furnaces. As if that were not enough, he ordered some commune members to burn straw in the open space of some larger courtyards behind locked gates. As a result, when the inspection team arrived they were immediately choked by the rolling acrid yellow smoke. With teary eyes and running noses, those big shots shook Old Jin's hand and dragged him out of the village to chant their praises: "Old Jin, your village is really marvelous at producing iron, really marvelous!"

But the more showy events were usually saved for the evenings. The rural night scene during the Great Leap Forward was strikingly beautiful. At wheat harvest season, Old Jin ordered the commune members to pack the cut wheat of dozens of *mu* into one *mu* (1 *mu* $\approx$ 0.16 of an acre) of land, while having stools concealed among the standing sheaves. When the county and people's commune inspection team came in the evening he would get children to stand on the stools and then brag about the bumper harvest: One *mu* of land was expected to yield 100,000 pounds of grain. Just look! How big and heavy the wheat ears were! The wheat stalks were so thick and sturdy that a child could stand on them.

Once while he was reporting, a child accidentally lost his footing and fell off his stool, and the other children fell off one after another with his infectious cries of alarm. As it was evening the inspection team couldn't see clearly what was going on. They probably thought that the children were putting on some kind of performance.

In autumn, in order to create a vibrant scene of building socialism, Old Jin had the production teams make a lot of paper lanterns and hang them up on the trees inside and outside the village, on grave mounds, hilltops, riverbanks and well sides. If there was no place to hang them, he demanded that lantern-posts be erected in the open fields. So, from afar the fields in the evening were starry bright. The following two lines are a description of the scene:

> *The Lord in Heaven stamps and asks:*
> *When does the Milky Way flow on Earth?*

In the lantern light, the commune members harvested sweet potatoes, sowed wheat and leveled the land. The most strenuous work was turning up the soil. Normally, if one digs spadeful by spadeful without leaving any soil unturned, an able-bodied

Half a century has passed since then. During that time I've been to many places and been through numerous nights, but none was so impressive as the night scene during the Great Leap Forward movement in my home village.

young man could do no more than half a *mu* in a day. But at night, especially according to the method taught by Old Jin, a person was able to turn up several *mu* in a night. His method was to dig up a spadeful of soil and scatter the loose earth over the surrounding area, and to prevent the inspection team from discovering the secret, when day was about to break he ordered the commune members to draw a harrow over the field to loosen the top soil. Therefore, if one took a casual look from a distance, the land looked flat and smooth as if freshly plowed and harrowed. But since there was only a thin layer of loose soil and the earth beneath was mostly solid and hard, the wheat seeds could not be sowed deep enough, and so they were either pecked out by birds or frozen and unable to sprout. The result was that when spring came the following year the wheat seedlings were thin and sparse, and at harvest time the output was even less than the seeds they had put into the ground.

As for harvesting sweet potatoes at night, the commune members didn't use spades, nor did they use hoes or picks. What they did under the feeble lantern light was give a few kicks at the root and then pull up the vine, and they collected only what came up with the vine. In such a wasteful way, one *mu* of land yielded little more than a hundred pounds of sweet potatoes. The majority of the sweet potatoes remained buried in the earth. But their enthusiasm and accomplishment in building socialism was able to seize the limelight, as one commune member could harvest three to five *mu* of sweet potatoes in one single night, and at the same time save the trouble of plowing the field for wheat sowing. That was the greatest agricultural wonder ever acclaimed in human history, and could be illustrated by a piece of doggerel posted up on the honor board at the production brigade office in praise of a member of the Eighth Production Team, Li Huzhan. It went like this:

> *Li Huzhan is an able man;*
> *In one night he digs tracts of land.*
> *Last night here grew potatoes sweet;*
> *Today it's turned to fields of wheat.*
> *The commune members are good hands*
> *At opening up wasted lands.*
> *Tomorrow night we plow again;*
> *Our fields will stretch to fairyland.*

The next spring, the starving villagers remembered the unharvested sweet potatoes in the ground. They sneaked out to the fields with spades and hoes, but the sweet potatoes they found were all frozen and rotten. And more unfortunate than that were those caught red-handed by Old Jin and his group. They were accused of sabotaging the production team's wheat field, debarred from the kitchen and paraded through the streets.

Half a century has passed since then. During that time I've been to many places and been through numerous nights, but none was so impressive as the night scene during the Great Leap Forward movement in my home village.

My Grandfather's Goats

My maternal grandfather used to raise about 20 goats, which he penned behind the main house of Grandpa Jinlin.

Grandpa Jinlin was said to be somewhat eccentric. He and his wife had no children, and they lived reclusively in a copse east of the village. They had no neighbors to their left or right, in front or behind. However, as he was on good terms with my grandfather, he agreed to let Grandfather use the lone thatched hut behind his house as a fold. The goats were then his only neighbors.

Grandfather worked in the fields in the morning and grazed the goats in the afternoon. Every day at around three o'clock he would come along one of the footpaths to the hut and open the gate of the fold. With the bellwether in the lead, the herd would push and squeeze through the gate and head for the dried riverbed outside the village.

As a matter of fact the river could hardly be called a river any more, for only in the rainy season would there be a trickle of muddy water flowing along its bed, but the trees lining the banks were old and flourishing. The trunks of the elms were thicker than an arm-span and the mulberries were twisted by age and weather. In early spring, the riverbed was a luxuriant carpet of soft grass.

Once the flock arrived, they would lower their heads and start to graze on the grass, the noise of their chewing echoed along the empty river. Tending goats was not a difficult task – one only needed to make sure they didn't sneak beyond the banks to eat the wheat sprouts. The goats would graze and move slowly along the riverbed under the lead of the bellwether. At the same time, Grandfather could find a sunny spot on the lee side of the slope, spread his sheepskin overcoat on the ground and take a comfortable nap.

All of a sudden, the goats stopped grazing. They raised their heads and gazed intently. Another flock of goats was coming from the opposite direction. This flock belonged to another villager, Gen, who was an even more carefree herdsman than Grandfather, for he often left his flock in the riverbed and went away to attend to other things.

With the scarcity of fresh grass in springtime and the militant nature of goats, when two flocks met, they would opt to fight. The kids baaed and sought refuge under their mothers' bellies as the flock marshaled itself into combat position.

The bellwether on each side was as large as a small calf, and sturdily built. He always walked ahead of his tribe like an intrepid army general. When the two came within three yards of each other, they halted and stared the other in the eye with their heads held high. After the momentary face-off, they each backed off a few steps, lowered their heads so their horns pointed forward, and charged. With a loud "bang," Grandfather's bellwether stood firm, while Gen's rebounded two or three steps. With his head on one side, his body aslant, he turned two circles, probably trying to gauge his pain or to muster his courage, before he was back into a dueling position. After a few more rounds of face-off and charging, Gen's bellwether was defeated. Drooping his head like a defeated dog, he quietly led his tribe away.

During the three years of natural disasters there was a severe grain shortage. With many children, my family was often on the verge of starvation. One day Grandfather dropped in, bringing us several chunks of boiled goat's meat.

"The children are at a growing age," he said to Mother. "They shouldn't be starved. Goat's meat is nourishing. Take this to make some soup. It's good for their health. Your Uncle Jinlin says a goat now sells for over 200 *yuan* at the market, but I'm not going to sell mine, no matter how much they can bring in. The children's health is more important."

And every other month or so Grandfather would bring us some goat's meat. Even decades after his death Mother did not stop reminding us that if it were not for his goats we might not have survived the hard times.

One day, not long after the beginning of the Cultural Revolution, Grandfather came again, this time with a full basket of goat's meat, but with a somber face. He sat down without a word.

"Pa, what's wrong?" Mother asked.

"My goats are gone."

"How come?"

"Erhan and the Red Guards butchered them. They said the goats were a remaining tail of capitalism and must be annihilated. This basket of goat's meat for the children is all that remains. There'll be no more." He left without even drinking a cup of water.

Even now I can still remember the grief and worry on his face. Later, my mother's brother filled me in with more detail.

Erhan had pushed a knife into the bellwether, but the goat managed to get free. With bloody eyes, it charged at Erhan with leveled horns. Erhan dropped the knife and ran for dear life with the goat in hot pursuit.

"The goat has gone mad! The goat has gone mad!" people along the street shouted in alarm.

"It serves him right!" some whispered. "It's no more than he deserves."

The bellwether caught up and gored him in the butt, sending him flying through the air. He fell face down, bloody and bruised.

For years afterward, his hands would tremble uncontrollably at the mere mention of butchering goats. The villagers said that was retribution. Don't think you can go unpunished if you mistreat a life, even if it is only an animal's.

Bathing

In the 1950s and 1960s the northwestern region of Henan Province had ample water resources, and bathing was not a problem in the countryside. Rivers zigzagged between villages, with limpid water flowing all the year round. Channels and ditches were dug to lead off the water to irrigate the vast stretches of cropland like the veins of a leaf.

At that time the water table was high. Well water was no more than two or three feet from the surface, and one only needed to bend low to fill a bucket. In the rainy season the larger pits in the village were filled. Peasants stripped to their underpants used the pits as natural bathtubs, and coming back from the fields in the evening they could jump into the river and swim to wash off both the sweat and dirt and the fatigue of a long day's work.

Children usually took their baths in the channels, which were about a yard in width and two or three feet in depth. The water there ran slowly, and abounded in small fish, frogs, tadpoles and shrimps. Children played there in groups, and then climbed up the bank, wiped themselves dry with their T-shirts, pulled on their pants and scampered home.

The well pool was a favorite bathing place for the brave. Wells were an important source of water for irrigation. Back then, the windlass, a device invented as far back as the Han Dynasty (206 BC-220 AD), was still a popular tool for hoisting water. A bucket was fixed to each end of a rope wound around a pulley. When one turned the handle, one bucket would come up full while the other would go down empty. On one side of each bucket was a ring looped around a long bamboo pole stuck down along the opposite sides of the well-shaft into the bottom. The poles served as guides to ensure the buckets did not get tangled up or bump each other and spill the water. The water was poured into a pool beside the well, from which it was led into the branching ditches. Water just out of the well was clean but chilly. Those who would rather indulge in a moment's pleasure than worry about long-term effects on health would jump into the pool, duck their heads under a few times and scramble out. As the sudden chill could trigger serious illness, parents strictly forbade their children to bathe there.

Quite a lot of families dug wells in their own courtyards. By fetching up a bucket of water in the morning and leaving it in the sun they could have a warm and refreshing bath – literally from head to toe – by pouring the warm water over themselves after returning from the fields in the evening.

One thing the country folk yearned for was to take a bath in a bathhouse like the townsfolk. Back then, there was only one bathhouse in the whole town. Though it was only ten *fen* for a bath, it was nonetheless considered a privilege for the moneyed. To children living in the villages, a bath in the bathhouse was a special treat to celebrate the Spring Festival, so long as their parents were ready to spend money on such things.

I had one such experience when I was five or six years old. My father begged a relative of my great-grandfather's generation to take me along with his other children to the bathhouse in town — a trip filled with excitement and expectancy.

The bathhouse was located on the northeastern corner of the T-shaped intersection at the town center. It was a large compound like those inns catering to the cart-drivers with their carts and draft animals. The room was also huge, lined with rows of narrow wooden beds with a low table between every two. On the table there was a teapot, teacups and two green pieces of some unknown things the size of walnuts.

The old man didn't seem to be a frequent client, for he picked up one of the green lumps and examined it. It felt soft in the hand and gave off a faint aroma when placed under the nose.

"Great-grandpa, what's that?" we asked.

"Cookie," he replied. "It's a snack. People are likely to swoon in the hot-water pool if they're hungry."

Taking that as good advice we each picked up a piece and put it in our mouth. But sweet as it might have smelled, it wasn't really palatable and was even sickening. And yet, since we village boys had never had a taste of cookies, we took it for granted that cookies would taste like this. And we swallowed it with a stretch of the neck.

"Delicious?" the old man asked.

"Sure," we nodded.

"That must be it. There's an old saying, 'Don't take a bath on an empty stomach; don't have a haircut on a full stomach.' Now, let's soak ourselves in the pool."

Just as we were about to move, an assistant walked over, ready to help granddaddy rub his back. He took a glance at the low table and asked, "Sir, where are the green pieces on the table?"

"The boys have eaten them."

"That's soap!" the assistant said in surprised alarm. "That's for washing the dirt off. How could you let the boys eat them?"

Our great-grandpa answered humorously, "Well, since they've put it in their stomachs, let it clean up their insides too."

The most dangerous place to bathe was in the Yellow River. The older generation often said, "The sea is boundless; the Yellow River is bottomless." If you stand in the river, you can feel the sands slipping away from beneath your feet. What was a flat riverbed a half hour before could be swirled by the current into a pool deeper than your height.

Once when I was a fifth grader, the school organized my class to take swimming classes in the Yellow River. The teachers had selected a safe place where the current was gentle, and stuck a circle of red flags on the circumference to prevent accidents, telling us not to go beyond the flagpoles.

Several bold fellows ignored the teachers' caution and were soon beyond the safe area.

"Come back immediately! It's dangerous!" the teachers shouted.

Fifty years later, water has become scarce in my hometown. The irrigation channels and ditches are all gone. The few rivers that remain have dwindled to sluggish trickles and the riverbeds are overgrown with wild grass.

But they turned a deaf ear to the warning and kept chasing each other.

"Don't worry. It's safe," the one in front even shouted back. "The water is shallow here. Look! It doesn't even come up to my knees."

But the next moment he disappeared. The other children splashed back horror-stricken, while several teachers who were good swimmers rushed over and made a number of deep dives, but none of them were able to reach the bottom.

Toward evening, a rescue team from the county town arrived by boat. They probed the river with long-handled hooks, but found nothing. When people came for a second search the next morning, the place was already a sandbar. The boy's corpse was never found, and we never dared to take a dip in the Yellow River again.

Fifty years later, water has become scarce in my hometown. The irrigation channels and ditches are all gone. The few rivers that remain have dwindled to sluggish trickles and the riverbeds are overgrown with wild grass. The water table has dropped 200 meters. Even the giant Yellow River dries up from time to time. On the other hand, water towers have been erected in the villages, so running water is available. Water now, whether it is for drinking or bathing, is all pumped up from depths of hundreds of meters.

Spring Festival in the Countryside

As winter deepened, the longing of village children intensified because that meant the arrival of the new year and that on New Year's Day they could have new clothes to wear, good food to eat, and a hearty time to play without the need to do any work.

The winter nights are clear and transparent. There is a dense group of stars hanging in the northwestern sky, called the "Boat Handle." And in the southeastern sky there are three large and bright stars in a row, which the locals call the "Sparkle." In the evenings, you can hear children chanting a rhyme:

> *New Year's just around the corner,*
> *When Sparkle catches Handle.*

But as the lunar New Year approached, I often forgot to check if the Sparkle really caught the Boat Handle.

The New Year season begins with the Kitchen God's Day, on the 23rd of the 12th lunar month. Every year every household buys a portrait of the Kitchen God and pastes it on the wall by the main kitchen stove. As the years go by and one new portrait overlays the older one, the pile grows thicker and thicker, and it is believed that the thicker the layers the wealthier the household. Beside the portrait there is always a pair of couplets. The one on the right reads, "Speak well for us in Heaven," and the one on the left says, "Keep silent when on Earth." The horizontal scroll above reads, "Head of the family." As I see it now, the Kitchen God is actually a mere ornament – how can he be a competent household head if he only talks about the good things in Heaven and keeps his mouth shut on Earth? But my grandmother insisted that the Kitchen God was always watching, and so kids should not steal food from the kitchen. If they did, the Kitchen God would report it to Heaven.

Once, terribly hungry, I sneaked into the kitchen and filched a sweet potato. I had just bitten off a mouthful when Grandma's warning buzzed in my head. I glanced over my shoulder, and was shocked to find the Kitchen God staring at me. Horror-stricken and with the sweet potato in my mouth, I tried to hide from his sight, but wherever I went I found his eyes riveted on me. That kept me worried for quite a long time for fear that he was going to report my bad deed to Heaven.

The traditional offering to the Kitchen God is sweet pancakes. No matter how poor a family might be, pancakes stuffed with sugar had to be made and placed in front of his portrait in order to sweeten his tongue, in case he should speak ill of the family to Heaven. That seemed to be the happiest time in the year for the Kitchen God.

The 25th and 26th of the month are the time for thorough cleaning. Tables, chairs, trunks and other large pieces of furniture that have been inside throughout the year are all carried out into the yard for wiping and washing. The walls are dusted and the ceiling is swept clean of cobwebs. Although one can't help getting dirty doing this, no one can quench his excitement about the New Year and the whole family remains high-spirited.

A rule to observe in cleaning is that one must not break anything, or it will bring bad luck in the coming year. It happened that in the winter of 1970, my elder brother had been recommended for admission to Kaifeng Teachers' College and was waiting for his enrollment notice which was due around the Spring Festival. That year, Mother told us to be especially careful when doing the cleaning. Ironically, the more one is afraid of something, the more likely it is to occur. I broke off the spout of the oil jar while wiping it. Hardly had Mother finished scolding me when my elder brother tripped over something while carrying the rice-cooker and it shattered into several pieces. Mother raved and clapped her hands in annoyance, "Oh, no! You boys! One of you broke the oil jar, and another smashed the rice-cooker! You want to go to college? You'll stay forever in a cottage!" These incidents upset the whole family throughout the festival season. But unexpectedly, on the fifth day of the new year, the postman was heard to shout outside our gate: "Feng Junqing, come and get your enrollment notice!" The whole family beamed with happiness. We made fun of Mother by imitating her admonition: "You broke the oil jar and you smashed the cooker! You want to go to college? You'll stay forever in a cottage!"

Mother blushed, "That's an old belief. It probably no longer works in the new society."

From the 26th through the 29th every household was busy steaming buns. It usually took more than half a day for one family to have all its buns steamed for the whole festival season. In those years, as only a few households in the village had large steamers, a sharing schedule had to be arranged months in advance. It was often the case that one family would start to steam buns before daybreak, and then the steamer was passed on to a second family around noontime, and to a third in the evening. If a family thought it needed more time than usual it would send members over to the user family to help it knead the dough or tend the kitchen fire. When the steamer was finally returned to its owner, it should never be empty; a few buns had to be left in it, for an empty cooking vessel could be a bad omen of food shortage. On reflection, it must have been a kind of courtesy for the loaning.

Steaming buns was a big event, in which every family member was engaged. The adults were responsible for making the dough, and the children tended the fire and refilled the wok with water. The buns were of various kinds – plain buns, buns stuffed with beans or vegetables, rolls with fried cicada pupa, and a special kind of big white buns with a decorative red date at the top, called the "family bun" and made one for each family member. A coin was inserted in one or two of those buns, and if you found a coin in your "family bun" it was believed that there was good luck in store for you in the coming year. After the buns were finished, it was time to cook meat, fry dough-sticks and meat balls, and prepare the fillings for *jiaozi* (dumplings). In short, all the food for the whole family during the festival season, including the buns to take along when visiting relatives, had to be prepared in these few days.

The first thing to do on the 30th was to put up Spring Festival couplets on door panels and gateposts, and paste scrolls bearing good wishes on every available space in and out of the house – such as "Good luck greets you" on a wall or tree facing the gate, "Spring fills the yard" inside the courtyard, "Endless resources of water" on the water vat, "Plump pigs in the sty" on the pigsty, "Animals breed and thrive" on the cowshed, "Bumper harvests every year" on the grain bin, "Inexhaustible flour and rice" on the rice and flour jars, "A thousand miles a day" on the cart shed, "Look out for fires" where the kerosene lamp stood, and "Watch out for the sharp blade" on the chopping board. Scrolls were also put up at places of worship. For example, where sacrifices to Heaven were offered a scroll with the characters "Heaven is Supreme" would be pasted above the portrait of the Lord of Heaven, "Shrine to the Lord of the Millstone" at the mill, "Shrine to Zhong Kui the Door God" on the gate, and "Shrine to the Earth God" in the courtyard. All in all, on this last day of the old year, every family looked fresh and clean, and the spring scrolls written on red paper filled the village with an air of jubilant expectation.

On the evening of the same day, that is, the New Year's Eve, *jiaozi* was the main course at dinner in every household. Some cooked *jiaozi* had first to be offered to the gods and placed respectfully in front of their memorial tablets. Incense sticks were lit and firecrackers set off, as the whole household kowtowed to the gods. People usually stayed up late that night. In the years when there were no radios or TV sets, the whole family would sit around a fire in the central room, reviewing the past year and making plans for the coming one. Children would stack their new clothes at the head of the bed and then go out into the streets to play while waiting for the arrival of the new year. Before going to bed, the family elders would place a wooden stick, known as "the wealth-protecting stick," across the doorway of the house to prevent the family's wealth from going out. They had to have everything needed for the next day well prepared, because on the first day of the new year it was forbidden to use scissors, needle or thread, or even to sweep the floor or take the garbage out.

New Year's Day was the jolliest time of the festival season. Since no wake-up calls were allowed, Mother told us before we went to bed that we should get up as soon as firecrackers went off in our own courtyard. We would lie in bed without daring to fall asleep, keeping our ears pricked up for the wake-up boom. Right after midnight, firecrackers started to sound off here and there in the village and were followed by more and more. But anxious as we were we could only stay in bed because the noise did not come from our courtyard. Then at around two o'clock we finally heard Father let off three loud bangs in the yard. We immediately jumped out of bed, put on our new clothes and rushed out into the pitch-dark yard.

On the altar table in the central room, Grandma had arrayed several wooden tablets of our ancestors. The "tablet of Feng's ancestors" was placed in the center, with those of my great-great-great-grandparents, great-great-grandparents, great-grandparents, and grandpa spread out on both sides like wings. Besides the various kinds of offerings on the altar table there were two big red candles – their flames shooting three or four inches high – and a bunch of incense sticks in a burner, from which smoke spiraled upward and pervaded the whole room with an atmosphere of solemnity. A mat was spread out on the ground in front of the altar. Grandma took the lead in performing kowtows to the ancestors, followed by my parents and us children. After that, we knelt down to welcome the return of the Kitchen God, who was believed to leave for Heaven on the 23rd and return to the mortal world at around four o'clock on the first day of the new year. A new round of firecrackers began to go off and the crackling and banging resounded throughout the village.

There were four meals on New Year's Day. The first one started right after the sacrificial rites and welcoming the gods while it was still dark outside. The staple food was rice, a luxury which we could only enjoy once or twice a year, because in my village people lived mainly on wheat. But on New Year's Day the main dishes were starch noodles cooked in stewed cabbage, and braised pork. Everyone could have a bowl of rice topped with the stewed cabbage plus a ladle of pork – a really appetizing breakfast, and the most sumptuous and delicious feast of the year, which children in those days were always looking forward to.

The day was dawning by the time breakfast was finished. Father then took us to pay New Year calls on the other Feng families, while Grandma stayed at home to receive well-wishers. There were groups of people everywhere on the streets. Adults raised their clasped hands in front of their chests and shook them in greeting when they met each other, saying, "Happy New Year!" or "Good luck to you in the new year!" The younger generation would kneel and kowtow to the elders, and the seniors would give them a ten-*fen* bill or a handful of walnuts, dates or peanuts in return.

The second day of the new year was for visiting new relatives in other villages. Young parents took their little children to their maternal grandmother's home. The roads between the villages were thronged with groups of people. Children in their colorful new clothes and with toys such as pinwheels in their hands skipped and frolicked after their parents. The road rang with their laughter.

My maternal grandmother lived in Y village, about three miles away. Early in the morning on New Year's Day, my maternal grandfather would wait at the village entrance to meet us. Upon arrival, we would first pay our respects to our grandparents and uncles, and they would give us a small amount of money wrapped in a red envelope as a New Year gift. Then we would be free to run outside and play.

Two Spring Festival recreational events in my grandma's

village impressed me most: the swing performance and the opera singing. A swing was set up on the village's main east-west street. Two people stood face to face on the swing and collaborated to push the swing higher and higher, drawing bursts of thrilled applause from the audience. The opera singing was performed on an open space, for there was no stage. Several people took turns singing highlights from the Henan and Huaiqing operas, accompanied by such stringed instruments as *banhu* and *erhu*, a wind instrument called *sheng*, and gongs and drums.

What attracted me most was the *banhu* player. He was a blind man and had no knowledge at all of musical scores, but he was an expert at playing the instrument. Not only could he coordinate perfectly with the singer, he could also sing along and imitate the chirping of various kinds of birds. His example actually made me resent the music classes at school. Since without any knowledge of music notes he could be an even better musician and singer than my music teacher, why should I try to master the weird tadpoles floating on the stave?

That day almost all the kids running around in my grandma's village were from married-off daughters' families, because the local children had all gone to visit their own maternal grandmothers. The mothers, who had spent their girlhood together in the village, could only meet this one day in the year after their marriage, and they always had a lot to tell each other.

The third and fourth days of the new year were for visiting old relatives – women who were now grandmothers or even great-grandmothers went to visit relatives at their maiden homes. So on these two days the travelers on the road were mostly old women, tottering on their bound feet with the help of a walking stick. You could almost always see a young man (a son or grandson) carrying two full baskets of gifts on a shoulder-pole walking behind.

The New Year season ended on the fifth day of the first lunar month.

(Translated by Xu Zhenyu)

Accusing the Old Society

During the Cultural Revolution a political movement was launched in the countryside to "recall the sorrows of the past and savor the joys of the present." To recall the sorrows was to recall the sufferings in the old society. The activities included eating a specially prepared coarse meal, living in a shabby hut, and holding accusation meetings. To savor the joys was to savor the good life of socialism, including the collectivization road, the people's commune and the happy life introduced by the Cultural Revolution. The revolutionary committees at the county, commune and production brigade levels organized these activities to make the commune members deepen their hatred of the vicious old society by recalling their past sufferings and enhancing their love for Chairman Mao and socialism, and strengthening their determination to carry out the Cultural Revolution by savoring their present happiness.

Every time such an activity was going to be held the production brigade's loudspeakers would repeatedly broadcast a heartrending song specially composed for such occasions by an unknown musician:

> *In the star-studded sky*
> *A crescent brightly shines.*
> *A meeting's held by the production team*
> *To pour our grievances out.*
> ...

As the plaintive song and the mournful melody hovered over the village, people would soon be cast into a gloomy and forlorn mood.

In order to re-experience the past living conditions of the poor the revolutionary committee of the production brigade carefully picked out a few ramshackle thatched huts built before liberation and assigned the Red Guards to lead the commune members and school students to visit the place to get some personal experience.

The hut my class visited was on the east side of the village and owned by a man of the Zhang family. It stood by itself. Battered by years of wind and rain, the mud walls on three sides had crumbled, and the remaining side of the wall was leaning dangerously on a pole and most likely to collapse in the first gust of wind. There were several holes in the roof, through which the sky could be clearly seen. The dirt floor was littered with straw, firewood, and the dried excrement of chickens, dogs and humans. In one corner of the room was a stove built of sun-dried mud bricks. An old man in his seventies, Zhang Wang's pa, was standing beside the stove and talking about the miserable life he and his family suffered in this very hut before liberation.

The old man's narration was choked by sobs. From his broken sentences we learned that his family of seven had lived in this hut. There was no bed, no mattresses or quilts, no tables – no nothing. And they spent the winter nights huddling in the straw on the ground.

We entered the hut from the remains of the door and squatted for a while in front of the mud stove to learn how food was cooked in those days. Then we stretched out on the moldy straw on the ground to get a feel for the sleeping conditions in the past. When we emerged at last from an opening in the dilapidated wall with dirt all over our bodies, straw in our hair and tears on our cheeks, we were all wiping and rubbing our eyes.

Back at school, students and teachers were gathered on the sports ground to listen to a speech given by a member of the poor-peasant propaganda team supervising our school.

"Just now we experienced the living conditions in the old society," said the man, named Zheng Wangqiao, up on the platform. "I noticed that many of you have shed tears. That's good. That means you have class feelings. Although so far not many of us can live in brick houses and many still live in thatched houses, the thatched houses now are very different from those of the old society, for now they have walls on all the four sides and are thatched with a thick layer of straw. People now have beds to sleep on, and have mattresses and quilts. Such houses are cool in summer and warm in winter. We owe all these to Chairman Mao and our socialist society. Though we live in a thatched house, we should have the whole world in mind and follow Chairman Mao to make revolution forever!"

Just then, there was a commotion among the students. Before I could find out what was going on I saw several tall six-graders pushing a smaller one toward the platform. I recognized him as a student of the fourth grade. He was of middle-peasant origin, one of the Ma family. It turned out that he had been muttering in the audience while Zheng Wangqiao was delivering his speech on the platform.

"My grandfather said the thatched house he lived in when he was young was also cool in summer and warm in winter," he was heard to say. "What Zhang Wang's pa said in the old thatched hut this morning was not true. The hut was my family's. My grandfather lived there when he was young. How could he say it was his?"

His grumbling was heard by the students beside him, and judged as a direct attack on the movement to recall the sorrows of the past and savor the joys of the present. He received a harsh beating and was pushed onto the platform to be criticized by the students and teachers of the school.

In response to the call of the poor-peasant propaganda team to criticize him, a young teacher ascended the platform and said, "On page 29 of *Chairman Mao's Quotations* our great leader Chairman Mao teaches us: 'The middle peasants wavered in the initial stages. It is only after they clearly see the general trend of events and the approaching triumph of the revolution that the middle peasants will come in on the side of the revolution.' Since he's from the middle-peasant class, he's blind to the great triumph of the proletarian Cultural Revolution. What he said is proof of his wavering and that he's not standing firmly on the side of the revolution. Since he viciously attacked the movement to recall the sorrows of the past and savor the joys of the present, he's made himself a target of the revolution rather than a person to be united with. We must criticize and denounce him till he's beaten flat and smells like a hog and will never be able to turn over!"

The poor fourth-grader thus became an infamous example of attacking the movement to recall the sorrows of the past and savor the joys of the present. Young revolutionaries swarmed onto the stage to beat him till blood trickled from his head. And then he was ordered to quit school and reform himself through labor in the production team.

When I went home in the evening and asked my father whose thatched hut it really was, my father said that what Zhang Wang's pa had said was not entirely true. Many people in the village knew he was not a native of our village. In fact he was a beggar and roamed to the village during the land reform movement. As our village was already liberated at that time, he wanted to settle down here. Since he had no place to stay, the Ma family lent the thatched hut to him and his family. So the time he was talking about was the land reform movement, not *before* liberation. In the newly liberated areas at that time, most families were living in shabby thatched huts and there were few good houses in the village. There was nothing wrong with what the boy had said, but my father just couldn't explain why he should be so ruthlessly beaten and even driven out of school.

More unforgettable were eating the specially prepared coarse food and the meetings to recall past sufferings. The two activities were usually held together. At the village center seven or eight giant woks were set up beside a big pit, and a group of middle-aged women busied themselves around the woks preparing the special meal by putting into the wok dried sweet potato leaves, turnip leaves, the outer leaves of cabbage and some corn seeds.

When the meal was ready, the whole village, including middle school and elementary school children, would each receive a bowl and listen to the speaker while eating the food. The speaker stood at the center and poured out his or her grievance with handfuls of snot and tears.

At one such meeting, two old women chatted while eating the coarse food.

"This doesn't taste bad," one commented. "They've put salt in it! In the old society how could we afford salt? How could we get such good things to eat?"

"If we had had this in the locust plague in 1943, nobody would have had to flee home and go begging," the other agreed.

Their conversation was caught by Ma Xi, the team leader of the "Prairie Fire Combat Unit."

"Hush!" he hissed. "Laowu's ma is speaking about her bitter life."

Laowu's ma was born into a rich-peasant family. As her parents were denounced in the land reform movement, they had no choice but to marry her off to a poor peasant in my village named Wang Jisheng.

Though married to a poor peasant, she remained lazy and gluttonous. She was reluctant to work in the fields, because it was hard work and one was exposed to the weather. She preferred to bear babies, because a woman could have better food before giving birth and have someone to wait on her after delivery. So she gave birth to nine children in succession. As she had been an actress in her youth, crying and laughing was at her command. It was often hard to tell whether she was really crying or laughing, or whether she was simply putting on a show. She also had the nickname "the clucker," because she had a quick and loose tongue. She loved to show off and enjoyed being the center of attention just like an actress' craving for the limelight.

On that particular day, there had been no arrangement for her to speak, but before the predetermined speaker chosen by the village revolutionary committee had a chance to stand up, she sprang to the center of the meeting ground with a bowl of coarse food in her hand. She took two quick mouthfuls and held up a chopstick bearing leaves from the bowl and started to whimper like an actress on the stage.

"In the past," she babbled, "I had many children and we had no food. To fill our stomachs we ate all kinds of wild herbs, raw chaff, and even ground elm tree bark. If we'd had such a bowl of nice food, one of my sons wouldn't have died of dropsy." As she said that, she flopped down on her bottom and started to howl.

Sensing something wrong, the production team leader, Old Pao, went over and asked, "Laowu's ma, when was that you were talking about?"

"I was talking about the time of the collective kitchen," she said as she put the chopstick with the leaves into her mouth. She looked innocently at Old Pao as she chewed on the leaves.

Old Pao was outraged. He pulled her from the center and scolded, "Don't forget you're from the rich-peasant class. What do you think you're doing?"

"Old Pao," she said, also worked up, "at that time you were the production team leader. Are you afraid that I'm going to talk about the sufferings you brought on us? You're scared, aren't you?"

He didn't know whether that was intended to be funny or serious.

"Today's meeting is to recall the sufferings in the old society, but you're accusing socialist society," he reminded her. "Don't you know what you've just said is reactionary opinion? Are you out of your mind?"

At the intimidating accusation, she immediately quietened down, and a dead silence fell over the meeting ground.

Ma Xi maintained that although she was married to a poor peasant, she hadn't changed her reactionary rich-peasant class nature. She couldn't forget the good life she had enjoyed before her marriage in the old society and she was taking the opportunity of recalling the past to attack the Great Leap Forward, the people's commune and socialist society. She was therefore branded an active counter-revolutionary.

Thereafter, whenever the village held meetings to recall the sorrows of the past and savor the joys of the present and had coarse food meals, with tears bathing her cheeks Laowu's ma would be sweeping the streets with the other "four types of bad elements," accompanied by the song:

> *In the star-studded sky*
> *A crescent brightly shines.*
> *A meeting's held by the production team*
> *To pour our grievances out.*
> ...

The Iron-rod Yam

After President Hu Jintao and Premier Wen Jiabao's visits to the iron-rod yam production base in Wen County, Henan Province, the iron-rod yam became more fashionable and enjoyed greater prestige both at home and abroad. The iron-rod yam is the best kind of yam. According to the national geographical indications product certification, its place of origin is limited to the area within the latitude range of 34.48°-35.30°N and longitude range of 112.02°-113.38°E. That is exactly where my home, Wen County, is situated. The iron-rod yam has a long history and has high medical and nutritive values. It was delivered as tribute to the emperor in the old days and has been an indispensable herb for the renowned Tongrentang Pharmacy. It won a gold medal at the 1994 Panama Pacific International Exhibition.

In my childhood, the iron-rod yam was not widely grown in my village, because, as my father told me, its output is low and it exhausts the land. The same plot of land cannot be replanted with yams for the next five or six years. Besides that, its cultivation and processing are rather complicated. First, the land needs to be deep-plowed and finely harrowed, and given adequate basal manure. Then the land must lie fallow for a year. In the following spring, a special plow is used to dig three-inch-deep grooves in the land, in which four-inch-long yam seeds called "dragon heads" are laid down flat about one foot apart. After sprouting, the dragon head will produce a new root, which will strike deeper and deeper into the earth and grow thicker and thicker. That is the iron-rod yam when harvested. The new shoot above ground grows into a vine several feet long. The green leaves on the vine absorb the sunlight to nourish the underground yam. When the vine is more than a yard long, it will bear many "yam eggs," which are about the size of a date. Some may fall off onto the ground, and if it happens to be a wet season, they too can strike root and sprout.

It takes skill to dig up a yam root. Inexperienced young men are generally not allowed to do it. The first step is to clear away the vines and pick out the "yam eggs." Then you find the "dragon head" to locate the new yam root. The next step is to dig a deep groove about half an inch from the root. The depth of the groove depends on the length of the root. The toughest part is that the groove can neither be too far from the yam, for you won't be able to tell how long the root is, nor be too close to the yam, for you may damage the root or even break it, and thus waste a year of hard work.

If planted in yellow earth, the iron-rod yam will grow thin and long, and very straight. The longer ones can be over two feet in length, and look like an iron rod. Its texture is smooth, dry and fine-grained. If it is planted in black earth, however, the roots are mostly little more than one foot long and of varying thickness. They can be straight or twisted, and their intersections may be round or oval. Although they may not look very pleasant, this kind of yam is actually of the best quality. It tastes smooth and fine, soft and floury. It is so dry that scraps fall off while you're eating it.

In fact it is only after a series of complicated processes that the iron-rod yam can be as straight and hard as an iron rod. My father was a master hand at processing yams, and I had plenty of opportunities to watch him do it when I was a child.

He first rinsed the newly dug-out roots and soaked them in clean water. After a period of time he took them out and put them on a cutting board. Then he used a home-made peeler to scrape off the skin. The peeler was made out of a finger-thick hollow bamboo stick about a foot long. Half of the stick was shaved off two inches from one end to form a semicircle, the edge of which was as sharp as a knife. This was a simple but very effective tool for peeling the skin of the iron-rod yam. Father used to hold a yam root in one hand and with his other hand used the peeler to scrape off a very thin layer of the skin. His movements were quick and light. In a moment the yam was turned into a smooth, snow-white stick.

I tried to do it myself, but the result was unsatisfactory; I either peeled off too thick a layer or failed to peel the yam clean. My father said that I was wasting the yams.

The freshly peeled yams are placed in a fumigation hut

built specially for this purpose with sun-dried mud bricks, and bleached by a sulfur lamp. When cured by the sulfur smoke, the yams are placed in the sun to dry.

During the yam-processing season, you could see white yam sticks neatly spread out on racks made of sorghum stalks everywhere – on both sides of the streets, in open spaces and in the fields adjacent to the village. Thus exposed, the yams become soft and yellow in a few days. Then they are put back into the fumigation hut. After repeated fumigation and sunning, the yams would be completed dehydrated, and the white sticks as hard as iron rods.

The last step is to rub the yam sticks. Each yam stick is dipped in clean water and placed on a cutting board. The tips at both ends are cut off with a knife. Then one hand is used to rub each yam with the rough side of a wooden washboard which weighs several pounds, and then the yam is rubbed with the other hand while protecting the end with the forefinger. After careful rubbing and drying in the sun one last time, a beautiful snow-white yam rod would be produced, as hard and smooth as an iron rod.

Its tonic function is perhaps best borne out by the following widespread ad: "If a man takes it, the woman cannot stand his stiffness; if a woman takes it, the man cannot stand her softness; if the people upstairs take it, those downstairs cannot stand the shaking; if the people of the whole building take it, the seismological bureau thinks it's an earthquake."

As the yield of the iron-rod yam is very low, and its growing and processing are laborious, its market price is high. Therefore, the market tends to be flooded with counterfeits or substandard products. Some bearing labels testifying to their geographical origin may be not from that place at all. Some sellers deliberately mix vegetable yams with iron-rod yams, and some had fake iron-rod yams sliced or powdered to deceive customers, as a layman finds it difficult to tell the difference.

Once, when I was attending a conference in Beijing, I found so-called iron-rod yam products on display in a local shop. A young saleswoman approached me and blabbered about their efficacy. I picked one up, and examined it.

"Is this a genuine iron-rod yam?" I asked with a smile.

"I guarantee it." she said firmly. "If it's a fake, you'll be compensated with ten times its price."

"Do you know where I'm from? I'm from Wen County in Henan Province, the iron-rod yams' place of origin. I've grown them myself."

She flushed immediately.

"Then you won't need my introduction," she said sheepishly.

The growing of the iron-rod yam has a long history, and has gone through many ups and downs. One of the downs in my own lifetime was during the years guided by the policy that "agriculture should center on grain production." According to the instructions of the workgroup stationed in my village, every plot of land was to be used to grow grain crops, and such sideline produces as yam and glutinous rehmannia were strictly forbidden.

There was an old man of the Sun family in my village. He was suffering from a chronic disease, but he could not afford the medicine he needed. What he did was dig up a number of small trees of his own to open up a plot of land, and there he covertly planted a few score iron-rod yams, not for sale but for his own use. The following year he would dig up another patch of small trees and transplant them to the previous year's yam plot, so he could always have a fresh plot to plant yams on. He kept up this kind of rotation until the early 1960s, when peasants were allowed to have private plots. It was only then that he could openly plant yams in the fields. But since yams exhaust the land, he divided his private plot into six or seven small sections to plant yams in rotation. In that way he not only cured his chronic disease, but also preserved the seeds of the iron-rod yam species.

Nowadays, the iron-rod yam is not only in great demand on the domestic market, it is also exported to Japan, South Korea, Singapore, Germany, the United States, Canada, Australia and other countries, as a welcome high-grade tonic.

Dividing Up Vegetables

During the Cultural Revolution there were three levels of ownership in the rural areas, that is, the people's commune, the production brigade and the production team, of which the production team was the base. The policies of "more plots for private use, more free markets, more enterprises with sole responsibility for their own profit or loss, and fixing output quotas on a household basis" and "the freedoms of loaning money, of renting land, of hiring labor and of trading" adopted in the early 1960s were abolished. Peasants could no longer keep private plots, and growing vegetables and beans in one's own courtyard was regarded as the "remaining tail of capitalism," and was annihilated. Since staple grain was all allocated by the production team, then what about the vegetables? After some discussion, the village revolutionary committee decided to allow each production team to set aside a piece of land near the village exclusively for vegetable growing.

Although growing vegetables is not heavy work, it needs experience and skill. The grower must know when to plow the land and how deep, which type of basal manure is to be applied, when to apply the topdressing fertilizer, and so on. He must know when to raise seedlings, when to replant and when to harvest each and every kind of vegetable such as cabbages, turnips, peppers, pumpkins, green beans, eggplants and tomatoes.

According to the above standards, Grandpa Zhang and another old man of my clan were elected by my production team to grow vegetables. Both of them were respected old men in their 60s, and they were experienced in growing both grain crops and vegetables, but their temperaments and dispositions were opposite to each other in every way.

Grandpa Zhang was a jovial and affable man. His family had been doctors for generations, and he himself was a good acupuncturist. The villagers respectfully called him Acu-Zhang.

The other man was stubborn and unsociable – a so-called stiff neck. He used to walk with his eyes on the ground, and would not greet others or stop for conversation. But when he was with his three-year-old grandson, he was an entirely different person. He doted on the boy, and they seemed to have so much to say to each other. Cuddling the boy in his arms, he said one day, "Little darling, let's go home."

"Old darling, we're not going home," the boy said as he played with the old man's beard.

Since then, people would refer to him as "Old Darling" behind his back.

People thought it was a wise choice to have Acu-Zhang and Old Darling in charge of the team's vegetable supply. And, sure

Although growing vegetables is not heavy work, it needs experience and skill.

enough, that very year under their diligent care the dozen *mu* of vegetable garden was a picture of colors – yellow pumpkins, red chilies, white turnips, green leeks and purple eggplants. A good harvest was in sight. But to everyone's surprise, the two old men got into a bitter quarrel one day and even wrestled with each other. As they rolled over on the ground, a patch of young green-leaved cabbages was crushed into a mess of pulp.

No matter how the team leader Old Pao stamped his feet in annoyance, he just couldn't separate the two. As a last resort he had to send for Grandpa Feng Qin, who was over 80 and senior in generation and whose shouting and scolding finally stopped their fighting. Upon inquiry, people learned that the fight was caused by the division of the vegetables.

As is well known, to weigh things a steelyard is indispensable. Its importance in daily life is beyond question, and no one could have imagined that in the late 1950s, when the countryside was dashing toward communism and the collective kitchen was the rule of the day, the steelyard in each family was confiscated and destroyed at the order of the workgroup leader Old Jin, because peasants were no longer allowed to have private property and bartering was forbidden. Each production team was permitted to keep only one steelyard so the cook could measure out the grain for each meal according to the rations. With the beginning of the Cultural Revolution, even that one steelyard was considered an instrument of capitalism, and was destroyed. The consequences of this became apparent when the vegetables were harvested and needed to be fairly apportioned out among the households.

Without a weighing instrument, the apportioning could only be done by visual judgment.

Old Darling fetched a bundle of foot-long sticks. He sharpened one end of each stick and whittled the other end flat, on which Acu-Zhang used a writing brush to put down the name of the head of each household and the number of family members. Then they stuck the sticks in the ground and drew a circle around each stick. The vegetables allocated to that family were to be placed in the circle. Only when all that was done could they get down to the business of apportioning out the harvested vegetables.

Without a steelyard fairness depended entirely on one's eye and experience. And that was what had sparked off their quarrel.

At first, Acu-Zhang asked Old Darling to do the apportioning. "One of your eyes is smaller than the other," he said jokingly. "Now you can make good use of that. Use the smaller one to judge when giving vegetables to the smaller families, and use the bigger one for the larger families. You will be a better judge than me in doing that."

"You've been doing acupuncture all your life," Old Darling replied in his usual stiff-necked way. "Since you can even distinguish something as fine as a needle tip and an acupoint, you must have sharp eyes. You do the dividing and I'll watch you."

Realizing that Old Darling could not be dissuaded, Acu-Zhang gave in and took up the job of dividing up the vegetables. According to the numbers written on the sticks he placed a relevant amount of vegetables in each circle. With sweat streaming down his face, he carried the pumpkins, eggplants, leeks and turnips here and there as he used his eyes as a measurement, and kept adjusting the amount of each variety in the circles. It was hours before he had the vegetables satisfactorily apportioned out to the 30-odd families of the production team.

All the while Old Darling kept a close eye on him, walking around with his hands behind his back and his head tipped to one side. The more he observed, the more he felt Acu-Zhang's portioning was not fairly done. How could a family of two have almost the same amount in the circle as a family of three? How could a family of three have almost the same amount as a family of four? And there was hardly any difference between what was in the circle for four members and that for five members. The closer he looked, the more he doubted Acu-Zhang's fairness, and the more certain he became. He started to grumble and question Acu-Zhang's visual ability and fairness. Then he tried to make adjustments himself by taking out some vegetables from one circle to put in another, and taking out some from that circle to put in still another circle. It was almost time for the team members to return from the fields to pick up their shares when he suddenly felt that his adjustments were not fair either, and was going to make some further adjustments.

Acu-Zhang interrupted him, "My judgment is not bad," he said. "But without a steelyard we can only do it by estimation. It's roughly fair. No more adjustments. That'll only make things even more unfair."

"A man's eyes are a good balance and can't be cheated," Old

Darling said in all seriousness. "You've been doing acupuncture all your life. Do you decide on an acupoint by rough estimation? Have you been a quack doctor all your life?"

Acu-Zhang was already tired by the apportioning work, and now he found not only his efforts was slighted, but even his acupuncture skills was brought into question and his reputation insulted. Unable to contain himself, he lifted his hand and gave Old Darling a slap across the face. The latter stretched out his neck and rammed his head into the other's chest. The two were then locked in battle.

Having learned of the cause of their fight and watching the ludicrous scene, Grandpa Feng Qin couldn't help laughing. He said to Old darling, "A man's vision starts to deteriorate when he gets over 50, and you're over 60, not to mention that one of your eyes is smaller than the other. How good do you think your visual judgment can be? And how much of a difference do you think one person can make between families? Are you sure you can make accurate estimations?"

Then he turned to Grandpa Zhang and said, "Don't think you have sharp eyes simply because you've been doing acupuncture all your life. Last year when you were treating me with acupuncture, you stuck the needle in the back of my hand and missed the proper acupoint. Have you forgotten that?"

Everybody laughed.

At last, Old Pao accepted Grandpa Feng Qin's suggestion that Acu-Zhang and Old Darling would only be responsible for growing vegetables, and the team's bookkeeper and two middle-aged team members were to take care of the allocation. That solved the problem once and for all. However, some people heard Grandpa Feng Qin muttering to himself on his way home, "Despite all my eighty years of life I just can't understand why peasants cannot have steelyards. Will that tip the balance of socialism?"

Village Nights

The night scenes in my home village were beautiful. They changed with the season and were different from day to day. Night quieted down the hectic hustle and bustle of the day, and brought peace and tranquility to the world. It also nursed and nourished the land and all the living things on it so that the village and the fields would wake up fresh and energetic in the morning. In my childhood it brought me joy, dreams for the future, and at the same time embedded sentimental memories in my mind.

The night scene in spring was somewhat ambiguous. It contained both the bleakness of winter and the vigor of spring. During the day one already found the winter jasmines in full bloom, young buds on the greening willow twigs, caterpillar-like filaments dangling from the poplars, the peach trees blossoming, and though there seemed no change yet with the elm, a closer look would reveal that tiny buds the size of mung beans were already popping out on the twigs.

Nightfall was always preceded by plumes of smoke rising from the kitchen chimneys, which gradually merged into a thin veil of mist over the village. Then, without being noticed, the curtain of night slowly descended to conceal the daytime signals of spring. But for a moment light lingered in the higher part of the sky. In the shimmering twilight the village and its objects were still blurrily visible. The warmth of the day had not yet completely dispersed, and so the evening breeze, though cold, had not yet been so piercing. Past midnight, as the temperature dropped, moisture seeped out from the earth where snow had once covered it and diffused into the air. The fading stars and the lone moon in the early hours still bore the chill of winter. If it happened to be a wet spring, the cold could make one reluctant to stretch out one's bare hands.

My Seventh Grandpa told me about his younger days' experience in catching wild geese on spring nights. On their migration from the south to the north, they would often stop for the night in the wheat field to the north of the village. After setting up the sentry, the leader and the whole flock would go to sleep. On rainy nights, the sky would be pitch-black, so dark that one couldn't see one's outstretched hands. Seventh Grandpa and his pals would stealthily crawl toward the geese's resting place. He would have a lighted incense stick hidden under his coat. Coming upon the flock, he would pull out the incense stick and give it a quick wave before hiding it under his coat again. The sentry geese would not fail to notice the light and give the alarm to wake up the whole flock. Since nothing disturbing was noticeable, the leader would peck the sentry and go back to sleep. An hour or so later, Seventh Grandpa would take out the incense stick and flash

The night scenes in my home village were beautiful. They changed with the season and were different from day to day.

it again. The sentry's cries of alarm would again alert the flock. But as it was all dark and quiet, the enraged leader and the larger geese would peck the sentry and then go back to sleep. After repeated pecking, the sentry would no longer let out a warning when it noticed danger, but would quietly fly away alone. Seventh Grandpa would then sneak up on the flock, grab a wild goose by the neck, give it a twist and tuck its head under a wing. The goose would be stuffed into a bag without it making a sound.

Aroused by Seventh Grandpa's story, I called together a group of boys, and we waited for pitch-black rainy nights to go to the wheat field north of the village to catch wild geese ourselves, but we failed to find any wild goose, not even a feather. Some thought Seventh Grandpa was only telling tales; others speculated that the wild geese had all been caught by Seventh Grandpa and his pals; still others said the wild geese had learned to avoid our village. Seventh Grandpa died many years ago. It's a pity that I didn't ask him whether his story was true or not when I had grown up.

On summer nights as it was usually stuffy in the low houses and enclosed courtyards, most people preferred to take their meals outside to eat. Naked children, bare-chested men and topless older women would be squatting at the sides of the streets with a bowl in one hand and a pair of chopsticks in the other, eating their meal while joking or swapping gossip.

The village back then had lots of trees, but the blazing sunshine could still penetrate their dense canopy to heat up the ground and form a steaming cage. In those days nothing could get on people's nerves more than the cicadas' incessant chorus of "I see...I see...." So after dinner while the womenfolk stayed at home to clean up, the men would lead a gang of children to the loudest tree and build a bonfire beneath it. After a while they would knock the branches with long bamboo poles. The startled cicadas would take wing and fly toward the light. Some plunged directly into the fire; some hit the ground and kept flapping their wings. The children would pick them up and drop them in a bag. By the time the fire had burned out, the bags were nearly filled.

Some men with rolled-up reed mats under their arms would take the boys to the threshing ground for the night. The threshing ground was usually an elevated place on the edge of the village, gently swept by the moist night breeze rising from the fields. It was the coolest place in the village. The entire threshing ground was often covered with spread-out mats. Some adults gathered in a circle to smoke and chat, while others stretched out on the mats to gaze at the moon and stars. The children chased each other around, laughing and shrieking. As the moon climbed toward the zenith, people began to doze off, and the threshing ground quietened down.

Some bigger boys were naughty. They would join hands to carry sound-asleep younger ones into the fields nearby and leave them there. So when the younger ones woke up in the morning, they would be amazed to find they had been sleeping in the field all night and wonder how they could have moved there in their sleep.

On autumn nights before the moon had climbed up from behind the trees in the east, the village was enveloped in a thick shadow, though light still glimmered higher up in the sky. On the ground, the direction of roads, the outlines of houses, the contours of people and trees were still discernable. It was time for birds to return to their nests, chickens to their coops, dogs to their kennels, cows and goats to their sties. It was also time for both adults and children to go home. The village was then filled with vitality, especially by that of the children, who ran wild around the village, shouting and grappling, as if a brood of hens had been kicked out of their coop. The streets then seemed filled with life.

In those years, rural families usually had many children. The population was large and so was the number of trees. As the night grew deeper, a bright moon ascended the sky to shed its silvery light on the trees and scatter mottled silhouettes on the houses and the ground. By then the streets were almost empty. As the trees swayed in the light breeze, shadows flickered. Walking along the street at that hour, one could feel like walking on jelly, and even feel a bit dizzy.

As autumn nights were neither hot nor cold, people easily fell sound asleep. And yet it was also a time when people slept uneasily, because autumn was the rainy season. People were most worried about late-night rains, for spread out like white scales over vast stretches of the newly seedling wheat fields were their sweet potato slices. In those years the major part of the freshly dug-up sweet potatoes were sliced on the spot and spread out on the fields to dry before being carried home for storing. Once the slices were drenched by rain they would become sticky and turn yellow. And if there was no good sunshine in the following few days, they would go moldy and rot. So if it happened to rain in the night, the whole village would be thrown into chaos. Adults would carry baskets and sacks to the field to collect the slices, with children in their wake rubbing their sleepy eyes. In the drizzling pitch-dark night, family after family fumbled its way to where they had left their slices, and worked frantically to gather them in as fast as they could. Occasionally, some families would be upset the next morning to find that some of their sweet potato slices were still lying in the wet fields, though they had busied themselves all night. As it was so dark and they were in such a hurry, it turned out that they had collected the slices of other families who had not been awakened by the rain.

Winter nights were cold. As there were no coal fires in the houses and many children did not have cotton-padded jackets, we would go into the streets as soon as we had finished dinner, and gather in groups to play various kinds of games just to keep ourselves warm.

One of the games we played was called "squeezing piss." The participants would divide into two groups of equal numbers and line up against a wall. And then the two teams would push toward the center point in single file and cry, "Squeeze, squeeze, till you need to piss. Wet your bed or seek relief." The so-called "seek relief" referred to those squeezed out of the line. They could choose to go to the end of the line and rejoin the pushing or drop out if they could no longer stand the pushing pressure. The team with the fewer remainders was the loser. This game was a fast way to get warm. In less time than finishing off two bowls of noodles the participants would be sweating profusely.

Another game we often played was hide-and-seek. It usually started with the older children doing the seeking while the younger ones did the hiding. When it came to a younger boy's turn to do the seeking, the older ones would often sneak home to sleep, leaving the poor little fellow there searching high and low without finding anybody. It wasn't until the next morning that he realized he had been cheated. When playing this game, children would run amuck in the village, their young voices vibrating in the air and disturbing the dogs and chickens.

Winter nights were also a good time to catch sparrows. The children would take a flashlight and go to the place they had marked during the day. As they trained the flashlight on the sparrows nestling in the holes in mud walls or under eaves, they could easily grab them one by one, for the sparrows were too dumbstruck by the sudden beam of light to move.

Half a century has passed since then. All the big trees in the village were chopped down long ago and two- or three-storied buildings have shot up on both sides of the hard cement streets. Most doors remain closed during the day, and there are few people in the streets and even fewer birds in the sky. Choking smoke pouring out from the chimneys of the fertilizer plant and the plastics plant enshrouds the village. At night one can hardly see the stars and the moon. Although street lamps blaze brightly, one finds no dogs lolling around, hears no cats mewing, and hardly meets a person. It's all lifelessly quiet.

Old village folks told me that the young people had all gone to seek jobs in big cities, and their children went with them to attend schools in town. In the village there are only elderly men and women looking after the houses. With the youth away, how can there be vigor and vitality? It's not only like this at night, but also in the daytime, and not only on winter nights, but on nights all the year round.

(Translated by Xu Zhenyu)

Village Smoke

Village smoke is a special phenomenon in the rural areas of China. It is something inseparable from the memories of one's native home.

The smoke hovers above and around the village, and changes with the season, sometimes thin, sometimes blue, sometimes thick, and sometimes warm. The smell of the smoke fills the lungs of the villagers with the comfort of home. Espying the smoke from afar makes one eager to enter the village, because the smoke symbolizes civilization. From ancient times, when fire was made by drilling wood, smoke has accompanied the peasants from generation to generation.

The smoke in spring is thin, because after a winter of wind and freezing cold the firewood, plant stalks and straw have become very dry. They burn well, producing cheerful flames and little smoke. The thin wisps from kitchen chimneys curling among the young sprouts of the greening twigs and the blossoms of peach trees and apricots can almost make one believe one is strolling and living in the mist of fairyland.

In the early 1960s matches were in short supply in the rural areas. In order to light the stove for cooking, one would take a length of plaited straw rope to a neighbor who had a burning stove to "borrow" fire. When ignited, the straw rope would not flare up and burn away but would flicker and smolder, and leave a protracted trail of smoke in its wake as it was carried it home.

Rather than choking the people, the thin spring smoke gives off a slight fragrance of straw and grass. An experienced nose can tell with a sniff what kind of fuel the family is using.

The smoke in summer is blue, for by now the firewood and stalks from the previous year are nearly used up, while the grass and twigs collected in the new year are not yet completely dry and have to be mixed with the dried ones to burn. The smoke rising from the chimneys is entangled among the canopy of trees and tinted azure blue by the sparkling sunlight sifting through the leaves.

In summer, smoke can be used to drive off flies and mosquitoes. In the evening people will light a pile of straw in the courtyard or in a room, and lay a bunch of mugwort stems on top of it. The grilled mugwort gives out a pungent scent of medicinal herbs, and together with the smoke drives the insects away.

The droning of cicadas can be annoying on sweltering summer nights. People sometimes build a fire under the loudest tree and let the smoke slowly permeate through the crown. A couple of hard kicks on the tree trunk will jiggle the cicadas, and they will take wing with a sharp trill and dart right into the flames. In a moment, there will be a circle of crippled cicadas on the ground flapping their burnt wings around the fire.

The smoke in autumn is thick, because the firewood, plant stalks and straw are all fresh from the fields and difficult to burn. At cooking time, choking black smoke rolls out from the stoves. It can be so dense that it gathers in the yard and takes a long time to disperse.

If the autumn happens to be especially wet, dry firewood is hard to come by, and lighting the stove then becomes a misery. The common method is first get a bunch of dry straw to kindle a fire. When it starts to flare up, carefully add in the wet stalks so that the heat can quickly dry them. Then it will be easier to keep the fire going by feeding the stove with dry and wet firewood in turn.

Children are most afraid of tending the fire on wet days. They take a deep breath outside and dive into the smoke-filled kitchen, stuff a bunch of stalks into the stove and bolt out again into the yard. It is only when the fire is blazing steadily that they can sit in front of the stove and feed it with a mixture of dry and wet stalks.

Another function of the village smoke in late autumn is to dispel an oncoming frost to protect the wheat seedlings and the unharvested green-leaved vegetables. At nightfall, bonfires are built in the fields with fresh grass atop the piles so that, rather than going up in flames, the smothered piles produce smoke so heavy that it hovers over the fields to form a thick quilt of smoke which saves the crops from being spoiled.

The smoke in winter is warm. On cold windy or snowy days children are attracted by the smoke, because, as the proverb has it, "There's no smoke without fire," and where there's fire, there's warmth.

On especially cold evenings, Mother would light a fire in the room before we went to bed, and keep the smoke in the room to create a cloud under the ceiling, which she named "a smoke blanket."

In winter the children's favorite place is the stock barn, where the stockman has hung up heavy straw curtains over the door and windows, and keeps a cheerful fire to warm the farm animals. The villagers like to gather around the fire in the evenings to warm themselves, and to chat and spin yarns.

Production team meetings are intended for adults, but on winter evenings the meeting place becomes the children's playground, simply because there is always a bonfire at the center. Prior to the meeting, either the team's bookkeeper or the warehouseman would have stocked a pile of firewood in the center of the yard. The fire is lighted as the team leader opens the meeting. The flames turn the whole place bright, and the surrounding walls reflect the warmth of the red tongues. Smoke hangs above the yard like a huge overturned iron wok, blocking out the sight of the sky and stars. As a matter of fact, on such occasions, people's attention is more focused on the bonfire than on the team leader. Around the fire women stitch shoe soles, men puff on their pipes, and children frolic. Nobody seems to pay any attention to the team leader's monologue.

I've been away from home for years, and many things have faded from my memory, but I can't forget the village smoke in the old days – the smoke that filled my heart with warmth.

I've been away from home for years, and many things have faded from my memory, but I can't forget the village smoke in the old days – the smoke that filled my heart with warmth.

The South Yard and the North Yard

The South Yard

When I was a child I had a dread of the south yard, a deserted courtyard with no houses or huts in it. The weathered old mud wall facing the street on the south was only waist-high, while the dilapidated houses on its left and right served as its eastern and western boundaries.

The yard was overgrown with weeds and shrubs, and rising among them were a dozen or so ancient elms and pagoda trees with luxuriant leaves on their vigorous branches, which cloaked the yard in an air of mystery. It was a place frequented by hares, weasels, foxes and stray dogs, but seldom visited by people.

One summer my mother kept nattering about one of her hens that should have started laying eggs. It cackled day after day, but no eggs were found in the nest especially prepared for her, not anywhere. I chuckled to myself at my mother's complaints, and decided to spy on the hen to find the eggs. If there were eggs, there would not be just one or two, but many. If I could find them, mother would certainly be overjoyed and would probably give me one as a reward. In those days, eggs were a luxury, and a boiled egg was only given as a birthday present. As I thought of that, I seemed to see a heap of alluring eggs in front of me and I could even catch the smell of the mouth-watering boiled egg.

One day when we were having lunch, the clucking of a hen came from the south yard. As it sounded like our hen, I put down my bowl at once to follow the sound. Sure enough, it was our hen. It quieted down at the sight of me, pretending to claw leisurely at the rotten leaves and grass for worms. But where were the eggs? I looked around. There were merely shrubs, weeds and a haystack as high as two persons, but there was no sign of any eggs. Disappointed, I gave the hen a kick. It flew up onto the mud wall with a shriek and scampered into the street. Yet I didn't give up. I slashed at the shrubs with a stick and parted the weeds meticulously, hoping to find the eggs.

Finally, I was in front of the haystack. Heaped up by my father two years ago, the outer layer of it had turned dark brown but the straw inside was still golden bright. As I slapped at the stack with the stick, I seemed to hear muffled cheeps of baby chicks. Holding my breath, I gently swept aside the fallen straw. What a surprise! A brood of newly hatched chicks was huddling in a nest, little yellow balls of fluff with pointed beaks. They were pushing against each other and making urgent chirps of terror. There were about a dozen of them, and there were a few unhatched eggs at their feet. I was just congratulating myself on this unexpected discovery when something pecked fiercely at my bottom. Turning around, I found the hen had sneaked back. She was staring at me angrily and flapping her wings in a threatening way. Suddenly she flew up and tried to peck me again. As I moved aside to dodge her attack, she slid back to the nest and collected the terrified chicks under her outstretched wings. The yard quieted down instantly.

Looking at the ferocious hen, the haystack that sheltered a dozen little lives and the wilderness of the yard, a quiver of loneliness and horror went through my heart. I dropped the stick and fled from the south yard.

One day, Grandpa Hong of my clan took a wooden box to the south yard, and placed it among the bushes. The box was more than five feet long and about a foot wide and high, with both ends left open. The inside was separated into two parts by wire mesh in the middle. A chicken was stuffed into one end of the box and the opening was sealed. A slot was cut in the top board two inches from the other opening and a heavy square brick with a small hole in it was suspended in the slot. A stick about one foot long was fixed to the outside center of the box with a horizontal bar balanced on top of it. One end of the bar was connected to the suspended brick by a string through the small hole; the other end was linked to a treadle, which was skillfully placed inside the opening of the box.

It was an ancient device popular in rural areas for catching wild animals. The bait was often a chicken. When the animal entered through the opening to seize the prey it would step on the treadle and tip the balance of the horizontal bar, thus bringing down the brick to block the entrance. The trapped animal could only wait for the arrival of the hunter, for it could neither reach the chicken on the other side of the wire mesh nor push open the brick blocking the entrance.

Anxiously waiting to hear the thud of the dropping brick, I didn't sleep well that night, and as soon as day broke I hurried to the yard and found that the brick had already fallen into position. Something was dashing back and forth inside and scratching the board frantically, while the chicken was fluttering its wings and squawking in horror on the other side. I ran to impart the news to Grandpa Hong.

Covering the open end of the box with a sack, Grandpa Hong removed the brick and tipped up the other end of the box to dump the catch into the sack. Then he tied up the mouth of the sack and flung it against the ground several times. The animal gave a few piercing shrieks and became motionless. He unfastened the sack and emptied out the catch. It was a weasel.

Not long after that, a group of young men intruded into the south yard with saws, axes and ropes in response to the central government's call for producing more steel in the Great Leap Forward movement. They chopped down all the big trees and even grubbed up the roots for fuel. In order to transport the wood to the smelting furnace the southern wall of the yard was torn down. Without the shelter of the ancient trees, the south yard looked empty and barren, and it seemed to have lost its mysterious and primitive atmosphere of untamed nature.

As more fuel was needed to feed the furnace, after all the big trees in the village had been chopped down, abandoned houses were dismantled for their wood, and then even shrubs and weeds were collected. Thus deprived, the south yard was laid open, with only decaying leaves rotting in its aged soil.

It was not until then that we found there had once been houses in the south yard, because the foundations were exposed and broken bricks and tiles were scattered all around. However, with a gloomy face my father said that he had never heard from the older folks that there were houses there, when they were abandoned, or when the yard was deserted.

The North Yard

The north yard was not actually a courtyard, for there were no walls marking its boundary. With lots of small trees, it was referred to as "the woods" by the villagers. Among the trees were a dozen or so date trees. Every year at harvest season their branches would be bowed down with red and pale-green dates. North of the yard a weed-lined dirt road stretched east to west, the surface of which was a layer of fine dirt, soft and smooth to the bare feet, like walking on silk.

Though there seemed to be nothing separating the yard from its neighbors to the left and right, in fact its boundary was clearly marked by a cylindrical stone buried at each corner of the yard. Sticking out about half a foot from the ground, they were called "landmark stones" by the villagers. A deep hole was driven into the earth by an iron drill and filled with lime before each stone was buried, in case anyone attempted to secretly move the stone. So these landmarks had another name – the "lime stakes."

What I remember best is the large pit in the yard. It was about ten yards wide from east to west, more than 70 yards long from north to south and ten feet deep, formed by digging up the earth to build houses. A large amount of earth was needed to build an adobe house. In the olden days they had no vehicles, and had to carry the earth loaded into two baskets on a shoulder pole. This limited the place where you got the earth to somewhere near the building site. In consequence, when a house was built, there would always be a pit not far away. But the huge size of the pit in the north yard was by no means the result of building one or two houses, for the amount of earth dug out from it far surpassed what was needed for building the houses of my family. Where had the rest of the earth gone? Since there were no pits in the yards of our neighbors on both the east and west sides, was it possible that their ancestors got earth from the same pit behind my house? However, since that was not an important matter to a child, I never asked my father about it and, regretfully, it remains a mystery till this day.

Such pits were very common in rural areas. While providing earth for villagers to build houses, they also served as a kind of flood-control facility. During the rainy season, rain water flowed from the roofs and yards into the pits. Within days, the pits would be turned into ponds with scraps of wood, leaves, or tree branches floating on the turbid water. In wet years, all the pits in the village, big or small, could be filled to the brim, and some large pits never dried up all the year round. In spring, reeds sprouted up around the ponds, and gradually formed a green fence as they grew taller and taller. Birds sang and frogs croaked happily there. In summer, youngsters would strip naked and dive into the ponds to catch fish and frogs, or play in the water, turning the place into an amusement park. In autumn, villagers would use the reeds to make reed mats. It was only then that the pond was exposed to the naked eye. In winter when the ponds were frozen over, people would skate and play on the ice. The ponds then became skating rinks.

As the pit in the north yard was fairly shallow, it used to dry up after several sunny days, unless there had been a heavy downpour. Small trees and weeds flourished in the pit. In the early 1960s, when Liu Shaoqi was promoting the policy of "more plots for private use," peasants were allowed to plant vegetables around their houses. My father dug up the small trees in the north yard, and weeded the pit to grow sorghum, corn and pumpkins. In years of good harvest, the spikes of sorghum were heavy and red, the corn ears were as thick as one's arm and large pumpkins sprouted everywhere in the pit. All these supplied my family with plenty of food. My mother affectionately called the north yard "our family storeroom."

(Translated by Hu Liang)

Concerns about the Land, the Water and the Trees

About the Land

According to the village elders, there were only two families in the village who had migrated from the big pagoda tree in Hongtong County in Shanxi Province at the beginning of the Ming Dynasty. The Shi family lived on the west side and the Zhao family on the east side. They were the aboriginals. With only two families occupying such a large area, the land was literally "sparsely populated."

By the 1960s the population of the village had increased to over 1,500. But between households there were still open spaces and trees. In every courtyard, besides the houses, there were also pigsties, cowsheds and trees. Houses comparatively far from the village center were hidden behind trees, though the crowing of their roosters and the barking of their dogs could be heard all over the village. Beyond the village rich farmlands unfurled toward the horizon, dotted with tree groves and hillocks. Even the rooftops of the nearest neighboring village were blocked from view by trees.

What I remember most clearly was a stretch of wild trees north of the village. Tombs clustered in fives or tens were laid out in the woods and in the surrounding fields, perhaps belonging to different clans. On a low rise were scattered hundreds of unattended tombs, big and small. The inscriptions on the stone tablets were blurred by the erosion of weather and the passage of time, and there was no trace of memorial services performed by their offspring.

Leaving the village from the north yard of my family, one would soon run across a score of tombs. The elders said that they were the tombs of those who had lived on the flood plain of the Yellow River. As that low land was frequently flooded, having a permanent graveyard there was impossible. So they had bought a piece of land from my village to serve as the graveyard for their ancestors. Their tomb mounds were usually small and clustered together, and almost hidden by weeds and shrubs. When irrigating the fields, sometimes a small hole would appear in the ditches between the tombs and water leaked into the graves. The flow made the hole larger and larger, and water would soon cascade into the underground cavern. Villagers said that the grave had caved in and they would simply dump a few shovels of earth on the hole to stop the leak.

At that time, as land was abundant, each person had an average of several *mu* of farmland. The most strenuous work was carrying the dung of pigs and cows and human waste to the fields on a shoulder-pole. It was an exhausting task and one needed to take several breaks on the way. As for the farthest fields, even an able-bodied young man could make no more than five trips in a day. Women and children often did it in relays. In order to save time, lunch was often sent to the distant fields by the housewives in pots wrapped in old quilts to keep the food warm. The peasants would gather in a circle and gobble down the food. When they finished, they would haul up a bucket of water from a well nearby to drink a few mouthfuls and then go back to work again.

On the other hand, watering the fields was a relatively leisurely task. Though one row of crop land between the two ridges was only one to two meters wide, it could be several hundred meters long. After making a notch in the ditch side, one could go away to do something else and, returning, might find the water had not yet reached the other end. As the wheat row was so long, at harvest time two people would start from opposite ends, and move toward each other. But very often when they got close and raised their heads, they were surprised to find that they were cutting different rows, and sometimes they could be several rows apart.

As there was so much land to cultivate, the endless work kept the peasants busy all the year round.

I've lived away from my hometown for nearly 40 years. Though I returned from time to time to visit my mother and relatives, I stayed indoors most of the time and seldom went out of the village into the fields. However, I have a feeling that there were more and more houses in the village closely packed together, and less and less land.

When I went home during the Spring Festival of 2008, I deliberately made a tour of the village, and was surprised to find that the familiar trees, hillocks, gullies and tombs had all been replaced by pig farms, poultry farms, plastic sandal factories, animal-feed plants, polyester bag factories, repair shops, chemical fertilizer plants, cement plants, and so on. They all had red brick walls around them, each occupying an area from several *mu* to nearly a hundred *mu* of farmland. I couldn't help wondering whether this was the place where I had grown up, and I felt like a stranger.

As I recall, there were only two streets going east from the village center. The one on the south had houses on its north side and reed ponds, tree groves and a lot of open spaces on its south side. The one on the north had houses on its south side and trees, pits and graveyards on its north side. But now, not only are the two streets lined by buildings on both sides, there are three or four new streets beyond and parallel to them flanked by two- or three-story buildings. Upon inquiry, I learned that most of the house-owners are not locals. As my village is not far from the county seat, some people working in town bought land here to build houses to improve their living conditions, and some wealthy people in the more remote rural areas built houses here for the sake of their children attending school in town. In this way, one building rose after another and more and more families moved in.

In less than 30 years, not only have the wasteland, graveyards, groves of trees, pits and hillocks disappeared, but the farmland is also disappearing. One family has built a house in the flood-land people's graveyard. There is a story that once around the

Qingming Festival (when the dead are commemorated) the family found that the descendants of the flood-land people were swarming into their courtyard with wreaths and all kinds of sacrifices. They placed the offerings in the families' living room, kneeled on the ground and wailed broken-heartedly, because enclosed in the courtyard were their ancestors' graves.

Abundant land resources were passed down through generations. However, drastic changes have taken place in the rural areas during the last 30 years with the development of science and technology, the soaring of the economy and the acceleration of urbanization. Meanwhile, farmland is shrinking in face of the growing population.

Land is the lifeline of the peasants. "Without land, where does food come from? How can we survive without food?" These questions are causing serious concern in the rural areas nowadays.

About the Water

My village was rich in water resources in my childhood. Dig three feet down in the yard and clean water would gurgle out. Two perennial streams flowed behind the village. Surrounding the village was boundless farmland. Irrigation ditches crisscrossed the fields. Several big pits lay in and around the village. Collecting rain water during the wet season, the pits would never dry up throughout the year. Weeds and reeds flourished around them. When it rained for days in a row, worried villagers would look up at the sky and ask, "What's up? Are you leaking?"

Village leaders wearing straw hats would make the rounds inside and outside the village. Holding shovels, they would dredge the gutters and block the leaks, and ask people to guard against waterlogging.

When the work in the fields was done in autumn, the people's commune would organize its members to dredge the river and strengthen the banks in case floods drowned the village and crops in the next rainy season. In short, flood control in the past was an important issue in the village every year.

However, the ponds have gradually dried up since the establishment of a chemical fertilizer factory west of the village and a cement plant in the south. At the beginning, no one took this matter seriously. The pits were filled up to build houses and plant trees. Within a few years, all the pits were gone.

Then the volume of the river decreased and the quality of the water deteriorated. Poisoned by residue flowing through concrete pipes from the chemical fertilizer factory and the cement plant, fish and shrimps died out and the green grass on the banks withered and became yellow. In a matter of only a few years, the banks became barren.

Imperceptibly, the wells dried up too. At the beginning, villagers drew the water containing chemical fertilizer from the river to irrigate the crops, thinking that the fertilizer in the waste water was a free gift. In the first few years, crops did indeed grow luxuriantly. As time went on, however, the wells were ignored. Weeds began to invade the collapsing well walls, and finally, the wells disappeared altogether. Then, in less than ten years the soil became hard, the weeds sparse and the crops short. Some villagers came to realize that something was wrong. It was not until the water from the chemical fertilizer factory began to kill the crops that they exclaimed, "Damn it! We've been fooled! Water from the wells is better."

They remembered that there used to be dozens of brick-lined wells, mud wells and pump wells in the village, almost one in every ten *mu* of land. The pump well at the village center was the last survivor. Old Cui, the village electrician, installed a submersible pump in the well to pump underground water up into a water tower. In this way, the villagers were pleased to find that they could use running water at home like the town people.

Later, the production team organized young people to dig wells again, but no water was found several meters down, or even a dozen meters down. The villagers were at a loss of what to do. The production team called in a drilling team from the county town, and water was finally found almost 100 meters below the ground.

There was plenty of water in the past, but nowadays the scarcity of clean and safe water has become an everyday concern.

About the Trees

There were lots of trees in the village in the 1950s and 1960s. Every family had some trees, and the village was encircled by trees. Looking at an adjacent village from a distance, instead of rooftops one could only see a patch of green.

My village boasted many ancient pagoda trees, mulberry trees and elms. The trunks of some were so thick that they could hardly be encircled by several people joining hands. Nobody knew exactly how old those trees were. The tall trees provided shade for the villagers with their luxuriant branches and leaves, while the low bushes shielded the yellow earth. Villagers going to work had to wind through the woods before they could reach the crop fields. In spring, blossoming peach trees, apricot trees and pear trees vied with each other for beauty, giving out an intoxicating fragrance.

There were dozens of big trees in the yard of my family, and their branches often stretched toward our house. In spring, father would climb up onto the roof with a saw to cut off the branches which were too close to the house in case they did damage in a summer storm. A neighbor's boy about fifteen or sixteen years old was very skillful at this job. He only needed to climb up one tree near his house, grab a branch and swing from tree to tree like a bird to trim the branches. In that way, he could do all the necessary pruning without returning to the ground.

At that time, not only were there many trees in the village, there were many in the fields, too. Most of them were persimmon trees and Chinese toon trees. Some of them grew alone, some in pairs and some in groves. Family graveyards were usually surrounded by cypresses, and wild grass flourished among the closely arranged grave mounds, where hares, foxes and weasels built their lairs and bred their young. In my young mind, the graveyards were mysterious and scary places. One didn't dare to go there alone.

There were lots of trees in the village in the 1950s and 1960s. Every family had some trees, and the village was encircled by trees. Looking at an adjacent village from a distance, instead of rooftops one could only see a patch of green.

The tragedy of the trees began with the national passion for steel in 1958.

In order to solve the problem of insufficient fuel for the smelting furnaces, members of the Youth Shock Team cut down the big trees first, then the smaller trees and finally the shrubs. When the trees in the village were all felled, they went on to saw down the trees in the fields. Even the graveyard cypresses couldn't escape. Soon the whole village became barren, like a chicken plucked clean of its feathers, moaning nakedly under the sun. Without trees, the houses of adjacent villages came clearly into view. Though later on trees were planted again in the village, most of them were cut down to build houses, pigsties and cowsheds before they had time to grow tall and big.

Decades later, there are more and taller buildings in the village but fewer and smaller trees.

Once, when I returned to my home village, I saw a group of elders sitting idly at the entrance to the village in the sunshine. Their weathered faces were lined with wrinkles. Except for an occasional glance at each other, they seldom exchanged a word, but kept staring at the empty streets, the bare houses and the barren fields.

It suddenly occurred to me that the whole village in which I had been born and grown up was just like their withered faces, staring worriedly at their offspring, who had changed it to its present state.

(Translated by Hu Liang)

The Weeping Pagoda Tree

How old was the pagoda tree? Grandpa Zhang Peng was over 90, but even he didn't have any idea. He said that the tree had been there when he was born and day after day, year after year, it just stood there unchanged. He heard from the older generation that the tree was planted when our ancestors moved here from Hongtong County in Shanxi Province. It was also said to have been planted in front of the temple to the earth god. But now there is no trace of the temple, and nobody in the village can tell where it was and which direction it faced. Several years ago, a broken stele was dug up during road construction. Inscribed on it was "Commemoration of the Rebuilding of the Temple to the Earth God," and the date was the ninth year of the Jiajing reign period of the Ming Dynasty, that is, 1530.

The ancient pagoda tree was a paradise for birds, which nested, bred and sang on it. It was over 100 feet high, and its trunk could hardly be encircled by several adults joining hands. The branches on the south side stretched across the road, and those on the north side covered the old house of the production team and half of the courtyard. Though it had lived through countless years, it was still vibrant and flourishing. Once a bird, be it sparrow, turtle dove, cuckoo, oriole or hawk, dived into the crown, it would be completely hidden in the dense leaves. Sometimes, as if in agreement or being startled by something, the birds would take flight in unison with a loud boom, and scatter in all directions like colorful fireworks shrieking through the air and exploding in the sky. It was a spectacular sight. In the incubation season nestlings with little yellow beaks occasionally fell out of their nests in the tree.

In hot summer, the tree provided a shady and cool place for villagers to repose under, but the birds in the tree kept singing, arguing and fighting. Some people were annoyed and tried to shoo the birds away, yet the singing and quarreling could not be stopped. One day, a man, who had been a hare hunter, was trying to cool off in the shady breeze after a bad fall-out with his wife. The noise of the birds annoyed him more than ever. He went home to fetch his shotgun loaded with pellets and fired straight up into the tree's crown. The ground was at once covered with dead and injured sparrows and turtle doves.

The tree was the king of all trees in the village, for no other tree could match it in age and status. Old folks said that the local earth god, who is supposed to be responsible for good weather, bumper harvests, peace and health, had taken up residence in the tree after his temple was ruined. As long as the tree flourishes, there will always be a good harvest, it was said.

I still remember that when I was a child a naughty boy called

Tudan climbed a ladder to catch sparrows under the eaves of his house. He fell to the ground, and went into a coma. His grandmother went to the ancient pagoda tree, and knelt under it.

"Almighty Lord of the Tree, please wake up my Tudan," she prayed as she kowtowed.

Then she hung a piece of Tudan's clothing on a stick and waved it in the air. "Tudan, come home! Tudan, come home!" she chanted.

The adults said that she was summoning the spirit of Tudan, which had flown up into the ancient pagoda tree the moment he fell from the ladder. And sure enough, Tudan soon came round. Only a few days later, he was frisking about again as if nothing had happened.

During the national steel mania of 1958 one enthusiastic leader of the Youth Shock Team shouted, "Do away with superstition! Don't believe in ghosts and gods!" and climbed up the ancient tree to saw off a couple of boughs to fuel the smelting furnaces. To his surprise, the birds in the tree circled him with threatening cries, and a few brave ones even dashed at him and pecked at his eyes. Scared out of his wits, he fell down and broke a leg. Since then, nobody dared to lay a finger on the ancient pagoda tree, which remained upright and flourishing, though all the other big trees in the village were cut down for iron production.

Nobody knows clearly what the ancient pagoda tree has witnessed in its long history. My grandpa told me that the Red Lance Society had set up an altar under the tree to offer sacrifices; my father told me that during the land reform movement it was a place for criticism meetings and the public trial of the despot Liu Laoshan. I remember that during the Cultural Revolution the Red Guards used to put up big-character posters there, and it was there that they criticized the old Party branch secretary, who was denounced as a capitalist roader, and afterward a "Loyalty Platform" was built there, where all members of the production team gathered every morning to ask for Chairman Mao's guidance and to report their work to him in the evening. Along with the change of the political climate, different kinds of people gathered and dispersed under the old tree, and yet one phenomenon never changed. Every noontime and evening, men of half the village would gather there with bowls in their hands. Besides having their meals, they bragged, played chess and argued about this or that. It became a stage for wives to show off their culinary skills and a platform to swap news and anecdotes in the village. Friendly jokes and laughter drove away the fatigue of work, and days passed into months and years. The old folks said that it was exactly the same in the time of their grandfather's grandfather, and some predicted that it would still be the same in the time of their grandson's grandson. The shady ancient pagoda tree will forever be a cool and happy shelter for the villagers, they maintained.

But when I returned home years later, I was surprised to find the ancient pagoda tree had changed. Its leaves had thinned out and become grayish yellow. Mother told me that since the construction of a chemical fertilizer factory west of the village, a paper mill in the north, a plastic factory in the east and a cement plant in the south, a pungent smell of ammonia, caustic soda and polyvinyl chloride permeated the whole village from morning to night. Dust spewed out from the tall chimneys of those factories stuck to the leaves, and in just a few years, the ancient pagoda tree had withered. A few years later, when I was home again, the ancient tree was dead, its bare branches stretching painfully into the grayish sky as if pleading to Heaven. Dozens of nests were then exposed to sight, and yet there were no birds and no trace of life. Under the tree, there was no one having lunch, neither were there jokes or laughter. A gathering place for birds and people had become bleak and desolate.

Mother told me that the village was haunted by disasters after the death of the ancient pagoda tree. Several babies were born dumb or disabled. Zhang Wang, living in the east of the village, died of lung cancer, and Li Er, living in the west, died of stomach cancer, though they were only in their thirties and forties. Such things had never happened before.

Grandpa Zhang Peng told the villagers before his death that if they still considered themselves heirs of the ancient pagoda tree, they should never cut it down. Let it stand there to tell later generations about its glorious past and why it had changed into this sorrowful sight.

More than ten years have passed since then. The ancient tree is still standing tall and proud, though it hasn't sprouted any new branches or leaves. Its twisted dead branches keep telling people about its grief and sorrow. Though it has been dead for years, it shows no sign of decay, nor is it infested with worms or insects. The guess is that the poisonous gas and dust has not only killed the tree but the pests as well.

The villagers say that on windy days you can hear the old tree weeping.

(Translated by Hu Liang)

The Yellow River Flood Land

My home was less than three miles north of the Yellow River, but when I was small the grown-ups always warned us children not to go to the river alone, for between the bank and the mainstream of the river laid the dangerous flood land.

No one could tell for sure how wide or how large the flood land was. Standing on the slope outside the south gate of the county town and looking in the direction of the river, what came into sight was not the river or a sandy beach, but a boundless stretch of wild grass, reeds, rose willows and all kinds of luxuriant trees. Adults said that there was no road on the flood land except for intertwined, zigzagging footpaths trodden out by humans or animals. There were no signs or landmarks, and if children or strangers got lost in the labyrinth they might not find their way out for days. But usually that was not life-threatening, because one could live on wild melons and wild dates, as well as sweet potatoes and peanuts planted by the flood land wardens. And the shacks built by the wardens or the marooned could provide shelter from rain or shine and a modest place for the night. The most dreadful thing, however, was accidentally stepping into quicksand pits, which the locals called "cow-hide sand" because of its seemingly hard surface. Once a person stepped on one, he would find himself being sucked down. Inexperienced people would make a desperate struggle, but the harder they struggled, the quicker and deeper they sank till they were completely submerged.

The flood land was home to pheasants, wild ducks, wild geese and hares, as well as boars, foxes and wolves. Sometimes snarling boars, cruel-eyed wolves and silly-looking badgers would roam onto the slope. At the sight of them, men would threaten them with whatever tools they had in their hands, yell and chase them till they retreated into the flood land. To a small child like me, the flood land with its mystery and horrors was quite a temptation.

The first time I set foot on the flood land was in the summer of 1964, when I was in elementary school. Our physical education teachers decided to take us to a river fork on the flood land, where he had selected a place for the swimming class.

River forks are a typical geographical feature of the Yellow River flood land. As the river pours out through the Sanmenxia Gorge onto the Central Plains, the current suddenly fans out and cuts numerous channels in the mile-wide riverbed. The locals call these channels "forks," which, like the blood vessels of the human body, weave through and nourish the flood land before they finally converge back to the mainstream.

After lunch that day the teachers took us to the flood land. Walking along a winding sandy path, we passed many shallow ditches and reedy ponds. There were wild flowers and bushes everywhere. In some places the weeds were tall enough to hide a human being and trees grew unchecked. Our intrusion flushed out wild geese, pheasants and many nameless birds from the lush vegetation. The forks were not very deep and the current was relatively slow, sometimes forming into a string of pools, which made natural bathtubs. In scorching summers, men on the flood land would often jump into the forks to take a bath or simply to relieve their fatigue. Old folks say that the river forks on the flood land could be more dangerous than the river itself, because the forks are haunted by river demons that can drag people to the bottom and drown them. In many cases, the bodies of people who had bathed in the forks were never found.

We arrived at our destination in the afternoon. The teachers marked off an area in a broader fork for swimming, and set up red flags around to make a warning line. The pupils were not allowed to go outside the red-flag circle. As we jumped into the water and trod on the flat river bed covered with fine and soft sand we felt very comfortable, as if we were walking on satin. However, we felt that the sand underfoot was rustling and flowing with the water. The water might soon whirl a pit under your feet, and sometimes the pit would quickly become large and deep. Where the water had just reached your knee, in another moment it might have risen to your neck. No wonder that old folks say the Yellow River is as bottomless as the sea is boundless. And it was exactly this bottomlessness that was frightening.

Soon the boys began to splash each other, and they started to chase a boy called Li Lin, who dashed ahead and quickly ran beyond the warning line. The teachers shouted to him, trying to call him back, but probably because the water appeared to be increasingly shallow, he ran even faster. Suddenly, he disappeared. The other boys were scared, and yelled for help. Mr Xie, our physical education teacher, was a good swimmer. He raced forward and dived into the water, but came up empty-handed. He dived again, but again came up empty-handed. Other teachers joined in jumping into the water, but they did not find Li Lin either. As the water was too deep, they could not reach the bottom. When the rescue team from the county came to search for the body the next day, they found that the pool had already become a sandbar.

Though seemingly tranquil and placid, the river forks were actually dangerous and horrible. After that, I never dared to swim there again.

The next time I went to the flood land was with Uncle Tujing two years later, to collect a wild herb called *ququ*. Edible for both men and pigs, they grew in large patches on the flood land. Led by Uncle Tujing, we fumbled our way in the waist-high weeds for a long time before we came upon a large expanse of *ququ*. They grew close together, about one foot tall with thick stems and fat leaves. Before long, each of us had collected a large bundle, but on our way back we lost our way. Instead of returning to the slope, we found ourselves right beside the mainstream.

A boundless expanse of turbid and torrential water swirled and roared, and churned along with it masses of weeds and branches. The tempestuous waves licked at the bank and ate away at its base. From time to time huge chunks of earth would collapse into the river with thunderous booms and splash up a wall of muddy waves. Then there was only a patch of white foam floating down the stream. We winced at the terrifying sight and retreated into the relative safety of the dense undergrowth of the flood land.

Could we get out of the flood land before nightfall? What if we couldn't? All of us were very anxious when, unexpectedly, we spotted at a short distance a thatched shack, in front of which was a threshing ground with corn, sweet potatoes, cabbages, turnips, peanuts and other crops planted around. Tired and hungry, we made for the shack and dropped our bundles on the threshing ground.

The door was unlatched. We pushed it open. No one was in, but there were some simple daily necessities.

"This is the flood land warden's shack," said Uncle Tujing, who had seen the world. "Let's see what we can get to eat. He won't mind."

We dug out handfuls of sweet potatoes from the field and fetched water from a well beside the threshing ground to wash them clean. We also plucked a few ears of corn, and placed all of them in the huge wok at the door. We made a fire and began to steam the food. When it was almost cooked, a middle-aged man wearing a twig-woven sunhat appeared. He was carrying a home-made hunting gun in one hand and two newly killed wild geese in the other. We were embarrassed to find that he was the owner of the shack. Uncle Tujing stepped forth to explain our plight.

"That's all right," the man said with a grin. "Go ahead to eat when it's cooked, but don't stuff yourselves with sweet potatoes. They hurt the stomach. I'll boil some noodles for you."

That day we had a hearty meal of corn, sweet potatoes, and noodles cooked in wild-goose meat soup.

"You'll not be able to walk out of the flood land tonight," the man said when we'd eaten our fill. "You can stay here. Lots of people have spent the night on the threshing ground."

Uncle Tujing and the other adults went to fetch wheat straw to make beds on the ground, while the warden took us children to the river fork behind the shack to catch fish.

The warden stood in the sunset on a small wooden boat with a bamboo pole in his hands and several cormorants perching on the boat's sides. From time to time he would wave the pole to drive the birds off the boat. When they emerged from the water each had a fish in its bill. The warden would let them land on the pole and bring them back to the boat. Then he would take the fish out of their mouths. As we wondered why the cormorants did not swallow the fish, he told us that he had tied a string around each of their necks so they were unable to swallow their catch.

At night, the warden built several bonfires on the threshing ground, and placed mugwort stems and wet grass atop the piles to produce heavy smoke to drive away the mosquitoes. From his conversation with Uncle Tujing, we learned that his name was Wang Shu and he was a bachelor. He once lived on the slope, but because it was too crowded there he had moved to the flood land a few years previously. The soil here was fertile and had a sufficient water supply to ensure a good harvest of whatever he grew. There was no need to worry about food. If he wanted to eat eggs, he could go and pick some from the weeds and reeds where pheasants and wild ducks had their nests. If he wanted to have fish or shrimp, he could catch them in the river fork. The flood land was a quiet and pleasant place to live. Self-reliant, he lived a carefree life. He told us there were many others like him living on the flood land, but you had little chance of meeting any of them because the flood land was so large.

During this second trip, the flood land revealed to me its other side – apart from the hidden dangers, there were hard-working, kind and generous people like the warden living there, leading a primitive but idyllic life.

Thirty years later, I returned to my native place in winter and rode in a car to visit the flood land framed in my childhood memory. The car drove out of the county town along a broad tarmac road bustling with trucks, motorcycles, tractors, tricycles, bicycles and pedestrians. Both sides of the road were lined with multi-storied houses and some large but seemingly empty yards encircled by red-brick walls. The plates by the gates revealed that they were chemical factories and paper mills. I was trying to figure out the locations of the slope and the flood land, and searching for the rose willows, woods and the river forks when the car suddenly stopped right beside the Yellow River. The whole trip had taken a mere ten minutes.

"Where's the flood land?" I asked in astonishment. "Have we missed it? Are you sure this is the right place?"

In face of these radical changes, I could not believe my eyes; I could not believe that this had really happened.

"Sure," the driver said firmly. "We've just passed through what used to be the flood land. There's no flood land any more."

He went on to tell me that the Yellow River had scarcely flooded since the Sanmenxia Reservoir was built. And after the Xiaolangdi Reservoir was constructed, not only had floods become history, the river itself sometimes completely dried up. Where there used to be the flood land was now a safe place, and people had moved down the slope, bulldozed the river bank, leveled the river forks, and turned the lot into farmland. They had also built houses and factories here and even set up villages, transforming the entire flood land into a place similar to the slope. County officials called this the "unification of slope and flood land," and applauded it as a significant strategic achievement.

For a long while I remained speechless. Looking at the Yellow River, I felt helpless. Its former magnificence was gone. On a riverbed that was almost a mile wide the stream was now less than 100 meters in width, flowing meekly, without waves and without even a sound. A breeze swept up from the river and rolled a cloud of yellow dust into the distance. The sky looked dusty. There were no birds or wild geese any more. The memory of my former classmate Li Lin and the warden Wang Shu suddenly popped into my mind. The flood land was gone. Gone too were the tragedy of Li Lin and the idyllic life of Wang Shu.

In face of these radical changes, I could not believe my eyes; I could not believe that this had really happened.

(Translated by Dai Yuliang)

Undying Love

On his deathbed my maternal grandfather caught hold of my mother's hand, and uttered his last words, "You must take good care of your mother after my death. You know, she once saved my life."

"Put your heart at ease. I will," Mother nodded, blinking back tears.

Then Grandfather left us forever as his family and relatives mourned and wailed around him.

Everyone in the family and in the village knew that my grandparents had been on very good terms. Grandmother was rather introverted. She was not the talkative type and her emotions were rarely revealed on her face, but she was industrious and there was nothing she could not do, no matter whether it was house or farm work. In contrast, Grandfather was an easy-going and straightforward man, a jolly soul with a perpetual smile, and there was a touch of frankness and joy in his voice as if he were free from difficulties and troubles. He had bright and observant eyes, and once he found Grandmother was offended, rather than reasoning with her he would crack a joke to amuse her and then walk away with a laugh without waiting for her to smile back. And by the time he came back, it would seem nothing unpleasant had ever happened. For this reason, the old couple rarely had a tiff. Yet we never heard that Grandmother had once saved his life. Many years after my grandparents' death, I mentioned Grandfather's last words to my mother when we were chatting one day. Mother, then in her eighties, recounted that a long while before she became related to us a moving and tragic story about the old couple.

Henan Province suffered an unprecedented famine in 1943. A rainless spring followed by a stormy summer made the harvest almost a complete failure. The peasants in their desperation placed all their hope on the autumn harvest, only to be hit by a plague of locusts. According to Mother, clouds of locusts came out of nowhere, so thick that they even blocked out the sun. As they descended on the crops, the sound of their chewing could be heard far away. In no time at all, the corn was left with bare stalks and the sorghum grains nothing but empty shells. The hunger-stricken people began to eat tree barks and grass roots, and even saline alkali soil. Those who could still walk started to "go west," that is, to flee the village and beg their way to the Xi'an area in Shaanxi Province. Some collapsed while walking and were never able to stand up again. There were corpses everywhere – beside the road, in the fields and under the eaves. The stink of decomposing bodies permeated the houses, yards and villages, for there was no one to bury them. It was exactly like what the old poem says:

> *Hundreds of villages choked with weeds, men wasting away;*
> *Thousands of homes deserted, ghosts chanting mournfully.*

It was just at that time that my grandfather fell seriously ill. He was unconscious and on the verge of death.

Grandmother went to a village about three miles away to invite a doctor of traditional Chinese medicine, but the old man refused to come. Grandmother went down on her knees to beg him to save a life.

"It's not that I'm unwilling to go, but I'm over seventy and I'm too hungry to walk that far," the old doctor explained.

"That won't be a problem," Grandmother answered. "I can carry you on my back."

Though Grandmother was tall and big-boned in her youth, hunger and the weight of the old man on her back made her stagger and pant. She had to stop and rest every now and then before she finally reached home.

"He's not really ill," the doctor said after feeling Grandfather's pulse. "It's caused by hunger, and I can't do anything about that. Never mind him, just go away with your daughter while you still can."

Grandmother said nothing. She stuffed two handfuls of chaff in her mouth, washed it down with the help of water, and carried the doctor home on her back.

It was after midnight when Grandmother returned. Watching Grandfather at death's door, she held my mother in her arms, and said, "I'm afraid your father can't get over this. Let's make one last effort. You wait here. I go dig up some carrots for him behind the village."

My mother was terrified, for she knew that although there were a few rows of carrot roots left in the field after the locusts had eaten away the leaves, the place was marked off by the Japanese soldiers stationed in the nearby blockhouse as a military reserve and they would shoot anyone who dared to approach. Right on the previous night two people who took the risk had been shot dead on the spot. Mother clung to Grandmother's leg and begged, "Ma, please don't go. The two shot last night are still lying there in the field."

"If I don't try it, your dad may not live till morning," Grandmother said. "Since two people were shot last night, the Japanese sentries will probably think no one will dare to come to steal tonight. It's a chance. We can't sit here waiting for death."

Grandmother took up a digging tool and insisted on going.

"Stay at the back door and count the time," she told my mother. "If you hear gunshots, that means I'll never come back. Remember: Don't go to retrieve my body. Just leave this place as soon as your father breathes his last. If you don't hear gunshots, I'll probably be safe. Open the door for me when you hear my footsteps."

They cried in each other's arms. Grandmother opened the back door and walked out into the darkness.

Mother was only ten years old then. She waited at the back door in suspense, fearing the sound of gunshots. Time crawled slowly by as she kept anxiously peeping through the cracks in the door. Nothing could be seen, for it was completely dark outside. The stillness was terrifying, but also a consolation, for it meant Grandmother was safe.

Finally came Grandmother's footsteps. Mother opened the door hurriedly and was relieved to find Grandmother safely back with carrots in her arms.

Grandmother sliced the carrots, and boiled them in water. She first fed Grandfather with the soup, then a few boiled slices. Gradually, Grandfather came round. So it was those carrots that pulled Grandfather back from the threshold of death, and Grandfather nurtured his gratitude toward Grandmother till the end of his life.

More than 60 years have passed. Under the care of Mother, Grandmother lived happily to a ripe old age. Though she had left us for years, Mother still couldn't hold back her tears when telling us the story. We too were moved to tears. But what puzzled me was why in all the years when my grandparents were alive no one ever mentioned the story.

"People of their generation believed the old saying that 'Better to die of anger than go to court; better to die of hunger than be a thief,'" mother explained. "They thought stealing was not a proud thing to talk about."

"What Grandma did for Grandpa was purely out of love," I said. "It's no stealing at all! Her noble deeds we will always remember. And those rows of carrots were not planted by the Japs!"

(Translated by Dai Yuliang)

Father's Burial

I was not at his side when Father died. When I arrived at home, his cold body was already placed on that cold bed board. Father lay there, dressed in a black wool overcoat over a Chinese tunic suit, a cotton-padded jacket, a lined jacket, a shirt, and a cotton jersey next to the skin, complete with a blue cap on his head. From outside to inside and from head to toe my father was dressed in brand-new garments. Kneeling on the ground, I held his cold, rough hand in mine and touched his stiff, bony face. As I looked at him a question suddenly flashed across my mind: Is this man really my father? When, if ever, did he wear such nice clothes and look so decent?

In my memory, Father wore no more than a pair of shorts in summer. Whether he was harvesting the wheat, working on the threshing ground, pulling a cart, loading sacks onto carts, digging the earth or carrying manure, he was always naked to the waist. His stout body was tanned copper-red by the sun. When he was at work, beads of sweat sparkled on his body, and his waistband was soaked with perspiration. Every now and then he would wipe off the beads with a towel he carried on his shoulder. He did not wear a shirt or even a T-shirt in summer, not because he had none, but because he thought it was a waste. How could a working man be particular about his dress? It was not easy to make clothes. So he saved whatever he could. Sometimes, he even saved the towel. He would scrape off the beads of sweat on his forehead with his forefinger and flick them onto the ground. During his lifetime he had never worn a piece of clothing made of fine cloth, which could only be bought in town with ration coupons for the urban residents. His clothes were all made of home-spun cloth. Mother spun the cotton into yarn, and after starching the yarn Grandmother would sit at our century-old loom and weave it into cloth, one weft after another. With the cloth, Mother made clothes for us, and sewed them up stitch by stitch.

There was a time when imported urea fertilizer from Japan was available in the countryside. The fertilizer bags then became the top-grade and most fashionable material for making pants, and even that was a privilege limited to the families of production team leaders. The imported bags were thin, soft and light, and were beyond the reach of ordinary villagers. The leaders' families would dye the bags, and two bags could be readily turned into a pair of pants. However, the material was not easy to dye, and the housewife's simple dyeing method often resulted in uneven patches. Sometimes the color at the pants bottom was not deep enough to cover up the two large characters which made up the word "urea." We also wanted to have urea-bag trousers, but there was no way for Father to get the bags. Instead of admitting his inability to get them, he told us that since the bags were used to hold urea, they would give off the unpleasant odor of urine when you wore them, and he wouldn't bring such smelly things home.

Father could wear a single item of clothing for many years. I guess he had never imagined that he could wear so many fine clothes on his journey to the other world.

He was laid in a coffin, which was placed in the center of the funeral shed erected outside the gate. Villagers came in an endless stream to offer condolences and funeral cloth, paper objects and other funerary items. At night, Mother took us to keep a vigil beside the coffin, inside which lay the body of my hard-working father, who, having been through so much, was to be buried in the yellow earth. Father, our family and the yellow earth had a tie that could not be severed. The yellow earth gave life to him and on the yellow earth he gave birth to us, and now he had collapsed on the yellow earth, which would eternally separate him from us. Such coldness and cruelty brought us infinite helplessness and sorrow.

Throughout his life on the yellow earth he experienced too much distress and hardship. Born in 1928, he spent his ill-fated boyhood in a miserable period in China, suffering from warlord fights, bandit infestations, the killing, burning and looting committed by the Japanese invaders, and the large-scale famine in Henan in 1943. To escape from war and famine, he slept in graveyards, on wild mountains, and in caves and shacks, begging his way through Anhui, Hubei, Shanxi, and Shaanxi provinces. To earn a little food, he helped people dig wells and graves, and carry heavy sacks at an early age. So much pain did he experience that even many years later, when those who had survived the hard times were recalling the past, he would shed tears in silence.

After liberation, a succession of political movements swept over the countryside, such as the land reform, the movements against the three evils and the five evils, the Great Leap Forward, the establishment of the people's communes, the Four Clean-ups, and the Cultural Revolution. Though at a vigorous hot-blooded age, he showed neither enthusiasm nor opposition, and behaved like a tame sheep among a flock obeying the command of the shepherd and never getting ahead or lagging behind. In fact, he was no fool. He often made his point to us in private. In his view, a good peasant works with his face to the earth and his back to the sky, raising crops and delivering tax grain to the state. If no one cultivates the land what can people eat? Political slogans cannot bring water up from the well, nor can political movements raise crops. What's the use of all those irrelevant activities?

After the three years of natural disasters, the peasants were allowed to grow their own plots of land. Father worked for the production team in the day, and in the evening he went out with his farm tools to open up small plots of waste land in some remote graveyards, along road ditches, on the river banks or in empty pits. When thirsty, he drank from the ditches; when hungry, he took a few bites of the food he had with him; when tired, he just lay down on the ground and pillowed his head on the handle of his hoe. More often than not, he would not come home till after midnight. One night he did not return even after the first cockcrow. Mother woke up my elder brother and me, and asked us to go and look for him. With a lantern, we searched high and low in the open land and finally near an abandoned railway we found him sound asleep on a newly reclaimed plot. He didn't even know how long he had been sleeping there.

After we were allocated a private plot, Father worked as diligently as ever – for the production team during the day, and on the private plot in the evening. At the time, my brothers and I were too young to lend him a helping hand, so he had to do all the farm work himself, turning over the soil, pulling the harrow, carrying manure, sowing and harvesting. The harrow should have been pulled by a draft animal, but at the time all livestock belonged to the production team. One night, he was harrowing our private lot. Exhausted he would lie on the ground for a little while before struggling to his feet to work again. As it was too dark, he didn't realize that the teeth of the harrow were pointing upward till the work was almost finished. So he had labored all night for nothing!

In severe droughts, the wells could not provide sufficient water for all the families to irrigate the land. In order to get water for our private plot, Father would sleep on the rugged ground beside the old well as he waited patiently in line.

During the slack days in winter, he would go some thirty miles to cart coal, sand or gravel from the mountain. To save every penny, he never stayed in a lodging house no matter how cold the day was. What he did was spread out a bundle of wheat straw on the ground to make a bed, and he would resume his trip after a brief nap. Like an overloaded bull, he worked and walked on the yellow earth night after day, year after year. He and the yellow earth were intimately inseparable. During his lifetime, even he himself couldn't tell how many times he had slept on the yellow earth, but this time he would sleep in it for all eternity.

Around Father's coffin, we discussed where to bury him, and finally decided on the village graveyard, which was on a high slope about a mile to the northwest of our village, where a Buddhist temple once stood. Father often said that the temple had many worshipers in the old days, and the tolling of its giant bronze bell could be heard a dozen miles away. When he was a child he often played there, and when the Japs invaded the village to kill, burn and loot, he hid there with his grandmother. The temple was pulled down in the steel fever of 1958. With the other commune members Father fed the wooden beams and pillars into the smelting furnaces, used the bricks and flagstones to build bridges and smashed the old mud walls to fertilize the fields. In just a couple of years the grand temple compound was turned into a wasteland. Father opened up small plots in the ditch in front of the temple to plant sorghum. On the west of the original temple there was a pump well, the water from which was sweet and cool. When tired or sleepy in the fields around the place he would go to wash his face in the well pool and have a drink of the refreshing water. In his few leisure moments, he would tell us old stories about the temple. It was situated on high terrain. In Father's view, the *fengshui* (geomancy) of the place must be exceptionally good, or our ancestors wouldn't have built a temple there. Though ruined, it was still considered a treasured place, and the villagers all wanted to be buried there. The funeral reform in the 1990s leveled all private family tombs, and the wasted temple site became the village's collective graveyard.

On the second day, my elder brother and I went to choose a grave site for Father in the graveyard with Uncle Tong, a foster-brother of his and a local expert on geomancy. The graveyard was crowded with grave mounds, and knee-deep wild grass filled the spaces in between. We looked here and there, and finally located a vacant lot. But after measuring it with his feet, Uncle Tong turned it down, because it was too close to the other graves and would likely break into the nearby ones. We continued the search until we thought we had found a suitable site. Yet we dug no more than two feet down when we came upon the top of an earlier grave. No one had any idea whose grave it was or how long it had been there, for there was not even a mound above the ground. So we had busied ourselves for half a day without being able to find a place for Father.

On the third day, my brothers and I went to the village leaders to settle on a place for Father. They told us that the old graveyard had already been fully occupied the previous year, and where to open up a new graveyard was still a question for further discussion. Several days passed, and the discussion reached no conclusion. The village head said that if the problem only involved my Father, it would be easy to solve, for no production team would refuse him a small piece of land. But since his burial place would decide the location of the new village graveyard, people could not reach an agreement. The key point of dispute was *fengshui*. It certainly had to be the most auspicious place. But which place was the most auspicious?

The land to the west of the old graveyard belonged to the first production team, but the team leader insisted that the land was high in the east and low in the west. It was inauspicious to lie facing west. That would increase the death rate of the village, especially of the first production team.

The land to the north of the old graveyard belonged to the sixth production team. The team leader said that with the south higher than the north, the negative principle prevailed, and that was even more inauspicious.

The land to the east of the old graveyard belonged to the seventh production team. The team leader said the land there was all black earth, hard and full of small stones. If the dead were buried there, they would meet too many obstacles in their afterlife and would be eternally uncomfortable.

The land to the south of the old graveyard belonged to my production team and the team leader was a junior uncle of my clan. He said that since it was our land, we could choose anywhere we liked, but the older generation had a saying that "Trees are not to be planted behind a temple and the dead are not to be buried in front of a temple." If the new graveyard was to be in front of the original temple site, he was unable to predict what calamity might occur.

A few more days passed, but still no agreement had been

reached. The whole family grew anxious and a bit angry. Father was born and raised in the village, and he had worked on the land his whole life. He had left his footprints and his sweat in and out of the village, in the fields, in the woods, on the slopes or along ditches and rivers, but at the time of his death he could not even have a resting place. Mother said there was no use being angry. After all, it was a problem of *fengshui*. We'd better consult Uncle Tong, for he was an expert in that. To my surprise, after knowing the purpose of my visit, Uncle Tong's eyes blazed, and he said, "*Fengshui*? Forget it. A person can be buried anywhere. Emperor Zhu Yuanzhang's parents were buried in a landslide. They didn't even have a tomb. But did that prevent him from becoming an emperor? It's a good place wherever you're buried. All that talk about *fengshui* was just excuses. People are worried about their shrinking farmland."

Uncle Tong was the most authoritative person in the village on *fengshui*, and I had never heard him say anything like that in public. His words were enlightening. Since Father's burial place would be the first of dozens and even hundreds to come, the production team that provided the grave site would therefore lose a large piece of fertile farmland. In the previous few years, chicken farms, pig farms and all kinds of factories, as well as new houses built by the villagers and townspeople had occupied vast tracts of cultivated land. The peasants were faced with a crisis of diminishing farmland, and land is as dear as life to the peasants. Father had an ardent love for land and it could never have occurred to him that his folks, who loved the land as much as he did, would deny him a resting place. A dead person needs a grave, and a grave will occupy a plot of land, and that affects the remaining amount of the village's arable land, which in turn affects the interests of the living and future generations. Father was just an ordinary man in the village and never quarreled with others over personal interests. I wonder what he would think if he knew that his death could affect the interests of so many people.

The deceased could lie at peace only when the body was returned to the earth. In order to let his soul rest in peace as early as possible without affecting the interests of the village, my family decided to bury his body in our ancestral graveyard, which lay on elevated ground less than half a mile from the village. That is where my great-great-grandparents, great-grandparents and grandparents were all buried. The graves of the three single-son generations were arranged in a straight line from south to north. To the northwest of my grandparents' grave lay my uncle and aunt, who died many years ago. When Father took us to sweep the tombs, he once drew a circle with his toes on the northeast side of my grandparents parallel to my uncle and aunt's graves, and told us that would be the place for him after his death – a place appointed by his father.

My grandfather said that my great-great-grandfather had consulted a geomancer when choosing a place for the family graveyard. The geomancer told him that this was an auspicious place, for it sloped down from Mount Qingfeng to the Ju River. According to the geomancer, after three single-son generations, the whole clan would prosper, with plenty of offspring who were bound to hold high positions in the government. It was said that the geomancer had even mapped out the tomb pattern for the following five generations. The tombs of the three single-son generations would make up the crane's head and neck, and as the family prospered, the tombs would gradually spread out into the pattern of a crane spreading its wings. My great-great-grandfather was quite happy to hear that, saying it would be fine for the first three generations to suffer, as long as the future ones could thrive. So he willingly paid a high price for this piece of land, which was about two hectares, large enough for his descendants, even for the next twenty generations.

My great-great-grandfather might never have thought that the family really would have three single-son generations. It was only in my father's generation that there were two brothers with an age difference of 12 years. In my generation, there are five brothers, and more than a dozen in the next generation. Much less could my great-great-grandfather have imagined that in the past hundred years the land he purchased has changed hands several times. Its former shape is unrecognizable. Now, except for a road to its east, the space on the other three sides is all occupied by houses or enclosed in compounds. The tiny portion of land that remains is smaller than an acre, with the four lone tombs of my great-great-grandparents, my great-grandparents, my grandparents, and my uncle and aunt. Even those four mounds were later leveled in the funeral reform to increase the amount of arable land. At occasions for memorial services, their offspring could only make a guess at the exact locations and place a few strips of white paper on the spot. After our ancestral graveyard was turned into farmland, it was allocated by the production team to two families and the place which grandfather had appointed for my father was then in one of the family's vegetable gardens.

My younger brother paid the garden owner a visit and offered to exchange a piece of land with him so that Father could be buried there. The garden owner said the most urgent thing was to let the deceased rest in peace and it didn't matter whether there was compensation or not.

We then reported to our team leader, my junior uncle. He said that since the deceased must have a place to rest and since it was in our ancestral graveyard, nobody could raise any objection. When we finally talked about our plan with the head of the village, he smiled and said that that was exactly what the village leaders had in mind, but it would have been too brusque for them to propose it themselves. He said there should be no more delays. Better dig the grave that very night, so the burial could be done the next morning. Before we took our leave, he bade us not to tell anyone that we had sought his opinion.

So, more than ten days after Father's death, he was finally laid in the ground that his own father had chosen for him.

(Translated by Dai Yuliang)

Mother and Beijing

In February 1977 I was enrolled at Peking University. At the approach of every vacation I would write to my mother and invite her to come sight-seeing in Beijing. I told her that this was a hard-to-get chance, for it would not be so convenient if I were to be assigned to work elsewhere after graduation. Mother had spent most of her time in the countryside and the farthest place she had ever been to was the county town. And yet, she repeatedly declined my invitation, because she didn't want to interfere with my studies. After graduation I got a job in Beijing. I invited her again, but she kept declining for reasons that I had just started a new job and didn't have family or an apartment of my own. Later on, when I was married and had a child, I invited her many more times, but she still declined on the ground that since I had a family to care for and a low salary she didn't want to further burden me. So, it was not until I had been working in Beijing for 14 years that she made her first trip to Beijing.

At that time I was living in the Ganjiakou area. When Mother got off the train and learned that I only had a room of nine square meters, she changed her mind and insisted on going to my younger sister's place despite the distance and her tiredness. My sister had a slightly larger apartment in the Mentougou District in the outer suburbs of metropolitan Beijing, about 25 kilometers away. At that time the road to Mentougou was narrow, curvy and bumpy. Mother was carsick, and vomited many times on the way. She went to bed as soon as she arrived at my sister's place and stayed in bed for two days. It pained me to see her suffer so much. As that was her first time to visit the capital city, how could I get her to enjoy her time here and tour around the city without suffering from carsickness? I racked my brains, and finally hit upon an idea – I'd take Mother around on a flatbed tricycle! So I borrowed one, and my wife fastened a chair on the flatbed and placed a cotton cushion on the chair. Then I paddled the tricycle to my sister's to pick up Mother, while my wife rode along on a bicycle. To get to Mentougou took us about two hours, so we set off early and arrived at my sister's home before the sun was fully up.

With Mother sitting in the chair on the flatbed I paddled the tricycle, and my wife, my sister and her husband followed on their bikes. Every now and then Mother would ask to get off and walk along to ease her dizziness. In fact, she did not feel sick at all on the tricycle – she was just afraid that she was wearing me out. We told her that walking was slow and if we arrived late at the scenic site there might be very long queues.

The first place Mother wanted to visit was Chairman Mao's Memorial Hall. But when we got there, we found a notice at the gate, saying, "Closed for interior repairs." Mother was very disappointed. All we could do was make a circle around the hall. Then we took Mother to visit the Great Hall of the People, the National Museum of Chinese History, and the Imperial Palace. The next day we went to the Summer Palace. As we passed Peking University on our way back in the afternoon, Mother insisted on visiting the campus since it was where I had studied. So I paddled her around the Unnamed Lake, the university library and other places. We originally planned to go to the Temple of Heaven on the third day, but when I got up that day, I inadvertently mentioned that my buttocks ached. Mother probably caught my mumbling, for she suddenly told us that she felt rather tired and did not want to go out any more. All our persuasion could not make her change her mind, and I could hardly forgive myself for having mentioned the soreness.

After staying three days at my Ganjiakou home, Mother said she would like to go to my sister's place again, this time by bus. But considering her carsickness, I insisted on taking her there by tricycle, and she gave in. So I paddled her to my sister's, and later from Mentougou to Beijing Railway Station for her return trip. Mother's first Beijing tour was probably my longest experience of paddling a flatbed tricycle – in both time and distance.

Eighteen years passed, and during all that time whenever I thought of my mother, I would blame myself for her unsatisfactory first tour of Beijing. She was unable to go inside the memorial hall to see Chairman Mao, and there were so many other places that I should have shown her around. Every year when I was back home for the Spring Festival, my younger sister and I would try to talk her into making another visit to Beijing, but she always declined on grounds of age, health, carsickness, or the trouble she would cause us. But to my surprise and delight, in early October 2009 my younger brother called from my home village and told me that Mother herself had raised the subject of going to Beijing again. I wondered why at the advanced age of 85 she had had this unexpected change of mind.

On October 9, 2009 my wife and I went to Beijing West Station to meet Mother. We were caught in a traffic jam, and were 20 minutes late. When we finally arrived, we saw Mother already waiting on the square in front of the station. She was leaning on the arm of my elder brother. Her back was bent and her hair had turned completely gray. One of her eyes was completely blind and the other was very weak. Clutching my brother's hand, she shuffled along with the help of a walking stick, like a toddler learning to walk. Every move seemed an effort, and she had to stop to catch her breath every few steps. She was really old. However, we were all glad that she could have braved the long journey, her carsickness and poor health, and come to Beijing again.

Only when I chatted with her in the evening did I become aware of her real motive for making this trip. Two months previously my elder brother had lost his wife and was overwhelmed by depression. Night after night he just couldn't fall asleep. So Mother, regardless of her age and health, decided to take him to Beijing in the hope that a change of environment might pull him out of his grief. She also expressed her regret that she had not been able to pay homage to Chairman Mao the first time.

To fulfill her wish, the whole family accompanied her to Chairman Mao's Memorial Hall the next morning. We bought a bouquet of white chrysanthemums, which she held in her hands as she moved with the line toward the hall. With trembling hands she placed the bouquet in front of the marble statue of Chairman Mao in the lobby, and made three respectful bows. Leaning on our arms she walked slowly to the crystal coffin and stood there, while the other mourners in the line moved slowly ahead. As she stood and gazed at the Chairman lying in the coffin, tears rolled silently down her face. Her pious respect and deep feelings toward the Chairman must have touched the attendants and guards so that no one urged her to move on with the line.

Coming out of the memorial hall, most people quickened their steps. Some looked composed, some heavy-hearted, and some young people looked pleased, as if they had just visited another tourist attraction. Among the viewers few seemed to be over 80.

Mother stood on the steps outside the memorial hall, and looked back at where she had just come from. Tears were still moistening her eyes, which she kept dabbing with her handkerchief. Her deep feelings for Chairman Mao were quite understandable. In response to Chairman Mao's call, she had joined the village's Women's National Salvation Association in the War of Liberation. She made shoes for the People's Liberation Army and milled wheat for soldiers at the front. She took part in the land reform movement, the establishment of the mutual-aid group, the people's commune and the Great Leap Forward movement. During the three years of natural disasters, when adults suffered from dropsy and children were too hungry to walk, she made no complaint. Chairman Mao himself did not taste meat in those years, she said. No matter how hard life was, it was far better than in the old days before liberation, when people lost their homes in the maelstrom of war and famine. To this day, Chairman Mao's portrait is still hanging right in the center of the wall facing the main door of our old house.

"Chairman Mao was just like the head of a family," she said to us as we came out of the hall. "Our country is a big one with so many people. It's no easy job to run such a large household. He led us through good times and bad times. After all, there were more good times than bad times. We must always remember Chairman Mao."

She was also a devoted mother. I have many siblings and we were young during the three years of natural disasters. As there was never enough food, we were always hungry. Mother would start to cook for the family as soon as she was back from work in the fields, no matter how tired she was. When the cooking was done, she would first fill our bowls, and when our bowls were filled, there was often little, or even nothing, left in the wok. She would then add some water in the wok and drop in a handful of green leaves – that would be her meal. Even if there was some food left in the wok after each one had a bowl, she would not eat with us but would give each of us one more spoonful before she ate what remained. The phrase hanging on her lips was that we were at the growing period and should not be over-starved. In the evening when we were in bed, she would still be sewing or stitching shoe soles for the family in the dim light of an oil lamp.

I left home at 17 to join the army, and was probably the one Mother worried about most. She must have shed a lot of secret tears, as one of her eyes went blind. In the early 1980s, when I graduated from university and had a job in Beijing, Mother sent my elder brother and his wife to Beijing to see me with a 50-pound bag of wheat flour, which she had personally milled, because she was afraid I did not have enough to eat. After I was transferred to work in the municipal Party committee of Beijing, Mother told all the family members and relatives not to call me or write to me at my office, much less come to Beijing to visit me, in case they should interfere with my work. Every time I went home for the Spring Festival, she would remind me that as a public servant I must keep to the stand of the Party and selflessly devote myself to my job despite hardship or difficulties. She also encouraged me with the models in ancient stories and of historical figures.

Out of filial piety and to repay her love, my wife would prepare extra dishes at meals when Mother was with us. But at the table Mother often looked at the dishes without taking up her chopsticks, and remarked that it was a waste to cook more than one could eat. When there was fish, shrimp or pork on the table, she would say she was more used to vegetables and tofu at home. We knew the real reason was that she thought those dishes were too expensive. When she learned that it was ten *yuan* for a barrel of purified water on the dispenser, she exclaimed, "How can water be so expensive?" Afterward she and my elder brother would only drink tap water boiled on the stove. Winter days are short. Often when I came home from work in the evening, I would find my apartment in darkness and thought everyone had gone out. But when I turned on the light, I was surprised to see Mother and my elder brother sitting on the sofa. When asked why they didn't turn on the light, Mother would say that there was no need to have light when chatting and that could save some electricity. She must have thought that my brother and her stay at my place was an extra burden on us, and so she would save what she could. When my wife went into the kitchen to prepare dinner, she would find that the vegetables had been rinsed clean and the rice already cooked. When Mother was with us, the floor, tables and chairs, and window sills, as well as beds were always tidy and clean. When my wife told her not to busy herself with the housework, her reply got us all laughing, for she said, "You have busy jobs and should take a rest at home. 'We have two hands and should not be idle in the city.'" The last sentence was a Cultural Revolution slogan to encourage educated urban youth to go and settle down in the countryside.

Why do we say a mother's love is most admirable? It is not because she is able to do an earth-shaking feat, but because she turns her whole life into bits and bits of love, and selflessly devotes it to the raising of her children.

(Translated by Dai Yuliang)

图书在版编目（CIP）数据

江河日月：英文 / 冯俊科著；张光前等译. —北京：外文出版社，2013
ISBN 978-7-119-08530-2

Ⅰ.①江... Ⅱ.①冯... Ⅲ.①散文集–中国–当代–英文
Ⅳ.①I267

中国版本图书馆CIP数据核字（2013）第212564号

出版策划：徐　步
项目统筹：解　琛
英文翻译：张光前　代玉亮　胡　亮　许振宇
英文审定：Paul White　韩清月
责任编辑：蔡莉莉
装帧设计：北京夙焉图文设计工作室
印刷监制：冯　浩

江河日月

冯俊科　著

出 版 人：徐　步
出版发行：
地　　　址：中国北京西城区百万庄大街24号
邮政编码：100037
网　　　址：http://www.flp.com.cn
电子邮箱：flp@cipg.org.cn
电　　话：008610–68320579（总编室）
　　　　　008610–68327750（版权部）
　　　　　008610–68995852（发行部）
　　　　　008610–68996158（编辑部）
印　　制：北京信彩瑞禾印刷厂
开　　本：889mm×1194mm　1/16
印　　张：19.75
版　　次：2013年11月第1版第1次印刷
书　　号：ISBN 978-7-119-08530-2
04800（英）（平装）

版权所有　侵权必究　如有印装问题本社负责调换（电话：68995960）